J.L. DRAKE

QUIET EMPIRE

QUIET MAFIA SERIES

Cover Design by Spellbindign Design
Editing by Lori Whitwam
Formatting by RedDoor Author Services

Dedication

Liz Clark and Jamie Johnson for making this series a
blast to write.
I will always hold M and R close to my heart.

Chapter ONE

The shot echoed around the property and tore through the trees, sending the birds into a frenzy above me. Their wings flapped in panic, and their screams filled the air. It was the only thing that told me life was still happening around me. I held on to a tree trunk and waited to see who was hit. My stomach did a painful flipflop when Elenora slumped to her knees and Sienna gasped in Elio's arms.

Why couldn't she have been the one shot? Fuck!

I shut my eyes and cursed. Why was I always left to deal with the aftermath?

When I opened my eyes again, I saw Sienna kick the gun away from her mother's reach and slowly kneel next to her. She placed her ear next to Elenora's lips as though listening.

I swore to God, if Elenora told her something, I'd drive a bullet right into Sienna's skull in front of the lot of them. Who was I kidding? I was going to do it anyway, but it just had to happen soon instead of later.

Everyone just watched as the two whispered together. I supposed they were giving them a moment before the bitch took her last breath and died.

I whirled around and covered my mouth, hoping Theo would deal with her on the other side.

I loathed Elenora. She got what she deserved, and it was up to me to finish the rest. A tear slipped down my cheek when I saw Theo in front of me.

I let my head slip into the last time I'd seen him.

"Do I look like I'm going to stop asking?" I pulled my arm back and slapped Theo's consigliere across the face. I knew I looked like a crazy person, but I didn't care. Theo had left in the middle of the night to go after Elenora and their spawn of a daughter without his normal cavalry, and now no one would tell me where he was.

"Do that again," he towered over me and squeezed my upper arm hard enough to bruise, "and I'll squeeze that baby right out of you." I ripped my arm free and stepped back, feeling a painful ache deep in my stomach. I was glad I was just at the six-month mark, or I'd be concerned for my baby's safety. Stress was eating away at my ability to make wise choices. "I'm just following orders."

"Noemi," Pippo snapped at me, "it's probably best you return home." I started to protest, but he held up a hand. "Unless you have anything else to share with us about what Bosco is up to?"

I looked away, searching my mind for anything new I could share about the Capris, but at that moment, nothing came to me. I knew the only reason I was even allowed to be on the Coppola grounds with Theo was my agreement to share any news I had about the man I was dating and the father of my child. That and the fact that Theo still wanted me and not Elenora and that baby.

"There's a taxi waiting outside." He folded his short arms and waited for me to leave. His brothers, Betto and Lotto, were never far away, and it wouldn't take much for them to throw me out of the house if I protested any more.

With a huff, I gathered my belongings, but I did hear Pippo ask for an update on Theo. I dismissed them and headed out the door and to the car.

"Where to?" the taxi driver asked.

I could go to my mama's, I could go to Bosco, but I decided to head out of town and visit my aunt Giana. At least she wouldn't ask questions and would be happy to see me. Also, she was a nurse, so if these pains got worse, I would be in good hands. I prattled off the address, and he sighed at the distance but carried on, knowing there would be a good tip at the end of it.

Once we were on our way, I settled in the seat and leaned my head back, watching the lights of the homes we passed. I was so close to my happily ever after, of money, security, and power. I just needed to get Elenora out of the way. It was when we were on the outskirts of town that I spotted it. Theo's car was parked at the end of a driveway. If I'd blinked, I would have missed it.

"Hey," I sat up and looked back, wondering what in the world he was doing all the way out here without any of his men, "I need you to turn around."

"I'm under orders to report where I drop you off. Are you sure this is where you want me to say you were dropped off?" the taxi driver said over his shoulder, and I should have known Pippo would have spoken to him. After all, most of the city was under their watchful eye, and those who weren't didn't last very long.

"I don't care what the hell you tell them. I'll pay you double if you turn around and go down the driveway we just passed."

"You're the boss." Without hesitation, he whirled the car around, sending me against the door, then he jerked into the driveway.

"Stop here," I ordered, not wanting him to drive right up to the house. "Pull up behind those shrubs. I can't have you be seen."

I counted out some money, skipped the tip, and tossed it over his seat.

"You'll get the rest when I get back."

"So, I'm waiting for you, miss?"

"Yes." I quietly closed the door, hoping not to draw any attention to myself in case I was about to catch him here with another woman. "I'll let you know when you can go."

"I'm leaving the meter on." He pointed to the stupid

little box that counted every minute we were in the car.

I hurried down the driveway, holding my belly, and was pleased to find the side door was open. In fact, it wasn't even latched all the way. That was odd.

"You called, and I came." Theo's voice caught my attention as I stepped into the freezing cold house. I held my breath for a moment, glad they didn't hear me as my shoes squelched on the tile floor. "Now you're here, with him," he chuckled darkly, "and you think you're going to walk away from me, take my daughter, and, what, just disappear into the night?"

"I warned you that the next time you hurt me, we'd leave." Elenora's voice was cool and calm. Chilly, almost. "You've everything you want in life, so just leave us be."

"Give me my daughter, and you'll never see me again."

"Why? So she can be treated like dirt in that house? Be undermined by your mother and hated by your father? The only way you're getting her is through me."

"She's my blood, and that means something to me."

I peeked around the corner and saw Theo's back was to me, and over his shoulder was Elenora with a gun pointed at him.

No!

"I don't love you—"

"No one loves you, Elenora." Theo half laughed. "Not me, not your parents, not even your boyfriend Francesco, who let his family kill your sorry excuse of a brother. You have no one, so put the gun down and do

what you're Goddamned told!"

Oscar came into view, and he too was holding a gun that was pointed at Theo. Oh, my God, he's out numbered! Why did he come here alone?

"You're never going to leave us, are you?"

"Not while I'm living—"

Bang!

Theo's entire body jolted as he took a step toward her then collapsed to the floor with a heavy thud. I covered my mouth in horror and fear as she lowered the gun and let out a cry of her own. I quickly threw myself into a closet and pulled the door close to my trembling body, as tears streamed down my face.

"We need to leave now," Oscar yelled. "Come on, the guys will be here to clean this up, and we can't be here." I could hear them approach and prayed they wouldn't notice the closet door wasn't shut tight. I knew she wouldn't hesitate to kill me too.

The moment they stepped out of the house, I flung myself into the room and dropped awkwardly to the floor over his body. I struggled to roll him onto his back, and he blinked up at me in confusion as he made a strange sound.

"No, no, no, no..." I sobbed as I pressed my hands against the hole in his chest. "Stay with me."

"K-k," he tried to say, and I grabbed his hand and held it tightly.

"I love you," I choked through my tears.

"Kill her," he whispered with one last effort before his body went slack, and I knew he was gone.

I sat back against the wall with numb legs and cradled my swollen belly. The only thing that ran through my mind in that moment was he wasn't thinking of me. Even with his last breath he was thinking of her.

Chapter

TWO

I watched as my mother's eyes drained of life, her head slumped to the side, and her hand went slack in mine. I placed her still warm hand on her stomach and shifted my weight back on my heels as her words spun in my head. I looked up at Francesco, the gun hung as though heavy in his hand. His horrified expression told me this kill would haunt him forever.

"She could have killed you," he whispered, and I nodded, knowing he was right. Mama had been determined to hurt the Capri family, to make them pay for what she thought they'd done. It was only a matter of time before she succeeded. "I'm so sorry, Sienna."

"Don't be." I stood, brushing the dirt from my knees.

"You've done enough for me. I'm only sorry that you had to be the one to… to do it. I know you loved her."

He gave me a tight nod, then he stood and walked to Piero. He handed him the gun and continued to walk away.

"Sienna?" Andrea's soft voice found me. "*Cuoricino*, are you all right?" I looked at Elio's pale face as I took a moment. He didn't approach.

"I think…" I paused as I remembered my mother's last words. They repeated over and over inside my head. "I think I'd like to go inside."

"That's a very good idea," she said as she placed her hands on my shoulders and steered me in that direction.

Elio moved then. He stepped in our path and stood tall and dark. He didn't speak right away, so I looked up and noted his ticking jaw.

"What did she say to you?" His voice was cold and distant. Some might have been upset that he hadn't asked how I was, but I knew him better than that. Clearly, I was fine. The fact that someone had slipped by his people and tried to hurt us would have been heavy on his mind.

"She said Oscar killed my father."

"Mm," he grunted, and I could only imagine what was running through his head.

Something strange passed through me, as if the wind took a sudden change of direction and sent a breeze of cold air over me. The hair on my arms stood to attention.

I felt the fear just as shadows emerged from the tree line all around us. I reached out for Elio's arm.

"Who are they?" I whispered as a stillness draped

around us. All that could be heard was the sound of flexed leather as their weapons were being drawn.

"Elio." Piero pushed Andrea next to me, and the two men created a bubble of protection. "Four."

"I see six," Elio responded.

"There are another two behind the one in red," I croaked and swallowed through a dry mouth, hoping I was helping.

"Just like Sicily," Piero said harshly.

Niccola and Vinni gave their count, and I felt Elio tug on my arm to move me closer behind him.

"Vinni, take Sienna. Niccola, take Mama," Elio ordered.

"Yes, boss." Vinni reached out for my arm, and as much as I didn't want to leave Elio in this crazy scene from a zombie movie, I hesitated but knew I had to move. "Come on, Sienna."

"Take this." Elio, whose gaze never left the men who were walking toward us at a slow, steady pace, handed me a knife. "Always aim for the inner thigh and then under the arm. Don't stop until they stop moving."

"I love you," I breathed in his ear and grabbed the knife as Vinni shouted to run. As soon as we started to run, a frenzy broke out and everyone began to move fast. There was shouting, and bullets began to fly. The sound of it all sent the birds into a frenzy, and they took off into the sky in sheer panic. Some men were closing in on us as we veered off toward the cars.

"Come on!" I could hardly hear Vinni but saw his mouth moving. Andrea, who was just a few feet from me, pumped her arms at her sides as she suddenly tripped over a rock and tumbled to the ground. I quickly pivoted and went for her, but Niccola shoved my shoulder, sending me toward Vinni again.

"Go with Vinni!" he shouted as he scooped up Andrea and basically carried her off in a different direction toward a vehicle. So many things were going on at once. I frantically looked back. All I wanted to do was see if Elio was all right. Niccola shouted something as he nearly tossed Andrea into the car. Vinni was a few feet ahead of me and made it to the car first and opened the door. He shouted at me to move it. I was almost to the car when *Bang!* Vinni's face twisted in horror, and I followed his gaze toward his brother.

Niccola had been hit. Andrea jumped out of the car and dragged Niccola inside. Then, with her in the driver's seat, they peeled off down the driveway.

In those same seconds, someone grabbed Vinni and sucker punched him in the face, and I was grabbed from behind and dropped the knife.

"I've been wanting to meet you," the man grunted into my ear.

My fight or flight kicked in, and I lost it. As I leaned forward like I was falling, I sent my elbow backward hard and drove it into his ribs, and he let go on a woosh of air. I kicked back and got him in the crotch. I spun around and used the palm of my hand and drilled it into his nose. Then someone grabbed me and pushed me to the ground. I flipped over and managed to get my knee between me and the new attacker. With all my might, I kicked upward and was able to knock him off balance just enough to wiggle free from his hold. I flipped on my stomach and scrambled desperately to get onto my feet, only to have his hand wrap around my ankle and yank me back onto the ground again. I hit my jaw with a loud crack. My ears rang, and my vison blurred, but my subconscious screamed at me to stay focused, and I had a strong will to live. One of the men crawled on top of me and pushed my face into the dirt.

"No!" I screamed as my feet and arms kicked and pushed up desperately as he tried to pin my arms. I looked to the side and saw Elio racing toward me, then he suddenly stopped, and the man let go of me and fell beside me with blood running from his head. I was lifted off the ground from behind and pushed into the back of a car.

Panic ripped through me. I looked desperately back toward Elio, only to see him give a quick nod, then he turned and shot at the men coming up behind him.

"Belt," Francesco barked from the driver's seat. I didn't even realize I was obeying until he looked at me from the rearview mirror with a worried expression. "Are you hurt?"

"No," I huffed, trying to catch my breath. My face hurt like hell, and I reached up and touched my jaw. "What about Niccola?" I felt tears prickle but chased them away, I needed to be strong. Niccola was like a brother to me; I couldn't imagine what it would be like to lose him. I knew how close he was to everyone else, too.

"Gain got to him. He's on his way with Andrea back

to the Hill House."

"Hill House? He should be going to the hospital."

"There are doctors and a whole operating room in the basement, Sienna. He'll have the best care."

"Jesus." I covered my face, trying to get my head on straight. What a rollercoaster today had been. "Who were those guys?"

"I don't know, but I have my theories."

"Do you think it was Greta?" He took a turn hard, and I had to hold on to the door and seat to keep from sliding around.

"No," he finally said, "I don't. Right now, I need to drive and get us out of here in one piece."

I sat back in the seat and held on as I tried to stop my head from spinning out of control. This was crazy. My mother was dead, we'd been attacked by God knew who, Niccola was shot, and I had no idea if Elio and the rest of them were okay. My hands twisted between my legs, trying to hide my shakes. My arms and legs were filthy, and my dress was wet from rolling about on the damp ground. My mind kept going back to try to make sense out of it all.

Once we got onto the open highway and merged with the other cars, I took my first deep breath. Francesco had an earpiece in, and it sounded like he was talking to someone. He was speaking quietly as his eyes flicked to the mirrors every few seconds.

After a little while more of driving, I grew impatient with the murmurs that were too low for me to hear. I wanted to know what his plan was. I removed my shoes, tossed them in the front seat, then climbed over the seat, careful not to bump Francesco's arm as he held the wheel. He eyed me as I situated myself and clicked the belt across my chest. He finished his call and glanced at me.

"You'll keep me in the loop with Niccola?" I asked quietly, and he nodded. "Are Andrea and Vinni all right?"

"Yes, they are."

"Good, and the rest?"

"I'm waiting for a call." I noticed he stretched his fingers on the wheel, and I knew he was just as nervous as I was. He didn't know what was going on either.

"Okay." I rolled my arm to inspect my throbbing elbow. "I appreciate your help back there."

"I'm just glad I was there in time."

"Me too," I agreed, hoping I still had some fight left in me if I needed it. "Where are we going?"

"We need to keep moving until told otherwise."

I eyed him, wondering what that meant. "Am I being tracked?"

He held up a finger and answered the phone that went straight to his earpiece.

"Remember to let me know if you hear anything. I need to know if he's okay."

He nodded.

That was all I got from Francesco as he took multiple calls, and I found my head shutting down, needing to reset. I pulled a suit jacket from the back seat and carefully folded it to use as a pillow against the window. I wasn't sure how far away we were from wherever we were going, but I knew if I was going to keep it together, I needed some sleep. I closed my eyes and drifted off to the sound of the engine.

The sun was just starting to set by the time Francesco nudged me awake. He looked the way I felt. Drained physically and mentally. He came around and opened my door, took the makeshift pillow, and draped it over my shoulders.

He whisked me past the hotel's receptionist and into the elevator then hit the button for the top floor. I wondered if we looked funny checking in without any luggage. I caught my reflection in the only shiny spot of the worn double doors and cringed inwardly at my appearance. I looked like I'd been scraped up off the side of the road. Oh, wait, that was pretty much what had happened to me. I closed my eyes at my sad joke and decided some big changes needed to happen. I refused to go backward because of the choices I'd made up until now. I'd worked incredibly hard not to be that person, all battered and full of secrets and sins. I stood up straight.

"Have you spoken to Elio?" I whispered through a sore jaw.

"No, not yet."

"I need to know when you do."

"I promise."

I nodded as we shot upward in the tiny box.

Thankfully, the walk from the elevator to the room

wasn't far, just two doors down. Once inside, I was surprised at how large it was. My impression so far hadn't been great, but it was a nice room. Perhaps the darkness had made it seem small and rundown from the outside.

Bed called my name, but at the same time I was wired and full of confusion.

"Shower is over there." He pointed to a room tucked in a corner. "I'm going to order us some food, and we'll figure the rest from there."

"All right." I liked the sound of that and disappeared into the bathroom.

The water was hot and soothed the aches and scrapes from this morning. I scrubbed my nails and the dirt from my hair and took a few moments to collect myself under the heavy steam.

Once I was dried off, I slipped on the robe that hung on the back of the door and ran my fingers through my hair. How I wished I had my toiletries.

I rubbed some of the complementary lotion over my skin then left the still steamy bathroom.

I heard talking and waited for what I hoped was the person from room service to leave before I entered the main room. Francesco was alone and sat nursing a cup of espresso in one of the common room chairs.

"Here." Francesco picked up a bag that sat on a small table next to him and handed it to me. I peeked inside and saw fresh clothes. "Two of our soldiers were still in town, so they were able to get those for you."

I wanted to ask more questions, but I decided it was

probably best I didn't know where they had bought a bra and panties or how they knew my size. Some things were better left unsaid.

"Thank you." I whisked away to get dressed and felt mildly better once I was cozy in the soft jeans and sweater.

On my way back out of the bedroom, I flipped over a magazine on the hall table. It was about the local nightlife, and I was puzzled to see where we were.

"We're just outside of town? Why can't we go to the Hill House?" I held up the magazine to him and pointed out our location.

"Piero just wants to make sure we don't lure who ever that was to the house. Once it's clear, we'll be heading back."

"All right." That made sense.

"Everyone is fine, just some scrapes and one clean bullet hole. Niccola was lucky, and, knowing him, he'll be back to work in a couple days." He used a tiny spoon to stir his drink as he crossed his legs. "It was Elio who called. He's fine. I told him where we are." He wouldn't look at me, and I wondered what was going through his head. "You should eat."

"Yes, I should."

I lifted the lid on the *Allesso di Bollito* and felt my stomach grumble. I wasted no time collecting a napkin and settled myself at the table where I could face him.

Silence fell over us as he slipped off in thought, and I filled my body with some much-needed fuel.

"I'm sorry," he finally said but still wouldn't look at

me. "I hope you understand why I did what I did." I felt his pain deep in my chest, and it mingled with my own as it oozed through me. "She wasn't always that way." He cleared his throat as emotion flooded his expression. "But she was dealt an unfair hand in life." He placed his espresso down on the table and folded his hands on his lap. "Sadly, she let her revenge against Piero for her brother's death consume her, and no matter how many times I told her he wasn't behind it, she just couldn't see it. I knew the Coppolas had filled her head with nonsense when Antonio died. They preyed on her in her weakest moment. She was still the girl I fell so in love with, but when she pointed her gun at Elio and you, I just…" He paused and shifted in his suit jacket. "I took an oath to protect you and Elio until my time here on Earth is finished."

I put my glass down and pushed my chair back from the table and sat on a footstool next to him.

"I don't blame you, Francesco. Mama came there this morning knowing how it was going to end. She might have been driven by hate, but she knew she wouldn't be walking away from this. You gave me a chance at life today, and it only proved who my real family is." I covered his hand with mine. "You could have given me up, handed me off and never looked back, but instead you kept me close, pointed Elio in my direction, and have protected me ever since."

He finally looked at me, and I almost cried at his expression. The worry and fear that I might never forgive him for what he'd done was written all over his face. I also knew he'd killed the love of his life so I could have a chance at mine.

"Blood means nothing to me, Francesco. It's who fights for me that counts. That's who family really is. "

"I took away the one person you looked for your entire life. Your mother."

"It took me a while to see it, but I wasn't looking for a parent. After all, that's been here all along." I squeezed his hand and felt a tear slip down my cheek. "What I've been looking for are answers. She wouldn't even give me the answers I so desperately needed without making me work for every tidbit. Even then, she never gave me the whole truth." I looked directly into his eyes. "Francesco, please, now that she's gone and she's not dictating our lives, would you be able to fill in the blanks?"

He hesitated but nodded. He knew I needed the whole truth. It was the only thing that could cure my fractured past.

"Okay." I smiled and moved to settle into the seat across from him. Not wanting to push my luck too quickly, I started slow. "When you found out what the Di Vaio house was really like, did you and Elio go and pay Andrew a visit?"

"Yes, Elio and I both did." His expression turned hard, and the lines around his eyes creased. "I thought I was leaving you in good hands when you were young. I was told you were going to be safe there. Little did I know that my contact was paid to look the other way when it came to the children of that house. I kept away. I couldn't risk drawing too much attention to you, and I failed you."

I nodded encouragingly, then I asked another question.

"So, you did send Elio to the pond that day?"

"Yes. He needed someone just as badly as you did. Though he had no idea why I sent him there. When I found out you were sneaking off the Di Vaio property, I knew I needed to find out what was going on. I didn't know what was going to happen between you two, and honestly, I couldn't be happier."

"Okay." I liked his answer, but I had more questions. "When I was living on the streets, did you have me watched?" He nodded. "Did they report back to you on things that were happening to me?"

"Yes."

Tears filled my eyes without warning.

"What about…" I cleared my throat. I needed to ask the one question that had haunted me for years. I just needed to know. "Was it me, or was it your guy that… you know…"

"What do you want the answer to be?"

"I want the answer to be the truth."

He leaned forward and studied my face then leaned back and seemed to consider. "Do you think the truth will make a difference in who you are? Do you think it will set you free?"

"No. I'm way past thinking anything will set me free, Francesco, but I deserve to know if I killed Renzo or if your guy finished him off that day in the alley."

"You did."

"Okay." I nodded, letting that sink in. "Thank you for your honesty."

"Anything else?"

"Yes." I got my mind back on track. "Do you really think Mama would have shot Elio?"

"Yes, and you as well." His face was a study of conflicting emotion.

"But why?"

He leaned forward and rested his arms on his thighs. "Because of what you did," he countered, and I shook my head with disbelief.

"You know, don't you?" I asked, almost afraid of the answer.

"Who do you think told me?"

I stood up suddenly, no longer able to sit, and bit the end of a nail. "She thought I betrayed her by what I did at the church," I said more to myself than him.

"You accepted the ring. You gave your oath and signed the papers."

"But it meant nothing. I mean, it meant something, but not what she thought. I did this for us, for all of us. Besides, it wasn't like I could say no—"

"No one is blaming you, Sienna. We just need to think about what the next step will be, and fast."

I glanced at his phone and lunged for it.

"I need to call Elio. He needs to know the truth."

"No," he swiped it away before I could reach it, "not yet. He has enough to deal with there. Give him a little more time."

"If he finds out and he didn't hear it from me first,

I've been down that road…"

"Just, please, wait. We need to talk first."

I sank back in the chair and covered my face. I had an urgent need to gather everyone up and put them in a room and share everything with them.

"Take these." He handed me two pain pills and a glass of water as he examined my face. "Just take the night, and we will figure this out in the morning."

I complied, as my jaw was quite swollen and painful. As I swallowed back the pills, I took a few deep breaths.

"Mama told me about Oscar." I said the words quietly.

"What? That he loved her?"

"No." I shot a glance over at him. I'd never really paid much attention to Oscar. He was kind of like air, always there, but never did much to catch your attention. Perhaps he stood out a little in the beginning but then seemed to fade away to the point where he never entered my consciousness. "She just said he was an excellent shot."

Francesco let out a sudden burst of laughter that shocked me, and I found myself intrigued to find out what was so funny.

"Oscar couldn't hit a wine barrel if he was standing next to it." He ran a hand through his hair with a chuckle. "No, it's your mama who was an excellent shot. That woman could shoot a white feather in the middle of a snowstorm eight miles away."

My stomach plummeted and the blood drained down to my toes, leaving me uneasy.

"What?"

"She told me Oscar killed my father." His humor faded away just as fast as it arrived. "Francesco, this is the time where you need to fill in the blanks for me. The time to prove you'll be honest with me."

"She did kill him, yes." He held up a hand to stop my reaction. "Your father wasn't a good man, and it was her or him. If I'd been in her shoes, I'd have done the same."

"Her last words to me were a lie." I leaned back in the chair and realized she had managed to get in one last blow before she died. "What kind of person would do that? What vengeful, vindictive *mother* would do that?"

"It's the mafia life, Sienna. You take your secrets to the grave."

Elio

Once Niccola was stable and I was assured Mama was fine after her fall, I found Papa in his office looking over some footage that had been taken earlier. I stepped inside and quietly closed the door. He removed his glasses and rubbed the bridge of his nose as he blew out a puff of air.

"I've no idea who they were." He looked worn out, and I knew the constant battle we all had to fight to keep our family name at the top of the syndicate list was exhausting. "Vinni is running prints, but that will take a bit. Your mama is sore but all right, and Niccola," he shook his head, carrying the guilt of what could have happened on his shoulders, "he's going to be out for a few weeks."

"He'll be fine," I assured him.

"Then this whole Elenora thing." He shook his head slowly. "How's Sienna holding up?"

"I haven't spoken to her yet, but Francesco assures me she's fine. I think she's angrier and more betrayed that her mother pointed a gun at us than about her actual death."

"Yes, well, wait until things settle and she has time to think about it. It will more than likely hit her then."

"Perhaps, yes." I leaned over the back of the chair as I thought. "I spoke to Nonna, and for once, I believe she had nothing to do with what happened."

"Let's hope," he grunted. "I make no excuses for my mother. She's a product of her generation and sadly can no longer be trusted."

I nodded and took a moment to try to put myself in Papa's place. I knew it must be hard on him.

"What are those?" I pointed to the spreadsheets he was going over.

"These are the reports the guys were combing through."

"And?"

"And it turns out the Coppolas are broke."

"What?" I took the papers from him and scanned the transactions. "But they were bringing in massive amounts of cash. Where'd it all go?"

"That's why I'm here, trying to figure it out."

"Maybe that Mikey person is funneling money elsewhere and not into the family's accounts."

"That ran through my mind, too." Papa nodded as he thought. "Problem is the paper trail falls off from there. The account is untraceable, and there's nothing left to follow."

"I'll see what I can dig up." I handed the papers back and pulled out my phone as it vibrated in my pocket.

It was Gain. After a few moments, I put the phone back in my jacket pocket and turned to Papa.

"I need to go deal with something. Let me know when the soldiers are finished clearing the area. I'll go get Sienna myself."

"Yes, go. I'll be in touch."

"All right. I'll check in later."

I got changed into jeans, a long-sleeved shirt, and a ball hat, something I'd normally never be caught dead wearing, but I needed to play a part. I needed to be unrecognizable. I left the house and jumped in my car and headed to the place where we'd stayed that morning. Gain was back there now with Harris and a few other soldiers. They'd been told to stay there to keep the house looking active. They were to watch for any more visitors, and one had just been spotted.

The sun was almost down, and the advantage was now in my favor. I knew the layout of all our properties; it was something Papa had taught me from an early age. "Draw your enemy into familiar territory and take the lead," he'd said.

And that was just what I did.

I called Gain once I'd hidden the car and raced into the woods. "I'm here. You have your night vision on?"

"Yes. Come east," he whispered from somewhere near the house. "He's wearing a t-shirt, jeans, sneakers, slightly shorter than me, maybe weighs twenty pounds less than you."

Keeping low, I moved swiftly, listening to Gain in my ear as I approached our visitor.

"I see you." I heard him moving, probably to see better. "He's just to your left."

"Got him." I took in everything as I raced along a few yards behind him. His sneakers were not meant for the woods, so I ran wide and came into his side view, steering him into thicker terrain. Darkness was creeping up on us, and he yelped as he tripped then started to run faster, unsure who I was and what I wanted. I ducked and jumped the ditch. I was prepared for it. I knew what was in front of me. I knew where I wanted him to go, and he was following my plan perfectly.

Jeans were hard to run in, which was why I lived in dress pants. They were light and weren't restrictive. You never knew when you'd have to move fast, and I was always prepared. In our line of work, it could mean the difference between life and death.

Shadows were becoming deeper, and an owl above us started his night call. The moon was bright and provided a sliver of light through the forest, just enough to keep eyes on the man.

Again, I used my body to steer him in a different direction. Quickly, I gained ground, closing the distance between us.

*Yes, keep running, because…*He tripped and flew

forward right into the thick sludge that always gathered in this small area. It had nearly caught me a few times when I was scouting the terrain.

I raced into the mud while he was off balance and wrapped my arm around his neck. I yanked him backward, using the sludge to hold his legs down.

"What were you doing at the house?" I grunted in his ear as he wrenched to get free. "Tell me or I'll snap your neck."

"I came here for Mikey!"

"Who?" I wasn't sure if I'd heard him right.

"I don't know—" He gasped when I punched his ribs. "I got a call from my boss," he coughed, "saying he got a lead that this Mikey was here, and I was to bring her back to him."

"Her?" Mikey was a woman?

"What else do you know?" I fixed my grip, tightening my arm around his neck.

"Just that she was siphoning money from my boss, and I'm not allowed to return until I have her." He fought to breathe.

Bang! The shot echoed through the woods. I strengthened my grip on the man and bent him back as I got low to the ground.

I got a quick glimpse of one of my soldiers. He moved his flashlight at a man across the way from me who was now lying face down over a rock. He must have been sneaking up on me. I gave a quick wave and went back to the man in front of me.

"There's no one left to save you now," I huffed.

"You think we're the only ones coming?" He half laughed. "My employer alone hired a multitude of men, and that's just us. I don't know who the hell this woman is. I just want to get paid, but the word's out and spreading fast that *Mikey* has surfaced, and they are out for blood. There's a lot of money to be made for whoever gets her."

Mikey is here?

"How do you know who you're after?"

"You should know. She's in the picture with you."

"What?"

"Phone." He struggled to speak. He awkwardly reached for his phone, and I let him open it. What I saw made my blood run cold.

No. Confusion tried to cloud my brain. Whoever Mikey was, I knew he or she had been making deals for years. Whoever they were, they would have to be much older than me.

"She's pretty, but orders are orders."

I saw black as I squeezed with all my might and jerked his spine to snap it at the base of his neck. I tossed him aside, scooped up his phone, removed the password setting with his limp thumb, and hurried back toward the house with my soldier protecting my back as I went.

I needed to change, and I needed to get the hell out of there.

I almost made it to the tree line when a whistle rang out. Gain motioned for me to follow him into the trees.

"You good?"

"No." I tossed him the phone, and he looked at it then at me, confused over the photo of me and Sienna.

"Do whatever it is you guys do and tell me everything that is on that phone."

"Yes, boss."

I made a brief call then ordered the soldiers to stay put and to report to me if anyone else arrived between now and the time I checked back in.

"Permission to shoot?" Harris, one of my top soldiers, asked as I was about to leave.

"They're after Sienna." I whirled around to drive my point home. "You have permission to slaughter."

Papa: We're clear and have tripled our protection.

I quickly called my father as I headed back toward the car and filled him in.

Vinni met me at the end of the road, and I tossed my keys to Gain and ducked in the back of Vinni's car.

"I have your bag and one Andrea packed for Sienna." He looked over his shoulder to check his blind spot as he eased onto the main road. "You good?"

"No." I tapped Francesco's number. He answered on the second ring.

"I promise you she's good." He must have stepped out onto the balcony by the sounds that could be heard over the phone. "She just fell asleep."

"How many soldiers do you have that can get to the hotel?"

Silence.

"I don't know." He paused. "Maybe three or five?"

"Find more."

"Elio, what's happening?"

"Someone's put a hit out on Sienna. They've named her as Mikey. That's why we were attacked at the house. I have a feeling they're heading your way."

"Mikey? That makes no sense. How could they think it's Sienna? The timelines of the transactions wouldn't even match up."

I thought about all those late nights when Francesco, Papa, and I combed the web for any dealings with someone named Mikey. We did find a couple of companies, but no one would agree to speak to us about it. I made a mental note that when they came under my rule, they'd answer to me or have consequences.

"I don't know. She was just named as Mikey. Maybe it's an organization."

"Jesus," he huffed. "All right. I'll make some calls. But hang on. I need to wake up Sienna, because, Elio, you need to hear what she has—"

A call came in, and I pulled the phone away from my head to read the screen.

What the hell kind of timing was this?

"I'm on my way. I'll call you back. Just get some guys there fast." I hung up and flipped over to the other call.

"I'd ask how you are, but something tells me I know the answer." Mariano chuckled, and I could tell by his slurred words he had probably had just taken a hit of cocaine.

"So, you finally sobered up enough to crawl out

from under a rock. What do want, Mariano?" I watched Vinni's head tilt at the name as he glanced at me in the rearview mirror. We hadn't heard from Mariano in a long time, and I was sure he was also wondering at the timing.

"Can't a guy say hi to an old friend?"

"And?"

"I wanted to hear your voice and find out if the rumor that she was dead was true, but the fact that you answered and aren't out on a killing spree with Tieri just told me my answer." I rubbed my eyes, massaging the tension that found me whenever Mariano was around. "I'd ask how my girlfriend is, but that's right, the two of you played me. You slept with her while I thought she and I were finally making progress as a couple."

"First, she was never yours to begin with. You knew who she was from the very beginning and tried to use her as a pawn to take me down. Of course, you failed because you can't keep your nose out of the powder, and she saw you for who you really are. An addict who can't keep his dick in his pants."

"You never let her give me a chance! You just stepped in and stole her from me. Every chance I had, there you were luring her away with your money and flashy suits." He snapped, and his angry rant morphed into a dark laugh. "But not this time." He paused. "This time I have the advantage because I've been watching her."

My blood ran cold. I knew he'd run to the Coppola house for protection.

"I've been watching how Salvo slowly sank his

claws into her while you weren't around. Their bedroom talks, their garden talks, my favorite was when Anna tried to get between them, and Salvo made sure he defended Sienna. It's always the subtle moments that you don't see right away that mean the most. How's it feel, Romeo? Now you might just lose your Juliet."

I closed my eyes, knowing Sienna and I had been parted for ten years and had still found our way back to each other. I knew a few weeks within enemy territory, as much as it pained me, couldn't affect us. "It's sad where you spend your energy, Mariano. Maybe you should be a real man and come visit me yourself. Or be a decent son and visit your parents."

Silence. There was a reason it was only Donte serving dinner that night. We'd made sure the rest of the staff were not on duty and were away from the house. We couldn't risk the news being spread about how we'd had the DeSimones over for their *last* dinner. Mama had sent the odd text to Mariano and to some of Bria's close friends from Bria's phone to make sure people thought they were still around. I made sure to say something just this once to plant the seed in his chaotic mind. It was just a matter of time before I played my cards on that one.

"You know what the best part of this is?" His voice strained like he'd just taken another hit. "There are people around you, people you know, and they're just waiting to make their move."

There were always going to be those people, which was why whenever we did anything big, like murder another Don and his wife, we did it with as few eyes as possible.

"It wouldn't be a crime family, Mariano, if everyone around you was loyal." I hung up, knowing he always needed the last word.

FOUR

Noemi

I'd slept for what felt like days, but in reality was probably only several hours. My eyes burned from all the crying I'd done the night before over Theo's death, and I rubbed them to get some relief.

"Well, I see you have finally settled down." Aunt Giana sat down next to me and reached over to tuck my hair behind my ear. "Want to talk about why you showed up on my doorstep in tears?"

"No."

"How about Bosco? Should we give him a call?"

"No."

"How about your mother?"

"No."

"*Why don't you start by telling me why you're pregnant with another man's baby, yet you've been seen on the arm of Theo Coppola?*" I closed my eyes again and tucked my legs up to my belly. "*I'm not one for judgements, dear. I mean, you do you, but you're playing with fire. If the Capris ever spotted you with Theo, they'd be racing to tell Bosco Capri.*"

"*Trust me, no one is looking for me right now,*" I whispered through the hole in my heart. "*I don't love Bosco. I love Theo.*"

"*Does Theo know it's Bosco's baby?*"

"*He did, yes.*" She looked at me, confused. "*Theo needed a boy, and that wretch of a wife of his couldn't even do that.*" I snickered and sat up. My head pounded, and my heart squeezed tight as I continued with the story Theo and I had gone back and forth on many times. "*Bosco and I met at a dinner one night through friends and ended up sleeping together. He was still dating Amara at the time, but that didn't seem to worry him.*" I paused to wet my dry mouth. "*I was so angry about Theo's wife, I wanted to make him jealous by dating the one person he hated the most. But when he found out I was pregnant, he wanted me back. Told me he'd always wanted me but needed a son to make it happen. He said if the baby was a boy, he'd get rid of Elenora and take this baby for his own.*" I shoved my trembling hands under the pillow and swallowed the knot in my throat, avoiding eye contact with her.

"*Noemi,*" Giana shook her head, clearly disappointed with my life's decisions, "*that's incredibly dangerous. If the Coppolas ever found out your son was a Capri, they'd kill him. It wouldn't matter what Theo wanted. You two need to end this now."*

"It has." I felt the pain bubble up my throat and steal any breath I had inside my lungs. "He was killed yesterday."

She gasped and drew closer to me as I leaned over in a heart wrenching sob.

"What? How?"

Hate coursed through me as I squinted at my aunt. I wanted to claw her eyes out for forcing me to speak the words. "Elenora shot him. I saw the whole thing. They didn't know I was there."

"His own wife shot him?"

"She's a monster. She was only after him for his money. She never loved him like I did, and now I'm on my own again, with nothing but pain and a baby with no father." I sobbed, ignoring my own words.

She stood, rubbed her face, then started to pace the room.

"Who is 'they?' Who else knows about Theo's death? Who else was there?"

"Oscar's her pet, but he's a nobody. I was hiding in a closet. Someone came back, but I got out of there, and I know they didn't see me." I rubbed my runny nose on my sleeve. "That bitch better hide because I'm coming for her and her stupid daughter."

"Your mother is going to lose it, Noemi. Does she even know what games you've been playing here?"

"Of course." I waved her off. She should know better

than to think her sister wasn't in on this. We weren't like my aunt. We didn't have any money. Papa left us broke when he died. We had to survive or die.

"Wow," she huffed like she couldn't believe my story, but she didn't fool me. I knew she was just as sneaky as the rest of us. "Your mother doesn't have the money to house you, let alone a baby!"

"She won't be." I bit my nail as I made up my mind. "I'm going back to Bosco. I won't live poor anymore. I'm not like my mother."

"Noemi," she gasped at my comment, "my sister tried to give you a good life. No one thought your papa had a weak heart."

"Well, lucky for me, my heart isn't weak." She shook her head at me and tossed her hands in the air before leaving me alone to mourn.

That evening, after Aunt Giana left for her shift at the hospital, I dialed the number from the back of a restaurant card that he'd given me on the night we met. I picked up the little outfit my aunt had gotten me that read "Mommy's little angel" and rubbed my thumb over the lettering.

"Bosco," he snapped over the line, and I rolled my eyes before slapping on a smile as though he could see me.

"Hi," I used my sweetest voice, "it's Noemi."

"Oh, hi." His toned changed a little, and I heard a door shut. "How is everything? How's the baby?"

Bosco had checked in with my mother a few times, but she'd stopped passing the messages along when I stopped caring to ask for them. Later, after a month in, I let him know I was living with Giana since she was a nurse, and I'd sold him on the story that I was a high-risk pregnancy. He agreed it was the best option until we both knew what was happening. It was no secret that he loved Amara. They were public with their relationship, and I knew he was worried about ever getting this call. I also knew Bosco was basically a good man and would do the right thing when it came down to it. I loathed the idea of living with Piero and his perfect wife, Andrea, but really, what other choice did I have? Theo was gone, and if this baby was a boy, it would secure my spot in that high-profile family. And if it was a girl, they wouldn't cast me aside like Rosa would. At this point, Bosco was my only option.

"He's getting big." I let the bait linger in the air.
"He?"

"My gut is telling me it's a boy. My aunt even had a doctor look me over, and since the baby is sitting so low, he ran an ultrasound and predicted it's a boy. And," I paused to sniff dramatically, forcing more lies out of my mouth, "he's healthy, I'm healthy, and even if he comes out tomorrow, they'll be able to save him." I swallowed down the bile that crept up the back of my throat. "I think it's time we shared the news with everyone."

"Jesus," he half laughed, half choked. I knew I was dangling the one thing that would make his father and family proud. He could roll the dice with Amara, or he could have his silver platter with me and a son.

When he went suddenly silent, I tossed one last

thing at him. "I know this wasn't what either of us was expecting," I whispered coyly, "but we have a responsibility to this baby, and I for one am going to love him more than anything in this world. I only hope his father feels the same way." I rolled my eyes and dug deep. "What do you say? Can we try to give this little boy a family?"

"Wow," he let out a long breath, "I'm having a son."

I closed my eyes and leaned back in the chair, knowing I'd hooked him.

Chapter FIVE

Sienna

I knew I was dreaming, but it felt so real. The wind kissed my face and whisked my hair around my cheeks. I smiled up at Elio as he wrapped a warm arm around my waist and pulled me into him.

"I love you." He kissed my temple, letting his lips linger there, sealing his words. "Come. I have something to show you."

When I turned, I saw my mama with her gun pointed at me.

"What have you done?" she shouted, then she pulled the trigger and sent a bullet through Elio's chest.

I woke with a jerk, grabbing my chest as my heart left bruises on my ribcage.

"What were you dreaming about?" Elio's voice found me, and I squinted to find him in the dark. He leaned forward, and the moonlight outed his position.

"You scared me." I ran my hand through my hair with a huff. "I was just reliving my mother's last few moments on Earth. When did you get here?"

"A few minutes ago. We need to talk." He dove right into it. "You need to know that they were after you."

I slowly tugged the blankets up with me as I rested against the headboard.

"The men at the house? Why me?" I wanted to hear what he had to tell me before I dropped my bombshell on him.

"Someone spread the word that you're this Mikey person, and now all of Mikey's clients are out for your blood."

So many things ran through my head at once that I zoned out for a few seconds while it all come crashing down around me.

"That friggin' old bat…" I trailed off. "Oh, my God…I walked right into it and never saw it coming." I shook my head, unbelievably upset that I hadn't seen it. I had been played like a fool. "I thought I was so clever, but she outsmarted me, and now look." I laughed even as I admired her.

Elio stood like stone as he watched me, and I realized I was only speaking in half sentences. I rubbed my face and knew it was time to tell him all of it.

I crawled out of bed and stood in front of him. I reached into his coat pocket and removed his cell phone, but when I reached for his weapon, his hand clamped down on mine.

"What are you doing?"

"I'm about to tell you something, and I'm nervous of your reaction."

"Sienna," he warned as he removed my hand, "don't think I didn't notice you changed your family ring to your right hand, and you never said yes to my proposal. If you're about to tell me you married Salvo, taking my gun won't help you."

"Elio," I reached up and cupped his face, "you think I married Salvo? No! God, no."

"Then what the hell's going on?"

"Remember you asked me to find out who Mikey was? I never got to tell you what I found out. It's important because Mikey was my grandfather's nickname. He used that name to make side deals. After he died and Stefano took over, Rosa manipulated him, and they used her husband's nickname to continue to funnel money into her own accounts. Rosa Coppola is Mikey. Anyway, the point is that one day she had me go with her to a church, when I was there, I told her I knew she was Mikey. Moments after that, the uncles were killed, and she disappeared in the confusion. My guess is it's her trying to get out from under the spotlight and telling people that Mikey is me. I bet she owes a lot of people a lot of money."

"Jesus," he let out a puff of air but then looked up at me, "the sheer stupidity of them stealing from such powerful people. Did they really think it wasn't going to come back around?"

"I don't know, but here we are."

"But she must have been stealing as Mikey for years. It wouldn't take long to figure out you'd be too young."

"Elio, there's more." I cleared my throat, and he went still and studied my face. "That day I went with her to the church, I was legally sworn in as the Coppola Donna."

Elio shot straight up and towered over me, vibrating.

"Repeat that to me again."

"The reason I was at the church that night, it was because Rosa had me sworn in as the new Donna for the Coppola family. Salvo was the witness, along with the minister."

"Sienna, no." His face fell, and I wasn't sure what to do. He looked up at me, his expression unreadable. "That wasn't the plan. You were supposed to bring the Coppola kingdom down, not step into the seat of the Don."

"Donna," I corrected him. "I thought it was a good move at the time. What better way to tip the scales than to have me step into that role?"

"Did you ever stop and think why Rosa Coppola would do that?"

"Truthfully, I thought she saw that Stefano had gone missing, thanks to you, and that the uncles liked me. I thought she saw me as her only move, but now I'm seeing I was played. She outsmarted me at my own game." I got angry all over again.

"Sweet Lord, I need to get my head around this." He paced then came back to stand next to me. "Okay, take a breath, Sienna." He placed his hands on my shoulders, as now my head was running like a hamster wheel.

"Elio, she's been making dirty deals forever, and who knows what my grandfather was doing before that. Come to think of it, Ugo mentioned to me after the fire that he overheard her *consigliere* talking to Rosa about getting rid of emails, and later that day, Rosa's things were gone from the house." His hands fell away as I took a turn to pace. "She was never going to return to the house. She had it all mapped out. Get me sworn in, kill the uncles, then slip away into the night with all the money and leave everyone coming after me for it."

"That explains where all their money went," he murmured, but I wasn't really listening.

"After the uncles were shot, Salvo got me in the car, and we took off out of there without Rosa." My brain ping-ponged all over the place. "I'm still trying to figure out if she knew what was going on at the house. Then there was Noemi." I wasn't thinking straight and just let my mouth run. "She was the one who soaked my bedroom in gasoline."

"What?" He grabbed my arm and pulled me from my tailspin.

"Yes." I nodded, feeling my eyes prickle, not for her but because I knew how much this news would hurt the family. "She tried to kill me."

I'd seen Elio upset before, but the anguish on his face almost brought me to my knees. I hated that I had to be the one to cause him such pain.

"Start talking," he nearly growled.

"I'm so sorry, Elio, but it's true. I found Anja, the

young girl who was planted in her house. She was barely alive on my bed. Noemi shot her, I tried to help her, but it was too late. Then Noemi came in. She had a gun and a candle, and she set fire to my room. She's the one who burned down the house."

His face went white, and I rushed to show him I understood his pain and disbelief. "I know. I couldn't believe what was happening either. What she was saying. She was crazed. She said Mama had killed Theo, which, by the way, is true. That's another thing." I shook my head, getting my thoughts back on track. "She said she was doing it for her sons and that there couldn't be any more lose ends. I only just managed to get out, but it was close."

Elio didn't blink. He just stared at me as he digested everything I'd shared. I knew it was a lot, but I didn't want to keep anything unsaid between us anymore. I had to let it all out. I stopped speaking then and studied his face. Just when I thought he was going to blow, he grabbed the sides of my head and kissed me hard. Then he pressed his forehead to mine, and we stood there a moment.

"We're going to get through this." His voice was gentle, and I took a breath.

"I know we are." I didn't miss a beat. I needed him to know I was strong enough to take whatever hits would come our way. "Elio, I know you want to act, but Noemi is the only link to so many unanswered questions. I think we should pretend like nothing's happened, like I never told you any of this. Who cares if she believes it or not?

I mean, the fact that the family hasn't kicked her out or worse means she still thinks she has a chance of getting away with it. We must keep this quiet, just for now. She's been talking to Rosa Coppola, so if we act like normal, she might lead us right to her."

"All right." He stood straight and stepped away as he rubbed his lips in thought. "I see what you're saying, and if even for my cousin's sake, I agree we need to tread very carefully here. This'll get ugly very quickly. But for now, we need you behind Capri gates. We also need to find a way around Nonna Greta."

"What if we tell Greta what happened? Maybe she'll see I'm not trying to hurt your family. I'm doing the exact opposite."

"No, she wouldn't believe it. She can't see past who your father was. We need something bigger." His hands dropped as he slowly turned to look at me.

"What?"

"You know you deserve the world, right?"

"Ahh?"

"You know that after everything that's happened up to this very moment right here that I've always loved you, right?"

"Yes."

"Okay, good."

"I'm not following."

"Grab your things, Bella. We have a celebration to plan." He grinned and swung me around.

Vinni's gaze flicked to me from the rearview mirror. I could feel his nerves from the back seat.

"I promise you, Nonna is far from the house. Piero made sure of it." He finally said something as we pulled into the wrap-around driveway and parked.

"I feel like I should be wearing a mask or something," I joked to Vinni when he opened the car door for me at the Hill House. Though I was looking forward to this evening after spending the last couple of days hidden away in Elio's house, I felt vulnerable out in the open. I would hate to be snatched up and sold to the highest bidder at this point.

"You have my word that Elio has everything under control." He helped me out of the car. "That is until he sees you in that." He grinned.

I smiled down at the green silk dress. It dove down into a deep V in the front, and the fabric draped gracefully down the length of my body from the gathers at the shoulders. A sexy slash stopped just inches from the top of my leg. I had paired a set of green beaded earrings so they would dangle from under my tumbling-curled hair and added dramatic green eye shadow to bring out my eyes. All my efforts had paid off when Andrea dropped in to see me earlier this afternoon. She had clapped her hands and smiled her approval.

"Well, you did say as a Donna I needed to make a statement."

"You look spectacular," She hugged me close then eyed me with one of her motherly looks. "How are you feeling?"

"All things considered, I'm doing fine."

"I'm very pleased to hear that, Sienna. You've been through a lot. Our family knows how important it is to watch our mental health. Bad thoughts can creep in out of nowhere, especially at times like these, so be sure to check in with me whenever you need to talk. I'm always here for you."

"Thank you." I hugged her again, incredibly pleased that Elio's mother was nothing like Elenora. Andrea was a hugger, and so was I.

Now standing with Vinni outside Hill House, I took a deep breath and knew I was ready for whatever I needed to face inside.

Andrea was the first to greet me with a big smile, knowing I needed her after this afternoon. I noticed Ugo hovered behind, pleased to see I was all right, but I could see something was gnawing at him.

"I have a little surprise for you," she practically sang.

"For me?" I couldn't help but wonder what she could have for me.

"God, I've missed that body," Wyatt said in English, popping out from behind her. For a moment, I stood, stunned. My best friend, looking mighty fine in a three-piece suit, stood grinning at me. "Hey, Sienna," he joked, his eyebrows going up and down as he whistled and pretended to check me out. Then shifted his gaze to eye up Vinni as he whisked by. "You look real nice," he said as his head twisted to follow Vinni's disappearing back.

I put my hands on my hips and waited for him to scoop me up in a big hug and sigh the way he always did.

"I'd ask how you're doing," he held me tightly, "but at the risk of sounding callous, I can see you're rocking your mother's death very well." He put me back on my feet. "And in green, I might add."

"I do miss the idea of having my mama, but the truth was she wasn't good for me."

Andrea excused herself, saying she had to see to the meal. She glowed at me, happy that I liked her surprise. She knew how much Wyatt being here would mean to me. I threw her a kiss as she left us.

"Look at you, being all grown up." Wyatt draped an arm around my shoulders and went back to gawking at Vinni, who had just reappeared. "Do you have any idea what is happening?"

"Not a clue, really. I just know it starts with dinner." I waved at Donte as I caught his eye. He waved back with a smile.

"I'll find you later," he mouthed, and I nodded, happy that I was among friends again.

"Sienna," Ugo called as he approached me hesitantly. "Excuse me for just a moment, Wyatt. I don't want to intrude, but I wonder if I could have a quick word with Sienna?" Wyatt gave a polite nod and stepped back a bit as Ugo turned me away, so my back was to everyone. "Now that I know you're here under the protection of the Capris, I want to share with you that I'm going to travel for a bit."

"Oh?"

"Yes. I've decided to take a page from your book and do some digging of my own into my father's family. I've already found out that I have some family scattered around northern Italy. I realize now how important it is for me to know more about who I am as well. You inspired me to this, but if you wish me to stay, I certainly will. I just think I need this."

"Ugo." I smiled and hugged him warmly. I thought how amazing it was that he'd thought to do that. "I think it's the most important thing to know where you come from. If you have the chance to find some answers, then run toward them." I squeezed his hand. "And when you're done with your search, don't forget your family here will be waiting." The lines around his eyes softened. "All I ask is stay in touch. I'm used to having you in my life now, and I don't want to lose you."

"You won't." He wrapped me in a hug. "Thanks for understanding."

"Of course, I do."

"I'll see you inside, then. I don't want to hold up dinner. Andrea's dinners are *bellissimo*." He kissed his fingers, then set off through the house toward the patio out back.

"So, enlighten me on something," Wyatt asked as he picked right back up where we were two minutes ago. "Ms. Greta tried to run you out of town, yet here you are at the Don's house about to have dinner. How's that happening?"

"Amazing how things change, isn't it? It's okay, though, honestly. Oh, Wyatt, I have so much to fill you in on later." I looked up as Elio approached with Piero at his side.

"You look lovely, Sienna." Piero eyed my dress. "You'll make quite the splash at the party tonight." I nodded my thanks as he turned to Wyatt. "It's nice to see you, Wyatt. I'm so glad you could make it." Wyatt and Piero began to chat about how Andrea was able to get him to come. Elio stepped close; I could feel the heat as he looked at me.

"Should I be attending a party if I'm supposed to be dead?" I asked Elio as I snatched a few grapes from a plate that was being carried by in an attempt to control my heartbeat.

"Oh, yes, with what I have in mind, you really need to be there," Elio muttered. His expression was positively smoldering as his gaze raked down my whole body. I felt a jolt of heat plow through me. "You look beautiful."

"Thank you," I breathed.

"You know what I think we should do?"

"I'm all ears." I pictured the fastest way to remove my dress.

"You should give me babies." I nearly choked on the grape. "I'm serious. We've discussed having kids before, and I don't know about you, but I love the idea of making them."

"I love the idea of making them, too, but now?" His gaze turned mischievous, so I held up a hand to stop him from steamrolling what we were about to do. "Why don't you feel free to fill me in on what's going on?" I took the glass of wine he handed me.

"I would," he kissed my lips, lingering over them, "but I wouldn't want to ruin the fun."

"Your idea of fun is very different than mine."

"Perhaps." He kissed me again, and I heard Vinni chuckle behind us. "But first, we have some business to attend to." He laced his hands through mine, motioning Wyatt and Piero to follow us. I was pleased he let the baby conversation go, at least for tonight. I had enough on my plate.

As we walked through the house, I thought how impossible it was that Elio was even more handsome in that moment than I'd ever seen him. He looked like he just stepped out of a men's mafia magazine. Three-piece suit like his father's, crisp white handkerchief with a splash of gold on the edge, engraved cufflinks, and his favorite Bontoni shoes.

In fact, everyone was dressed to perfection. Even poor Niccola, who struggled to hide the fact that he was still in some discomfort, looked the part. I smiled as Ugo helped him into his chair.

Yes, something big was definitely up. I hoped Elio knew what he was doing.

The outdoor table under the weeping trees looked beautiful. I'd forgotten just how much I loved this place. It all looked positively whimsical, all done in gold and black décor. The table runner was black and had golden designs woven through it. The black roses were nestled in tall, thin vases, the white plates had gold trim, and little crown-shaped chocolates peppered the empty spaces between the serving dishes. As I got closer, my eyes were drawn to a servant pouring red wine into glasses that matched perfectly with the shape of the vases. It was truly spectacular how much talent Elio's mother had for decorating. Something, however, looked totally out of place and stood vastly different from the rest of the décor. Two very old and grand-looking wooden chairs stood at either end of the table. They almost looked like medieval thrones with their odd carvings over the black leather padding.

Elio pulled out a chair next to one of the thrones and inclined his head to me. Once I was settled, Andrea did the same at the other end, then Elio and Piero stood at either end of the table and looked at one another.

It was Piero who spoke first as he raised a glass in the air for silence. "Let the crow fly high and watch over those who seek to harm. Let the loyal warriors fight with strength to protect our families. Let the crown rest on the head of who will rule our people and honor all that we stand for. For we are the dark crow who watch over all." Andrea's gaze found mine, and her eyes sparked with excitement at her husband's words. "Though tradition has been twisted this time around, there's nothing wrong with change. And with that change comes this." Piero looked at his son. "Your title is underboss, but I think it's safe to say that you've performed well beyond that position. You're a born leader, Elio, and now it's time for me to pass the torch and not limit your full potential. I have never been prouder to call you my son and now to call you Don of the Capri syndicate."

Oh, my…I took a quick glance at Wyatt, whose wide

eyes were already on me.

"Wow," I mouthed as the whole table cheered. I knew he was wondering what was going through my head in that moment. I was in love with a Don of a syndicate, but he still didn't know the biggest bombshell of all. He didn't know who I was.

"Thank you, Papa." He hushed the crowd, never liking any kind of attention on himself. "It would be my honor to accept the role. As Don, I can only hope to live up to your expectations and those of the family. With that, I'd like us all to drink a toast to my papa." Everyone drank, and a cheer rose for Piero, who dabbed at his eyes.

Elio then held up his hand to speak again.

"I would like to ask Francesco, if you would, to continue as my *consigliere*."

"It would be an honor." Francesco gave a small smile and inclined his head. It wasn't hard to see how much the last days had affected him. *Any emotion for my mama's death is still not there. Time of death of me caring, two days ago, sometime in the morning.*

"Niccola," he addressed his oldest cousin, "I would like nothing more than to have you as my underboss."

"I've always had your back, Elio, and always will." He nodded while his little brother Vinni congratulated him by holding up his glass.

"To new beginnings," Andrea added over the cheers.

I hopped to my feet and clapped with everyone else, grinning at the man who deserved this more than anyone.

"I'm really happy for you, Elio."

"Thank you, my *bella*." He leaned down and kissed

me gently. "Now we're going to rule all of Italy as one."

I felt a dark, exciting shiver as our eyes met, and the power that surged through me in that moment was incredible.

Chapter

SIX

Noemi

I peeled open my puffy eyes and attempted to blink the soreness away. I had been living in my car since the fire at the Coppola mansion. I'd needed time to try to figure out how to get myself out of this mess. I needed to know what Elenora had said to Sienna before she died so I'd know if it was safe to go home. Had that little bitch snitched on me to Elio? Or did she know nothing at all?

Why couldn't she just have died in that fire? Why do bad things always happen to me? I'm a good person just trying to survive in this crappy world. First, I lose my Theo, then that bitch kills him, ending any future I had.

I knocked the bag of chips off the passenger seat to make room for my legs. I'd been driving all over the place looking in every spot I could think of where that old bat could hide. Then I'd caught a break last night. Now it was a waiting—

"Ah ha, so there you are, you stupid old bat!" I'd spotted her. I tugged at the edge of my sweater to wipe the food off my face and did a quick fix of my hair. I knew I looked like I felt. Horrible. Living on gas station food and coffee had done a job on my stomach as well.

I kicked open the driver's door and marched across the road to the side door of a local church.

"I should have known you'd come back here," I hissed at her as I knocked her suitcase out of her hand. It hit the floor with a bang.

"I wondered when you'd show your face." She held a hand to stop her *consigliere* from stepping in.

"What did you do?" I shouted, not able to contain myself any longer.

"What I had to do." Rosa fixed her sweater to sit just right. "You have your memories, Noemi. They're just things."

"You took all his photos and belongings. Everything else of Theo's is now reduced to ashes and soot. You could have told me the plan."

"The last time we spoke, you tried to threaten me."

"You gave her power," I seethed at her.

"To a syndicate of ashes and soot." She snorted. "She won't last long. She's being sniffed out as we speak. Like a fox on a hunt. I may not have seen Alessia coming, but she's a good Donna who pivots and adapts to the unknown."

"You ran her right back into Elio's arms." I leaned over, bracing my hands on my thighs and feeling the world crumble around me. I had no one. "He'll protect her."

"Let him." She struggled. "I just tossed a grenade at the Capris' front doorstep," she replied calmly. "The uncles found out I was Mikey. It was only a matter of time before they realized I'd been funneling money and they were broke. I had to do what was best for me."

"I can see that." I snickered.

"Since Michael's and Theo's deaths, our syndicate's been failing." She continued to rattle on, not at all seeing I was close to losing it. "Stefano was nothing more than an easily manipulated boy with a ring, and the uncles were only powerful because of who they used to be. The fact that there were three of them made it harder, but I handled it. I was the one who carried the family name until Alessia showed up. I knew it was time to make a change, anyway. I'll still rule just in a different way."

"And what about me?"

"What about you?"

"I was the only one who truly loved your son for who he was." I stabbed at my chest. "The one who sacrificed everything to be with Theo, even though you married him off to her!"

"Oh, please, Noemi, you're being dramatic."

"Dramatic?" I laughed. "What did she have that I didn't?"

"Elenora may have had nothing, but she could get pregnant just by looking at a man. I didn't want Theo in love. Men in love only listen to one thing." She stepped closer. "I needed him to have a son. The rest was disposable."

"Disposable?" I couldn't believe her choice of words.

"Careful," she warned as I flirted dangerously close to her dirty little secret.

"What am I supposed to do?" I dropped my arms, needing some sort of direction.

She tapped her cane as she looked away then cleared her throat. She walked outside onto the street, and I followed.

"You go home and act like nothing happened. There were no witnesses, correct?"

I shook my head. "No, but I know she would have told Elio, and if she knew anything about my past, she'd have shared it."

"It's her word against yours. You're Niccola and Vinni's mother, who are well placed in the family. You've been in that family a lot longer than she has. You just need to convince your sons that she's a liar if you're accused of anything. The only thing that might make you look guilty is if you don't go home."

I rubbed my face, unsure of anything anymore.

"Don't cross me again, Noemi." She stood shoulder to shoulder with me, sending a chill across my skin. "Remember, I have a talent for making things disappear."

I held my breath as her *consigliere* opened the door to a car and helped her inside, then he put several suitcases in the trunk. He didn't look at me as he slipped behind the wheel, and they left, leaving me to watch them drive away. I got back into my car and sat for a moment. My pounding head flopped back against the headrest, and I fell into a memory.

Nonna Rosa woke me up from a dead sleep in the wee hours of the morning and ordered me to quickly pack an overnight bag. We got into a car with Elenora, and the three of us flew to New York while my head spun with unanswered questions.

"Where are we going?" I asked as I sat, still bewildered, on the edge of the bed in the hotel room while Elenora was in the washroom.

"You are staying here." Nonna swiped her finger in some eyeshadow and dragged a heavy line across her lid. All that did for her was intensify the cold look in her black eyes.

"Where are you going, then?" I was disappointed. I had never been to New York, and now I was here I really wanted to see Times Square.

"Eleanora and I have to be somewhere. You need to stay here."

"Can't I go out and sightsee by myself?"

"No."

"Then why am I even here?"

"Because I need you to be." She tossed Elenora a jacket and tugged her purse up over her shoulder. Elenora looked at me with a worried expression, but I looked away. I hated that woman.

I did nothing but wonder about what was going on. I tried to watch TV but couldn't concentrate and ended up staring out the window. I began to get angry and pulled on my sweater and stepped out the door, but a man blocked my exit. The old bat always planned ahead.

"Inside," he ordered, and I never tried to leave after that.

When the door finally opened hours later, I turned over on the bed to look at the time. It was seven p.m. I clicked on the light and saw Elenora dabbing at tears.

"What happened to you?" I rolled my eyes; she was always such a drama queen. She didn't say a word, just headed for the washroom.

"I'm hungry," I protested. "Can I at least go down to the restaurant and eat something?"

"Fine." Nonna nodded and opened the door to say a few quiet words to the guy outside. He would escort me. Oh, great, my company is Mr. Friendly.

As I took my time and admired the artwork on the wall next to the front desk, I heard a man ask for Rosa Coppola.

"She left this at the office today. I want to make sure she has it before she returns home."

"Excuse me. I'm traveling with Rosa." I looked at the receptionist. "Room 407." She clicked away on her keyboard and nodded that I was who I said I was. "Would you like me to make sure she gets it?"

"That would be lovely." He handed me the sweater. "Please let her know that Dr. Finley values her business and that we hope to see her again soon."

"I'll be sure to pass along the message." I smiled warmly and repeated his name in my head.

After my dinner, I went into the business center of the hotel and researched who Dr. Finley was. Rosa's soldier made a few annoyed sounds, but I ignored him. After all, he got to eat, too. It only took me a few clicks to figure out who he was.

"Oh." I dug a little deeper, and everything suddenly clicked. "Oh, wow."

I leaned back and thought what perfect timing it was that I'd run into that man.

"How much longer?" Mr. Friendly grunted from his post by the door

"I'm ready." I had an extra pop in my step. "It's okay, you know, to crack a smile occasionally, like this. Watch." I smiled widely, and he looked away, unamused at my sudden happiness.

I opened the door to the hotel room and handed Nonna the sweater. Though I couldn't care less about what happened here, I could only imagine what the repercussions of it would be if the other parties ever found out. Nonna's life would be taken in the worst of ways, and that excited me.

"Dr. Finley sends his warmest regards." I watched as her face slipped and her eyes widened.

That's right, Nonna, I know what you did.

Chapter
SEVEN

Elio

I sat at the end of the table and watched my family laugh and enjoy one another's company. Becoming the Don was something I had waited patiently for since I was a child. Even after my initiation at twenty, when I watched the life drain out of Marcello Angelo then tossed him in the river to join the rest of his friends, I knew this was the life for me. Killing had become an art for me, not a sport. I wasn't a total monster, but I made sure I kept up a certain level of finesse. Presenting a soul to the afterlife should be done for the right reason. That was why, when I killed, I made it count.

I strummed my fingers on the wooden arm and let my mind sink deeper into my thoughts. Tonight would be grand. I'd made sure of it, not just because of my new position, but because the world would know what was coming.

"Everything all right?" Sienna's soft touch drew me back, and I smiled lovingly down at the one woman I'd give up everything for.

"Actually, we should talk." I excused us and led her down toward the rows and rows of vineyards. We didn't have much time, so I dove right in.

"If we're going to make tonight count, we need to pull out all the stops."

"I agree."

"Good, because I'm going to come at this backwards, and I really hope you can see why."

"I'd say sex looks good on you, but damn, Si, you were only gone ten minutes," Wyatt joked as he matched his steps to ours as we walked toward the front of the house. "I'm all about a quickie, but—" He stopped talking when he caught my unamused expression.

"Vinni?" I called.

"They're here." He motioned for us to hurry. "There's six in total, not to mention the other two hundred who will line the property and check all IDs as they come and go."

A police officer turned and smiled as we approached the car, and it took me a half a second to recognize him.

"Officer Hector," I nodded, "nice to see you again."

"You as well, sir." He looked at Sienna. "You look lovely, Miss Sienna."

"Thank you." She didn't hesitate as she dipped low to disappear into the car. Wyatt hopped in the front seat with Vinni, earning him a chuckle from Sienna.

"Five cars will be with you at all times." Hector got right down to business. "Three are just like this one, and the two others are a different make but the same color. If anyone's following us, they'll have a hard time pinpointing which car is yours. You'll be the third car."

"Good. No stops until we get there. We'll be entering the party at the north gate. Only my family will be using that entrance. Understood?"

"Yes, sir."

"Vinni." I let him take over the rest of it while I got situated in the car.

"Anything looks out of the ordinary, we abort the plan and come right back here."

I closed the door and looked at Sienna, making sure she was up for this.

"Is that the same officer who helped us in the alleyway at the Sunflower Fields wine festival?"

"Yes." I shuddered at the memory of Sienna having to cut her arm as a decoy.

"How did he get in on this detail?"

"I'm not sure. Vinni set this up."

"Just seems kind of strange." She shrugged and went back to her conversation with Wyatt.

Once we left the protection of the iron gates, I went to high alert. I casually draped an arm over the back of the seat, pulling Sienna closer, and took a moment to inhale her sweet-smelling shampoo. I knew she didn't wear perfume, but she used other fragrant products that sent my body into overdrive.

"Where are we going, anyway?"

"Vincigliata Castle." I brushed her hair off her shoulder and kissed her warm skin. "The owner is a family friend, and they insisted we hold the celebration there."

"It must be nice to be so feared," Wyatt cooed from the front. "I have to sleep my way in, you know, to get into clubs."

"Yes, that's why you sleep around." Sienna rolled her eyes, making me smile. "I've never been there, but I hear it's beautiful."

"It is." I checked the time on my watch and knew we were getting close. "Are you sure you're up for this?"

"Are you underestimating me?" She cocked her head and threaded her fingers through mine. "I won't say I'm not nervous," she admitted, "but if we are going to do this, I agree this is the best way."

"Good." I kissed her hand. I constantly wanted to touch her. Maybe I was nervous, too. I motioned out the window. "Because we're here."

Vinni held the phone to his ear and waited a moment then hopped out, opening my door.

"All clear, boss."

"Wolves are never far away from their prey," I said in a low voice. "If you see anything…"

"If I see anything, you'll be the first to know."

I helped Sienna out and waited for Wyatt to join us. Officer Hector and his team escorted us over to the head soldier who would oversee everything at the castle for the event.

"Vinni, take Wyatt to the party and we'll join you shortly."

"Elio," Wyatt stepped in my way, "with all due respect, I'd rather stay with Sienna, if that's all right."

"You'll be leaving me alone, Elio, so I'd prefer Wyatt be with me." She reached for his arm, and I knew it was for the best.

"Fine, but you know what this moment means."

"I do, and I've remembered everything you've said."

I took her hand and led them both through the back corridors of the castle, up the winding staircase, and through another door that led to a maid's room.

"Right through there," I pointed to the door, "that's where we'll enter from."

"Okay."

I looked at the time again, hating to leave her alone at such a dangerous time. But if I was late, people would start wondering what was going on. We didn't need that tonight.

"Anything happens, call me."

"Of course." She leaned up and kissed me.

With one last glance, I headed out the door and over to the balcony that overlooked the party that was being held in the courtyard. The crowd below contained some of the most prestigious guests in all our land. Not to mention the top reporters, TV crews, and, of course, our close family and friends. I scanned the faces and listened to the buzz on theories of what was going to be announced tonight. We'd purposely kept the details vague about tonight's events. I knew that would draw even more hype and excitement to the evening. Everyone loved gossip, and tonight I fully expected to feed them all well.

"Elio." Niccola, who was stationed to keep out of the crowd tonight due to his injury, motioned for me to look at the far end of the courtyard.

There in the shadows, trying to blend in, was my nonna and Abramo. It was hard to blend in when you were one of the last remaining elders of a powerful syndicate.

Here we go.

I headed down the stairs and tried to be polite as I made my way through the sea of people. The whole time, I kept my eye on her. I had to smile as I thought about the last time I'd tried to keep my eye on a woman in a crowd. I ended up getting my life back.

"Nonna," I leaned in when I reached her and kissed her cheeks, "I'm very pleased you were able to make it."

"As was I. I won't lie, I'm very confused on what all the fuss is about."

"I'm here to make you proud."

A smile turned up the corners of her mouth like clockwork. The same smile that appeared during my youth when she was pleased with me because I'd behaved.

"You seem to be in a good mood."

"I am." I glanced at Abramo. "Thank you for bringing her home so quickly."

I knew Nonna loved it when I treated Abramo with respect. I knew respect was earned, and he never made any attempt to earn it. He thought he had some sort of authority within our family when, really, we only tolerated him. No one ever saw him as much more than Nonna's lapdog.

"Come," I put my arm through hers, "I have a surprise for you."

"For me?" She raised a curious eyebrow and looked back at Abramo, who quickly stepped in and followed us.

As we climbed the stairs, I caught sight of Vinni ahead of us. He dashed off the way I'd originally come in.

"The last time I was here, I think I was in my forties," Nonna prattled while I focused on moving her forward. "Things were different then, rules were always followed, and no one dared step out of line." I licked the inside of my mouth, trying not to snap at her. "I know you've been through a lot, Elio, with the loss of that manipulative woman, but you'll see it was all for the best. No one needs an enemy in the henhouse." She chuckled.

"Things have become much better, Nonna." I turned the handle to the door ahead of us and pushed it open.

Her gasp echoed along the stone walls as she took in Sienna. She sat up straight in her sexy green dress in a high-backed chair. Her legs were crossed, and her arms were draped over the armrests.

"What? Will you ever die?" she hissed and looked over at Abramo, but as he went to make a move, Vinni stepped into the room and shook his head.

"Not wise," he warned.

"I demand to know what is going on right now!"

"Nonna," I moved into the room and stood behind Sienna and rested a hand on her shoulder, "I'd like you to meet my fiancée."

Nonna's face fell and drained of color as she placed a hand on her chest.

"She's got the blood of a Coppola!" she snapped. "You dare mix our sacred bloodline with that filth!"

"Be careful what you say, Mrs. Greta." Sienna's voice was strong and crisp.

"Don't you dare speak to me in such an informal way! Who do you think you are?"

Sienna leaned forward, and I saw Vinni's smirk grow wide.

"Why, Mrs. Greta, didn't you hear? I've been appointed the new Coppola Donna."

If there was ever a moment in time that I'd wished I could have recorded to watch over and over, it would have been then. Nonna's head shot back like she had been slapped by Rosa Coppola herself. She reached out for the wall and let out a wail that could only be described as utter despair. Abramo wrapped his arms around her shoulders to help keep her upright.

"How could you do this to me, Elio? My own grandson betraying me for some long-legged Coppola witch!"

"You will not speak to my future wife like that," I boomed across the room, making her jump and yelp at the same time. "Times are changing, Nonna, and with that change will come happiness to all who join us." I moved around Sienna and tucked my hands in my pockets. "You can choose to be a part of this—"

"I would rather spit on the cross."

"Or I can drive you out to the middle of nowhere and leave you with a train ticket to Rome in your hand. We'll see how you fend for yourself."

The skin around her eyes tightened in shock at how I was speaking to her, and she saw I knew the truth of what she had done to Sienna.

"You're tossing away everything I've worked for." Her voice didn't match the glare of hate she directed toward Sienna. "All I taught you was for nothing."

"No, Nonna, the only difference is I'll now rule all of Italy, with the woman I love by my side." I reached back for Sienna's hand to have her stand next to me. "Vinni, escort Nonna and Abramo back to the party." I moved my attention back to Nonna. "Where both of you will embrace our marriage and swallow anything negative you feel toward our decision, because it *is* our decision." I kept my stare hard on her and dared her to step out of line. "Now, we have some news to share with everyone else."

I waited for Vinni to follow while Wyatt stood motionless in the hallway.

"Take a breath." I patted his shoulder. "It'll be okay."

He reached out and took her arm, stopping her.

"You…you're the Don of Coppola?"

"It's the Donna, but yes, I am." She smiled sympathetically at her best friend. "I promise you we'll have drinks later and I'll fill you in on everything."

"I better be in your wedding!"

"You got over that quick."

"I adapt to great changes." He laughed, shaking the nerves from his hands. "This is something else." He shook his head.

I walked Sienna to the edge of the balcony where she waited for my cue. I stood in front of a microphone and looked down at everyone. The castle was much too big for all to hear without a little help.

The music stopped, and the spotlight found me.

"Good evening, everyone." I waved, and the crowd give a little cheer. They were thirsty for the news. "I come tonight with big news. My father, Piero Capri, has appointed me the new Don of our family." The crowd erupted into a deafening cry of excitement. I gave them a moment then raised a hand to quiet them then looked over at Sienna as she ran her hands down her dress and lifted her chin. "Now for the fun part." I laughed, buying a moment to let them amp up again. "As most of you know, the Coppola syndicate has recently fallen on bad times. Their home has been destroyed, and three of their elders were shot and killed. Most must wonder what that will mean. I have a secret to share with all of you. Before Rosa Coppola disappeared into the wind, she appointed her estranged granddaughter to be the first ever Donna to rule a syndicate. And, my friends, that woman just so happens to be my fiancée." I held out my hand to Sienna, and she walked toward me and linked her fingers with mine.

The crowd grew quiet as they digested the incredible news, then to my shock, Sienna stepped up to the microphone.

"Good evening, everyone. I understand all of this must come as a shock to all of you, but I want you to understand something very important. I met the Capri family when I was a young girl. I was an orphan who was raised on their land and by their rules. Blood or not, my loyalty is with all of you. Elio and I will rule this land as one powerful empire. This has and will always be the Capri syndicate. Which means," she covered my hand with hers, "we'll be merging the syndicates under the Capri name. We will rule Italy together as one."

"I stand with both of you." Our local minister lifted his water glass and gave a respectful nod toward us. "To the new Don and Donna of Italy!"

That did the trick. The crowd went wild, but I held up my hand for one last announcement.

"I appreciate the loyalty, I truly do, but there is one more thing I'd like to address. It has come to my attention that there are some out there who think Sienna is also known as Mikey." I kept my story short. I knew whoever was watching the broadcast would know what I meant and would fill in the blanks. "I stand here before you and in front of God and say that she is not this person. To the business owners who have sent hit men to find Sienna, call off your dogs." I reached back and took the file from

Vinni, holding it high. I darkened my expression to drive my point home. "If you want to come after someone, you come after me." I paused as Sienna gasped. "But know this, when you do, I'll show you proof that the person responsible for the theft of your money is actually Rosa Coppola. She is the Mikey you're looking for." The shock and awe from the people below told me I'd been heard. Now, they just needed to get the word out.

"Now, my friends," I smiled widely, "we have a lot to celebrate!"

I pointed to the band, and the music started back up without hesitation. I looked down at Sienna and saw her free hand was shaking. I knew that speaking out the way she had took a lot of nerve. She was amazing.

"You just put yourself in the line of fire."

"Let them come at me." I stuck out my elbow, and she linked her arm with mine, and we made our way to the top of the grand staircase. The crowd turned and looked up at us. Their faces mirrored our own excitement and told me they were in awe of the whole situation. After all, we had not only announced that I was now Don of the Capri syndicate but told them that their powerful Don was now also engaged. Add all that to the shock of just exactly who my fiancée was, and it would just be sinking in as to what a powerful force we were going to be. I also congratulated myself on breaking the mold on mafia tradition. I had paved the road for our children to have the choice to marry because of their heart and not because someone told them they had to. If my parents had taught me anything about our world, I knew a syndicate run by a powerful couple would be a successful one.

The old original torches on the castle walls flickered warmly as I looked over the room below, and I leaned over to whisper to Sienna.

"Ready, my *bella*? Your country awaits you."

Her eyes sparkled as she took the energy I offered and gave me a nod. I was so proud of her; it constantly amazed me just how incredibly strong she was.

"Now I know how Laney Boggs felt," Wyatt cooed behind us, bringing an unladylike snort from Sienna. I brushed off his weird comment.

We took the stairs and slowly descended together with our heads held high.

Chapter

EIGHT

Sienna

Elio was amazing as he worked the room, shaking hands, smiling, and laughing. When women flocked toward him, he'd pull me forward and introduce me, then tell them something about me they could relate to. I fell in step with him and did my best to memorize faces with a smile and an interested word. One moment I'd be shaking hands with someone, and at the same time I'd be answering someone else's question. Faces blurred and names went in and out, but I kept up, not once showing my growing fatigue. When men gathered about me, Elio would pull me in a little closer as he continued to chat. I wondered if he even realized he was doing it. Everyone seemed kind and welcoming and full of congratulations.

Now and then, someone would pry a little too hard as they asked questions about my past, and Elio would step in and say that was for another time and change the subject. I was pleased, as I didn't want my past to be the topic for tomorrow's gossip. I wanted it to be about Elio and me and our future.

"I have to meet the woman who stole this guy right out from under me." A tall, blonde woman towered over me, and as she did, her gaze swung to Elio. He looked less than amused by our new guest. "Lara," she said as she stuck her hand out. All the while she kept her gaze on Elio.

"Lara," Elio pushed her hand away, so we didn't connect, "how is the family?"

"I'm not here to talk about my family."

"Well, then, how lucky are we?" He leaned over and kissed my head. "I would like you to meet my fiancée, Sienna."

Finally, she ripped her attention away from him and forced a gummy smile down at me.

"Elio's never spoken of you before, so you can understand why this would be such a surprise to me." She laughed falsely as her straight, fair hair shone in the light. She was very pretty; it was just a shame that her personality didn't match her exterior.

"For someone as attractive as you, Lara, you really don't wear jealously very well." Elio tried to hide his chuckle, but her glare told me she'd caught it. "I would like to get to know you," I smiled at her, "but perhaps right now isn't the time." I looked up at Elio. "Shall we?"

"You handled that well." He pulled my hand up to his lips.

"You're a heartbreaker, Elio. It's going to be my biggest challenge."

"Says the woman I can't keep my hands off of." His hand slipped down and cupped my butt and discretely caressed it. "Says the woman I can't stop kissing." His fingers lifted my chin, and he skimmed my lips with his. I instantly fell under his spell then blinked as people around us started to chuckle.

"We should keep moving."

"Not yet." He kissed me again, a little longer this time, and I didn't care if it was to set a precedent that we loved one another and wouldn't hide it or to draw the line with the women in the crowd to stay away. Either way, I was pleased and, despite those watching or perhaps because of them, I tossed my arms around his neck when he dipped me.

"You two certainly are making a statement." Piero came up behind Elio. "Would you join me in a dance, Sienna?" He offered me a hand, and I smiled and walked with him to the dance floor. He nodded at the band, and they began to play a smooth waltz.

I was pleased when Andrea pulled Francesco onto the floor to join us, so we weren't in the dance alone.

"I'm so proud of you tonight." Piero smiled down at me. "The way you handled yourself in front of everyone was impressive."

"Thank you." I stiffened in his arms, and he followed my gaze to Nonna Greta as she moved to the side of the dance floor. She looked like an angry cat on the prowl. "Piero?" I lowered my voice just as the song ended and the applause drowned me out.

"Not to worry about my mother, *caro*. I'll be speaking to her, and we have plenty of soldiers watching her, too." He kissed my hand. "Thank you for the dance." He gave me a slight bow and inclined his head. Then a waiter came over and offered me a glass of something bubbly. "Excuse me."

Piero whisked away, and I felt Elio at my side.

"Did you enjoy your dance?" The way he said it made me look up at him. "It's tradition for the new Don to dance with his mother, or in your case the Donna to dance with her soon to be father-in-law."

"Oh, I see." I drew the glass to my lips, thinking how sweet it was that they were bending tradition for me.

"I'll take that." Niccola snatched the glass from my fingers and dumped it in a plant. "Nonna thought you might be thirsty. She sent that over to you."

"Where is she?" Elio's sweet tone evaporated.

I placed a hand on his chest and made him look at me. "She wants a reaction, so don't give her one."

We spent the next hour visiting as many people as we could. Niccola and Vinni hovered, and Francesco seemed to always keep me in sight. At one point, I closed my eyes and turned to Elio. He instantly read me and knew I needed a moment of quiet.

"Wyatt," Elio called over my head, "would you let Niccola know we're going to slip out for a bit?"

"No, that's all right, Elio." I knew how important it was for him to stay and socialize. "Wyatt can take me. I won't be long."

"All right."

"Come on, little Donna." Wyatt grinned as he hooked my arm and handed me his water glass. I was more than pleased to have some water. I hadn't realized how parched I was.

"You were pretty amazing out there." He smiled. "This life suits you."

"You think?"

"Yeah, there was a time where you wore the same outfit to work for days and stole cherries from the bar top. Do you know how many people put their hands on those things?" He shuddered dramatically as we walked.

"When you're hungry, you're hungry."

"And now look, you're in a designer dress, heels, have fabulous hair, you're the queen of your land and are marrying Italy's most eligible bachelor. I mean, he's scary as hell, but sexy as sin."

"That, I'll agree with."

When we turned a corner, I spotted a familiar face. He was about to walk into a room off the hall but caught my eye.

"Hey, stranger." Tieri, otherwise known as Elio's Santoro brother, backed up and made a show of tucking his hands in his pockets as he strolled toward me. "That was a pretty impressive speech the two of you made."

"Thanks." I tried to smile. "Who are you here with?"

"Umm," he looked around and pointed at a young

woman in a blue dress with a fancy headpiece, "her."

"Pretty."

"Just a date, nothing more." His gaze came back to me, and I shifted as an uneasy feeling came over me. Tieri was one of those men who never stepped over the line but often flirted with it.

"Would you happen to know if any of these rooms are free?" Wyatt came to my rescue, and I squeezed his arm to let him know I was happy he'd stepped in.

"Yes, actually, this one's empty." He motioned for us to follow him to the room he'd been about to enter earlier. He opened the door then stepped back.

"Thanks." Wyatt waited for Tieri to leave and spoke quietly. "That man screams asshole and sleaze."

"That he does." We slipped into the room, and I took a deep breath for the first time all night.

"That was—"

"Intense," I interrupted him, "yeah." I leaned my butt against the windowsill and pressed my palms against my knees as I mulled over what we'd just done in front of our country.

"And you thought your gorgeous self on the *Fab Magazine* billboard was a lot of attention."

"Don't remind me."

"Tell me what's going through your head at this very moment."

"What if they hate me?" I gave him the truth because Wyatt was the only person I didn't have to prove anything to. "They love Elio—how could they not—but now I'm a woman with the blood of their enemy running through me, who has not only taken Elio off the market, but," I took a deep breath and continued, "I also come from the wrong side of the tracks. They won't be as accepting of me. To be truthful, if I was them, I'd feel the same way."

"You're right." He folded his arms and rested his shoulder against a pillar. "Even though you did a fabulous job tonight, you'll just have to show them who you really are."

"How?"

"Get out there, earn their trust. People are quick to judge what they don't know but are less likely to cast judgement if you let them see that you have a great heart in there." He tapped my chest.

"You think?"

"It worked for Princess Diana."

"We're not royalty."

"Maybe not in the normal sense of the word, but you are dark royalty." He chuckled. "Maybe you just need to off a few people in the street. All mafia-style like."

"Maybe." I laughed then covered my face, feeling overwhelmed.

"Look, you got this," his tone was more serious now, "because you have Elio, who will be with you every step of the way. He proved that downstairs when he made sure everyone knew who you were to him. He said something about you, showed you around with kindness and humor, and, let's be honest, you were born into this life."

"I'm scared." I hated to show weakness, but he would never use it against me.

"If you weren't, I'd be worried." He stood straight.

"Look, stay here, take a minute. I'm going to get us something to drink and maybe something to eat. It'll help."

"Thanks." I smiled, so incredibly thankful he was here tonight.

"Pasta? Wine? Or maybe just a heaping plate of carbs to get the blood pumping?"

"All of it." I laughed.

He granted me a sexy smile then headed out the door. I heard Wyatt tell Vinni I needed a minute alone and he was off to get food. I loved that my best friend knew just want I needed.

I turned and went to the window. The castle grounds were peppered with lights and torches. It really did look like something out of a fairytale. A woman stepped out onto the cobblestone path with a phone to her ear. I made sure the curtain hid me from her view. Something about her pulled at my memory.

"Where do I know you from?" I said through my fingers as I tapped my lips. Oh! It was the woman I'd seen during the fire at the Coppola house. We'd run into one another, and I remembered she was stealing things. She'd known my name. I'd almost forgotten about her. Why was she here? If she was in the Coppola house, she must have a connection with them, so how was she even allowed on Capri land, let alone at this party?

I didn't hear the door open, but I heard the floor creak. I didn't turn, thinking it would be Wyatt. I continued to watch the woman, studying her features.

"Green is a good look on you." I almost jumped out

of my skin at that voice. I turned and found myself face to face with Mariano.

"Shit!"

His once handsome face looked pale and gray. His cheeks were slightly sunken, and he looked like he'd lost about fifty pounds.

"Well, I guess congratulations are in order." He snickered, eyeing me up and down. "Funny how I was the one who brought you here to date me, but somehow you're now engaged to my partner."

"You knew who I was. I know that now," I snapped. I could feel my nerves creep into my throat like bile. "I was part of your sick plan from the very start."

"You were supposed to be mine."

"I was never yours." I shook my head, and at the same time I wondered when he'd last taken drugs.

"And now you're the Donna of the Coppolas." He slowly moved about the room then stopped to pretend to admire a few items on the table. "I heard Rosa left you with quite the gift." He peered over his shoulder at me. "A massive debt, a massive number of angry people, and a massive pile of rubble to clean up." His self-satisfied smile made me angry.

"Seems that way." I kept a good distance between us and eyed different things around the room that I could possibly use to hit him with if I needed to.

"Wait until Salvo hears about your engagement. He'll be so heartbroken." He let out a dark laugh. "I heard you two'd become close."

"We were friends, that's it."

"I thought you and Elio were friends too."

I cut my eyes at him, not wanting to his play games. This night had been a challenge in itself, and I didn't need this as well. As we talked, I slowly slid my hand into the purse that hung from my shoulder. I could feel it cold against my fingers.

"What are you doing here, Mariano?" I distracted him with a wave of my opposite hand. "You showed your true colors when you tossed me into Rosa's car, just like I showed you mine when I kicked your teeth out." I was still proud of that, even more so when I sent them to Piero. I'd been waiting for the right moment to tell him who they belonged to. "Unless you want to go down that path again, I suggest you—" He suddenly lunged forward and wrapped his hands around my neck and pressed me flat up against the stone wall.

"I'm here to show Elio that I'm untouchable." His breath smelled of brandy as he squeezed my vocal cords. It wasn't too painful, but it was enough to show me I couldn't get away. "I want him to know I now have connections and can slip by anyone, at any time. Not everyone is loyal to the almighty Elio Capri." He spat to the side, clearly disgusted with Elio. "I found you once, and I can find you again, protection or not." His face twitched. "You know," he sniffed and blinked rapidly, "the best part of this whole thing? You have no idea who *he* really is. But I do, and when you find out, that will be what will bring down the Capri syndicate."

I suddenly snapped my wrist under his arm and sliced down the side of his ribcage. It wasn't where I was aiming, but it did the trick.

His eyes went wide as he registered the pain and leapt back as he felt around then looked at the blood on his fingers.

"You bitch! You're never really alone, Sienna. Remember that." Mariano laughed like the crazy person he was. "Not even close." He shoved me to the floor then bolted for the window.

"Vinni!" I screamed as loudly as I could as I raced to look out the window. I saw him disappear into the shadows, instantly regretting not choosing an upstairs room.

Boom! The door flew open, and Vinni had his gun drawn as he came running in. I heard a crash and saw a plate of spaghetti hit the floor as Wyatt ran in.

"Mariano was here." I pointed to the window, and Vinni quickly made a call.

"Did he hurt you?" Wyatt had me by the arms as I shook my head.

"He just…" I took a deep breath, trying to settle myself. "I'm fine. He had me by the throat, but I'm okay."

"What happened?" Elio raced into the room and pulled me into his chest.

"I'm okay. Mariano was here and was saying all kinds of things. I cut him, though," I held up my little blade, "straight down his side."

"Vinni," Elio ordered, and Vinni was already out the window and retracing Mariano's steps. "Come on. We're leaving. You can tell me everything in the car."

"No." I stepped away from him.

"No?" His brows drew together. "It wasn't a question, Sienna."

"I know it wasn't, but tonight was about announcing the joining of our two syndicates. Leaving right now won't look good, and I won't let Mariano win. He banked on scaring me, and though he did, I'm not physically hurt. I say we go back out there and work the crowd as a team."

"I don't like that idea."

"Okay." I shrugged, not caring that he didn't like my pushback. "You don't have to like it, Elio, but you know I'm right. If we back down every time someone comes at me, what would that show the people? That I really am your weakness."

He closed his eyes and let out a curse while Wyatt tried to conceal his shit-eating grin.

"You never leave my sight. Do you understand me?"

"I wasn't planning on it."

"I'm serious, Sienna. I don't know how he got in here, but he just pushed my last button. I won't be held accountable for my actions if something else happens here tonight."

"Understood." I reached for his hand. He looked down at me, and I saw conflicting emotions run across his face. Then, after a moment, his eyes softened, and he nodded.

"Before you go, drink this." Wyatt handed me the glass of red wine he'd managed to save. "I'm afraid your dinner needs replacing." He chuckled as we all looked at the mess on the floor.

"Thanks, Wyatt." I kissed him and brushed at a small red wine stain on his jacket. I took a few steadying sips then put the glass on a side table. "All right, I'm ready." I smiled and took Elio's arm.

We went back to the party, and I tried to hide my growing anxiety as I scanned the faces to see if Mariano was in the crowd. With my subconscious so preoccupied, it proved to be more difficult to engage with people this time around, but I was determined not to let Mariano's sudden reappearance ruin my night.

"Drink?" Elio asked.

"Water, please." I gave him a reassuring smile that I was fine, then I reached out when I saw Tieri's date for the evening looking rather lost.

"Hey, are you looking for Tieri?" I asked her.

"Who?" She looked at me, confused, then glanced around the room.

"Tieri," I repeated, unsure if she heard me correctly, as the first time as the music was so loud. "Your date who brought you here."

"I came with Edwardo. I'm sorry, but I'm not sure who Tieri is."

I stood there staring at her, knowing she was the same woman Tieri had pointed out. At least I thought she was. It was the same dress and fancy headpiece.

"My mistake." I forced a smile and shook my head.

"What was that about?" Elio handed me a tall glass.

"Nothing, I guess."

On the way home, I filled Elio in on what Mariano had said, and by his silence, I could tell he was attempting to process everything. He held the door for me as we arrived at the house.

"Can I get you anything?" He tossed his keys in the silver bowl then used his thumb to unlock a hidden gun compartment.

"No, I think I just want to get out of this dress and have a shower."

"I need to make some calls. Why don't you join me when you're finished?"

"Sure." I wrapped my arms around his neck and drew his mouth to mine. "Look at us," I sighed with a smile, "under the same roof, together, just like the old days."

"A little more complicated, but we made it." He seemed to let go of the Mariano thing for the moment. He picked me up, swooshed my dress aside at the slit, and hiked my leg up on his hip.

My head flopped back as he kissed along my collarbone. His other hand gently palmed my breast. His phone vibrated in his pocket, and I groaned at the sudden intrusion.

"Don't answer it," I huffed.

"Shit." He looked at the screen and closed his eyes.

"It's okay," I almost moaned. "Let me shower, and I'll come find you later."

I couldn't stop thinking about what Mariano had said as the water flowed over me. When he said *he*, did he mean Elio or someone else? Suddenly, my head couldn't take the thoughts anymore, so I stepped out of the shower and changed into a bra, panties, and a simple dress. I never knew if the guys would stop by, so I made sure I looked respectable.

It didn't take long for Elio's tone to draw me down from the bedroom.

"You're my eyes right now. Tell me everything you see," Elio commanded as he stared out the living room window, with whoever it was on speaker phone. He listened as the voice prattled off what was apparently happening at the warehouse.

"A couple guys came to the dockyard looking for you. They were sent away but somehow found their way here to the warehouse. Now they're trying to get past the guards at the gate, and there's more of them coming around the back. Any idea who they are?"

"Yes. I think I might." Elio tucked a hand in his pocket and leaned against the window. "What's happening now?"

"They seem upset that they can't get in. One is calling your name and saying something."

"What's he saying?"

"Hang on." We could hear him move about. "He's saying, 'I know you're in there. Give us the girl, and the hunt stops now.'"

Oh, boy…

Elio stood and ran a frustrated hand through his hair while he thought.

"What do you want us to do, boss?"

I watched as he headed to the bar and poured himself

a stiff drink of rum. With a quick flick of the wrist, he downed the amber liquid and tapped his finger while his gaze shifted back and forth. Power and anger poured off him, and I found my body jolting alive.

"Find out who their employers are and start sending bits and pieces of them back with a message that Sienna is not who they should be looking for, it's Rosa Coppola. I'll email you the proof."

"What is—" He stopped himself and went quiet, realizing he was questioning Elio.

"Be sure to include one of my cards, so they know exactly who they're dealing with."

"Yes, boss."

"I want to hear their screams from here."

"Understood."

"One more thing. If anyone else comes, you deal with them the same way. I'm the Don now, and I'm setting the precedent here and now that I won't tolerate anyone coming for my fiancée."

I found myself grinning at Elio. The dark corners of his mind were both sexy and empowering.

He tossed his phone on the bar and leaned into his hands as they pressed against the smooth granite top. He must have felt my presence, so he turned to look right at me. He lifted an eyebrow as he caught my expression.

"What?"

"Just you," I shrugged, my smile spread wide across my lips, "and all this." I waved my hand in front of him. "Elio Capri, the big bad wolf, finally showed me some teeth today."

"Teeth, huh?" He stood, and his eyes darkened, making me feel the heat between my legs. "Why don't you come over here and let me show you what these teeth can do."

I bit down on my lip, gave him a 'come get me' sexy look, and ran out of the room.

Chapter
NINE

Elio

"You think you can run from me, *bella*?" I chuckled. I needed her body as a distraction from everything that was going on. I moved swiftly through the rooms as I removed my suit jacket and unbuttoned my shirt. "You know wolves are excellent hunters."

Suddenly, a lace bra fell from above and landed on my shoulder.

"Mm, I don't know, Elio." She leaned over the railing. "You're still down there, and I'm all the way up here."

Reaching up, I hoisted my body over the rail and dropped to the landing. She laughed from one flight above me.

"Is this how you hunt your prey?" She dragged the zipper of her dress back up a bit to stop between her bare breasts.

I pressed hard against the floor and leapt forward to land a stair below her. As I went to scoop her up, she ducked under my arm and raced back down the stairs and through a door that led to the basement.

With a smirk, I followed her, knowing she'd made her first mistake. She'd never been down there before and would never find the light.

"Where the hell am I?" she huffed to herself as I came up behind her. Her hands were out, feeling her way around, and I followed close behind her. "I know you're here." She half-laughed. "I can feel you."

"I assure you I am," I teased, and she whirled around and tried to find me.

"This isn't fair. I don't know where the light switch is."

"You want to talk about what's fair?" I slid my hands around her waist, making her jump. I pursed my lips and blew my cool breath over her shoulder then nipped at her skin as she shivered. "You're always wearing all these sexy dresses," my hand ran up her belly and then tugged down the zipper to pull the fabric away from her body, "making me want you every minute of every day."

"You don't think I feel the same way about your suits?" She ground her lacy thong into my painful erection. "Or the way people are scared of you?" She arched her back as I slid between her legs, nearly moaning at her heat.

"You like people being scared of me?"

"Mmhmm." Her head dropped back against my chest. "It makes me feel safe. Like no one can get through you."

I closed my eyes and relished that I could still make her feel safe. I promised when she returned that I would do everything in my power to make things right. This was progress.

"Tell me something else."

"I love your fingers," she shamelessly pressed against my hand, and I rubbed one of my knuckles gently over her greedy bud, "and when you do that." She dragged out the last word.

"Come here." I lifted her hips and helped her duck under the ropes.

"Am I in a boxing ring?" Her head moved around, trying to make sense of the pitch-black room.

"Mmhumm." I removed my shirt and gave a command for a tiny strip of light to flicker on below the ring.

"Wow," she blinked until her eyes adjusted, "this is amazing."

My gaze slowly slid down her bare back, sexy bottom, and sexy-as-hell heels. Backing her up to the corner, I watched her take in the basement. It was the one place I could go to work out my frustrations that was all mine. "Is that where you sit when you rest after a match?" She pointed to the stool behind me.

"It is."

"Just you? No one else?"

"Just me."

"Well, then." She pushed my hands away when she came near and undid my belt to slip my erection free. It pretty much had a heartbeat to itself at that point. "Sit," she ordered, and I obeyed more out of curiosity. She lowered to her knees and brushed her hair to one side. "Every time you sit here, no matter what's going on in your head, think of me between your legs sucking you into my mouth." With a sly grin, she leaned down and drew me in with her lips. I reached out and held on to the ropes as she took me to the root. I hit the back of her throat and nearly cried out when she started to hum.

"Yes, just like that," I moaned.

She flattened her tongue as she bobbed up and down, fast then slow, hard then soft. On each downward motion, her hands slid over my thighs and up my stomach.

Her hair fell from her shoulder, so I reached down and gathered it up in one hand and admired how damn sexy she was. They way her throat contracted, those pretty pink lips, and her hungry eyes as they lifted to meet my own. Her lips made a slurping sound, and I let out a primal moan from somewhere deep inside. She was perfect in every way. For her to do this for me, especially here, in the one place that was totally mine, the one place where I could find peace, was unbelievable.

I reached forward with my free hand and dragged my thumb from the top of her bottom up along her spine to her neck. Her groan nearly had me lose it right there.

"Deeper." I gently pushed her head into me, and I shuddered as she increased her force. I felt the buildup deep in my stomach, and as much as I wanted her mouth on me all night long, I needed to be in her.

"*Bella*, stand and turn around." She did and wiggled out of her thong as I backed her up and guided her down on top of my slick erection. She let gravity do the work and slid all the way down until she was flush with me. Moving her hips, I pressed into her, getting as deep as possible, and all the while, she moaned, rubbing her breasts between her hands.

"You're so fucking sexy." I ran a finger down her spine, massaging her lower back. I couldn't help but think how perfect it was that I was deep inside the enemy, deep inside the woman I'd loved my entire life, and we were about to make history and change the way Italy was run. I was never one for an audience, but I would pay good money to have Salvo witness what we were about to do.

Sienna lifted, and I shot upward, plowing hard from below. I pumped with everything I had while I directed the angle. She could do nothing but hold on. Her screams fueled my adrenaline, and my vison started to cloud. I needed more. I started to lose control. I could taste our sex in the air, and it was driving me mad. I let out a roar, giving into my desire.

"I need more!" I felt caged and desperate.

I bent her over, careful not to slip out, as I took her from behind on all fours. Her body shook and fought to stay with me. I held myself up on one hand while the other hand roamed between her legs, over her stomach, and then on to her breasts. My fingers slid around her neck. I squeezed lightly and gave in to the almost animalistic urge to take her like a savage. She didn't fight me, just let me have my way because we had trust. I'd never hurt her.

"I can't," she started to say but moaned instead. I knew the feeling. It was incredibly intense and overwhelming, but I was so close to the finish line, and by the way her stomach flexed, I knew she was, too.

"Ahh!" She bucked as she came. The vibrations trembled through my hand, and I shot off after her, pumping her with as much of me as possible. Sliding from her neck to her shoulder, I held on tight and pushed her body into mine while I did the same, resisting the urge to bite her shoulder. Heat burst through me, sweat broke out across my shoulders, and my muscles screamed as if I'd just had a shot of ecstasy. Slowly, she went limp, unable to hold herself up. I fought to catch my breath and couldn't remember the last time sex was that good. That was the thing with Sienna. Everything just kept getting better, intensifying my addiction to her body. If she wasn't nearly out cold, I'd flip her over and do it all over again.

I pulled her limp body off the floor onto mine as I flopped down, resting her on my chest.

"I think I just left this world and came back." She chuckled with an exhausted sigh. "We have pretty amazing sex."

"Agreed." I kissed her head as the nerves in my body still buzzed.

"If I'm not pregnant by that, I'm not sure what it'll take." She laughed but stilled when she felt my erection come back to life. "Seriously? I may not be able to walk anymore."

I wanted a lot of children, that was no secret, and I was more than willing to perfect the art of making children by whatever means necessary. "I guess you'll be at my mercy, then."

"Mm." She cuddled up closer. "It felt like we'd been apart for a decade when I was in Rome." Her hand rubbed over my shoulder. "I missed hearing your heartbeat."

"You're the only reason it beats."

She lifted her head and kissed over my heart.

I woke to my cell phone as it buzzed against the chair in my coat pocket. I rolled away from Sienna, who was sound asleep nuzzled into my side. I had carried her to bed last night and ravished her one last time before we both fell asleep like the dead. I was determined to be inside her as many times as I could. We had a lot of lost time to make up for.

"Were you asleep?" I could hear the smile in Vinni's voice.

"I was, yes, and I'd still like to be."

"Long night," he teased.

"Something like that." I yawned and glanced at the clock, only to find it was nearly 11a.m. I couldn't remember the last time I'd slept that late.

"Well, we're here, and all that's missing is you."

"Give me fifteen and tell Mama I'm on the way." I

hung up and crawled back in bed with Sienna, kissing her shoulder, neck, and cheek until she slowly woke.

"Good morning." She didn't open her eyes, just smiled as I cupped her breast.

"I have to be up at the Hill House for a meeting. Would you like to come? Or would you be all right here?"

"Not moving. Yes, I can promise you, I'll be just fine."

"Are you sure? It's kind of important, or I'd stay."

"Mmm." She was too tired to listen and just lay there looking perfect between the soft gray sheets.

"Is it wrong that I want you even more now?" I ran my hand down her stomach and enjoyed her nakedness. She flopped her legs open, and I groaned, feeling my erection stand to attention, begging me for another round. I knew once I got inside her, I would never make it to the house. Instead, I bent and swiped my tongue between her folds, and she granted me a moan that I would carry for the rest of the day.

"Join us if you want, but tonight you're mine again." I kissed the inside of her thigh then peeled myself away. I watched her roll into my pillow and pull it into her arms with a happy sigh.

I loved that woman.

With a painful grunt, I rushed to the shower, changed, and headed to the Hill House.

Once I stepped through the door, Mama appeared out of thin air.

"I'd ask how your night was…" She fussed with my tie, which we both knew didn't need to be straightened.

She was buying a moment alone with me. "But since you're late, it tells me it went well?" She lifted a hopeful eyebrow, and I leaned down and kissed her cheek.

"Better than well."

"Good." She stepped back. "Will she be joining you?"

"She's worn out, but it's all right. She'll join us for dinner later."

"Well, I've never known you to be late for an important meeting. You should get moving." She gave me a little shove, and her smile gave away how much she wanted all of this for me.

I hurried down the hallway and into the living room where everyone was gathered.

"My apologies for being late." I glared at my cousins, who were both grinning like fools. "Let's figure out this Mariano problem and then dive into the rest of the mess."

The meeting ran longer than I hoped, which normally wouldn't faze me, but knowing that Sienna was in our bed, naked, made it hard to concentrate.

"Mama, are you good to make your move when I give you the green light?"

"Yes." She nodded at me from her seat next to Papa. "I've been worried that people are starting to wonder where they went."

"I know. I guess there might be a few who would find the DeSimones 'missable.' Who? I have no idea," I muttered, thinking how much better our world was now they were gone. I fingered the edge of my tablet while

I tried to keep my face neutral with my next statement. "Vinni, I'd like you to spend a little more time at your house, keep an eye on what Nonna is up to."

"Sure thing." He nodded. I watched and waited to see if he was going to bring up anything that might allude to where his mother was. "Anything else?"

"Niccola," I moved on to him, "has Trigger settled in?"

"Trigger's here?" Vinni's face dropped. "When was I going to be told that?"

"You just were."

"You crooked ass hair." Vinni glared at his brother. "And you were sending me down there this weekend." Niccola smirked at me, and Papa started to laugh.

"Yes," Niccola answered me, "he and Tess got in last night and have everything they need."

"Good. Make sure it stays that way."

"Understood."

"Francesco," I turned to him, "get Ugo and Oscar to start questioning the Coppola staff. See if they can give you a starting point to finding out where Rosa could have run to. If they comply, offer them work here. They either work for us, or they're out on the street."

"Of course." Francesco smiled. Did I see pride there? Then he left with Niccola and Vinni, and Mama headed to her office to get things set for her part of the plan.

"Pretty impressive for your first official meeting as the Don." Papa sounded pleased.

"I was late." I sighed as I cleaned up my belongings

so the staff could clear the table.

"I think we can all agree that it was perfectly understandable." He smiled.

I checked the time and headed back down to my place, wondering if Sienna was still in bed.

Chapter TEN

Sienna

I was stuck in a sex trance. There was no other word for it. My brain was in a constantly delicious loop of pleasure. Many times, I tried to pull myself out of it but was unsuccessful, so I gave in and let my mind wander back to last night. My thighs flexed as blood heated my chest and neck. Visions of Elio's hands around me, the noises he made, and…

My phone broke the moment, and I glared, frustrated at the hunk of technology that buzzed at me.

I didn't recognize the number, but something told me to answer anyway.

"Hello?" I stood and made my way over to the window to look at the view from our bedroom.

"I wasn't sure if I should call, but I had to know if you were all right."

The air got caught in my throat as I registered the voice.

"Salvo?"

"Sorry it took me so long to call. Things haven't been the easiest since…well, it's been hard."

"What happened to you? Where did you end up going?" I tried not to push, but he'd just disappeared into thin air.

"Rosa gave me strict instructions before I arrived at the church that if anything was to happen to get you out of there then meet her in the next town."

"Is that where she is now?"

"She never showed. I gave it as long as I could. Later, someone called telling me to leave town and wait for further instructions. Those never came either."

"Where are you now?"

"Staying at a friend's house right now, but who knows where tomorrow."

"I'm sorry." I wasn't, really. I wasn't sure if I could trust Salvo or not, but he might be the key to finding out where Rosa was.

"If it's not too forward to say, I've missed you." He went quiet, and so did I.

I tapped the window as I thought of what I should do next. I wasn't about to lead him on, but I knew I might need him. Especially any information he might have. "Have you seen the news?"

"I have, so I guess I should say congratulations on

your engagement."

"Thanks," I said quietly, not wanting to sound too cheery.

"I should have known you were playing us."

"I wasn't playing you." That wasn't a total lie. "I wanted to know my family and where I came from. The fact that you and I met, well, let's just say I don't regret our time together."

"Mm, and I won't lie and say it wasn't disappointing to hear. Elio is a lucky man."

"I'm lucky, too." I waited for him to say something. "What will you do now?"

"Well, that's reason number two why I called you. I'd been groomed to be the eyes and ears of Rome for the Coppolas, and now that position is gone. Though you have no reason to trust me, I wanted to see if you'd be willing to take me on?" He waited a beat. "You know, to let me come work for you, under the Capri rule."

What?

"I get this might come as a shock, but I'm wasting my talent here and thought if you can't beat the enemy, join the enemy." I went silent. "I have no one left, Sienna, but I do have a head full of knowledge on the Coppolas that might help you out."

"I'll need to think about this." He was right. I had no reason to trust him, and I certainly didn't, but I needed time.

"I missed you," he sighed. "Let me try that again. What I should say is you were different than any woman I'd been with. You're more real and down to Earth. It was refreshing, and I just miss your company in general."

I wished I knew how I should play it out. Did I turn him down flat, or should I play him along?

"I really enjoyed your company too. I was thankful you were there for me to talk to." A reflection in the window had me whirling around to find Elio looking mad as hell.

I held up a finger to tell him one moment and to stay quiet, but he didn't like it. I shook my head and pleaded with him to just give me a moment.

"Well," Salvo misunderstood my silence and cleared his throat, "think it over, and I'll be in touch."

"I will. Talk to you soon."

"Bye, Sienna."

"Bye." I hung up, and Elio crossed his arms and raised an eyebrow at me.

"Oh, yeah," I laughed at him, "you think I'd be cheating on you after last night?"

"I know you're not cheating, *bella.*" He followed me out of the room and down the stairs and into the kitchen. "But I know what you do to men. So, who was that?"

"Oh? Please enlighten me. What do I do to men?"

"Hey," he trapped me at the counter with both hands on my waist and pushed his erection into my back, "this."

"Says the man who is in love with me."

"Mmm," he kissed the side of my head and moved his arms around for a hug, "so in love."

"Well, in that case, it was Salvo." One moment his front was to my back, and the next I was spun around to face him.

"Salvo called you?"

"Yes." I popped a grape in my mouth. "He wants to come work for us." He laughed like I was crazy. "I don't trust him either," I swallowed the juicy pulp, "but if he's desperate for work, maybe we can pull some helpful information out of him. Maybe we can find Rosa?"

"You'll need to come at that very carefully."

"Teach me, and I'll do it."

He smiled, and I knew he was impressed with my answer. "I'll tell you on the way to Beach House. Papa has a meeting there and we should fill him in on Salvo."

"So, you're basically telling me to be Tieri?" I grinned at him then closed the door and followed him to the front stairs of the Beach House. "Flirt, but not enough that anyone could call you out on it."

"I'm going to pretend you didn't just say that." He gave my butt a swat. "We have enough people on our kill list right now, and I don't want to add another."

"Speaking of which," he opened the door and urged me to go in first, "doesn't it seem strange that—" I stopped short when I came face to face with a man who looked just like Piero.

"Ah, Sienna," Piero smiled warmly, "you've never actually met Vinni and Niccola's dad before, have you? Bosco, this is Sienna."

"No, I've heard of you, though." I stepped forward to shake his hand. "To be honest, I thought you were dead," I joked, wondering where in the world this man had been. Bosco laughed heartily along with the others. Clearly, they got that reaction a lot.

"That would be because I don't live here full time. I only visit when duty calls. Truth be told, I stepped away years ago to follow my heart."

"Papa lives with Amara on the other side of town," Niccola explained as he tucked his phone away. "Our unofficial stepmother."

I tried not to look confused. I had no idea Bosco lived with his mistress. I guessed that would explain Noemi's bitterness whenever she talked to me about Bosco.

"Vinni," Bosco handed him a box, "Amara made these this morning. She thought you'd like some."

Vinni snatched it up and peeked inside. "She's really too good for you, Papa."

"She is, but don't tell her that."

Again, I tried to mask my expression. So, they were all okay with this arrangement? Honestly, I couldn't imagine living with Noemi, but why did she live in the family home while he lived elsewhere? Or was that by choice? Maybe Nonna Greta didn't approve. A cold chill ran up my back when I thought of that old lady. She sucked my breath away like a dementor from the *Harry Potter* books.

"Does Mama know you're here?" Vinni asked.

"Does Mama know who is here?" Noemi walked right by me, and I felt my knees go stiff. "Oh, you're home." She shrugged as her eyes slid quickly past me to Bosco.

Elio reached forward and slowly pulled me close. I wasn't sure if he was protecting me or if he was afraid I was going to attack her. Truth be told, I wasn't sure either.

Breathe, Sienna.

"There are some things Bosco and I need to discuss." Piero spoked kindly, but his voice lacked warmth. I wondered if Elio had told him the truth about her yet.

"And when are you leaving?" She flipped through the mail on the table.

"When I'm ready." Bosco's comment made my lips twitch, so I pressed them together before anyone saw it.

Noemi glanced in my direction and shot me a smile. "Sienna." She turned her attention on me, and all I could think of was the candle in her hand and the smell of the fuel that had soaked my bedroom at the Coppola house. "I was just going to saddle up the horses. Would you like to go for a ride with me? I'd love the company."

"No." I shook my head, trying to remain calm when all I wanted to do was jam the letter opener on the desk through her heart. "Not today." I needed to keep my head. After all, she was Niccola and Vinni's mother. I just wasn't sure how to negotiate my thoughts about what would happen once she was exposed for what she was.

"We have to prepare for the tour." Elio came to my rescue, and although I had no idea what he was referring to by a tour, I appreciated it. I knew he had to be having the same difficulty as I was, knowing what we knew.

I glanced over at Niccola, who watched me with a

strange expression. I peeled my gaze from his and turned it back on the woman who had tried to kill me. I decided two could play at this game.

"Yes, and Mama left me a ton of paperbacks she'd kept from her days in hiding. I want to comb through it all. She kept lots of journals too. I guess we had that in common, she and I." Though her smile remained, her eyes gave her away. *Yes, you two-timing psychopath, I can play games, too.*

"Papa," Elio spoke up, "we have something we need to discuss with you and the others."

"All right, let's get to it, then." He led the way.

I gave Noemi a smile as we headed into the other room to share what we had planned for Salvo. I couldn't help but wonder if she was sweating about what we wanted to talk about. She must have known I'd tell Elio. It was going to be interesting to see how all this would play out, though my heart ached for her sons.

Chapter
ELEVEN

Noemi

The moment the door shut, I sagged into the chair, letting go of the breath I was holding. I had no idea any of them would be here, let alone Bosco.

My legs shook, and I had to sit down. I cursed myself for not being able to hold it together. I'd been living this lie for years, but with everything that was happening, I could feel the cracks starting to form. All because of her. The offspring of the woman I'd loathed for years. How was it she was being welcomed back into the family circle? Where was Greta, and why hadn't she had her kicked off the land again? What the hell was happening? My memory was still scarred from the last time I'd been this unnerved.

I knew I wasn't welcomed by Bosco's mama. She made that very clear the day her son announced me to the family and told them I was carrying his child, but they didn't have much time to digest it, as it was only a few days later I gave birth to our son.

I held our little boy in my arms and gently stroked his forehead as he stared up at me. He was gorgeous for only being a few hours old. His dark eyes and long lashes would make the women swoon one day. I was exhausted after fourteen hours of labor and wished I could get into a shower, but there was no way I could move.

"Knock knock." Andrea's more than annoying voice was like a cheese grater on my last nerve. "There are a lot of people out here who would love to meet this little man."

"Sure," I hate you, *"come in."*

That was the problem with giving birth at the family home. There wasn't any damn crowd control. It was a free for all, they could all come and go whenever they wanted. Was it too much to ask for a little quiet and some damn sleep?

"May I?" Andrea waited for permission with her arms outstretched. I swallowed back the comment on the end of my tongue and handed him to her. I felt like I was handing him over to the enemy. I was barely tolerated; would he even be accepted? "Hello there, little one." She looked at Bosco with tears in her eyes. "He's beautiful, Bosco, just perfect." She sniffed, and I relaxed a fraction of a hair. "Elio, come meet your cousin, Niccola."

Piero lifted Elio up to see him better.

"Baby." Elio pointed at my son, and everyone nodded like he'd just solved the world's hardest math problem. I had to roll my eyes, but I was glad they didn't seem to reject my son. If only I'd gotten pregnant sooner, this situation would have been so different. Niccola would have been first born then, and his role would have been much better. I knew he'd never be the Don, as that was Piero's role, but Niccola would have been older and wiser than little King Elio. "My baby?" the little king asked.

"No, Uncle Bosco and Aunt Noemi's baby," Piero corrected him, and Elio looked at me with a smile then wiggled out of his father's arms and ran toward Francesco, who was, as usual, watching quietly from the back of the room. He did that a lot, and it creeped me out.

"Welcome to the family," Greta said as she popped out of nowhere along with that slimy Abramo. She handed something to Bosco and kissed his cheeks.

"Thanks, Mama."

"I will move in and help raise him," she announced, and I felt like the world just turned black. I stared at Bosco to try to burn my thoughts into his head, but he just nodded at her once and didn't have the balls to say, 'Hell no. Are you kidding me? No, no way is she going to move in with us. I forbid it.' "I have everything prepped. We'll start renovations tomorrow." Greta smiled.

"Mrs. Greta," I cleared my throat, "that's very kind of you, but are you sure you want to live in the same house as a newborn? I mean, they cry and keep you up at night, and..."

She glared at me along with the rest of them. You'd think I'd just cursed the Pope or something.

"Would I have offered if I thought I couldn't handle it?"

You didn't offer, you announced.

"I suppose not," I gritted through my teeth, and Bosco shot me a warning to shut up.

"Tomorrow, nine a.m.," she tossed over her shoulder and left the room.

Great, all I needed was Elenora to show up, and my hell would be complete.

My heart lodged in my throat as I pulled myself back to the present. I heard Sienna's voice grow louder. They must be finished. How long had I sat there? I leapt to my feet, grabbed my purse, and ran to my car. I decided I'd go back to the city where I could blend in and breathe.

As I sat outside, at my favorite table at Bagni Lido, the soothing ocean sounds calmed my wild thoughts. I ordered a seafood platter and sipped a glass of prosecco. I began to feel a strange pull and looked about. It felt as if someone was watching me. I slipped on a pair of sunglasses and let my gaze go over the few faces that were around me. I didn't recognize anyone, but a chill went over me as a shadow was thrown across the table from behind me. The sound of his polyester pants told me who it was before I even looked at his face.

"We need to talk." He sat across from me, and I glared at him.

"You might as well wrap yourself in reflective tape and blow a whistle to announce you're here, Hector."

"I think it's time." He dismissed my tone.

"It's not."

"Why?"

"Because even looking at your face upsets me."

"This face?" He removed his sunglasses, and I looked away, unable to control my anger. "I never asked for this."

"Neither did I," I snickered, "yet here we are."

"I've gotten so close, and I'm now on their tour. I've won their trust, and I want to finish what I started."

"A moot point now."

"Don't." His fist hit the table, and my fork clattered off my plate. "Don't say that."

"Look," I lowered my voice when a few people looked over, "give me a little more time to figure out how to handle my situation, and once I have that smoothed out, I'll let you know, then you can do whatever you want."

"How long?"

"A month."

"No."

I removed my sunglasses and tried to control my temper. I needed him to go away. He was going to ruin everything. I glared up at him and tried to keep my voice even.

"You need them to meet you at the Villa del Cardinale, correct?" I waited for him to acknowledge he was listening to me. His face was set like stone. "I can make that happen. You name the time and place, and I'll make sure they are there, alone."

"How can I trust you?"

"I let your mama live, didn't I?"

He licked his lips, and I knew I was in danger of pushing him to the edge, but it was true. I didn't kill his mother. I could have, and no one would ever have known.

"One month." He pushed the table as he got up then left in a hurry. I motioned for the waiter to fill my water glass and slowly counted to ten, doing my best to relax, and it worked until I spotted Greta watching me from inside the restaurant.

Chapter
TWELVE

Elio

I tugged at my dress shirt underneath my Alexander Amosu Vanquish suit. I hadn't worn this one yet. I'd been saving it for an evening like tonight. I admired the incredibly soft vicuna fleece, diamond inlay, and the nine-karat gold buttons that sat in a row on the sleeve and front. Using my thumb, I carefully lifted out two of the more elegant weapons from my gun box. After all, an elegant outfit needed to be paired with the correct accessories.

A flash of gold had my gaze focusing on Sienna who stepped into my view in the mirror. A sexy smile grew across her lips as she took me in. I did the same, admiring the gold Dolce and Gabbana gown that hugged her shape and showed off her perfect breasts.

"I'm not complaining about any of this," she twirled, enjoying the beautiful dress, "but now will you tell me where we're going?"

"I could." I turned around and took in her beauty. My heart skipped to a different rhythm whenever she was near, and tonight was no different. "But where would the fun be in you knowing?"

"That's cruel."

"No, my *bella*." I came closer and touched the thin chain that held my crow pendant. It seemed fitting to see it nestled next to her little bear. I never tired of seeing it dangle above her cleavage. Each time, it reminded me of the moment I'd given it to her. We'd been so young. "What's cruel is that I'll have to look at you all night and know I have to behave."

She draped her arms around my neck and smiled up at me. "When have you ever behaved?"

"This is true." I kissed her gently and stepped back, knowing the night could be ruined if I didn't control my head.

"Oh, a quick kiss and release. Tonight must be important," she teased and reached for her wrap. "Ready?"

"I am." I waved for her to head downstairs where the car was waiting.

She hesitated when her phone rang, and she glanced at the ID. She looked over at me, and I quickly went to her.

"Hi, Salvo." She put him on speaker phone.

"Have you thought any more about my offer?"

"A little, yes."

"Any conclusions?"

I mouthed for her to take a breath and not rush her words.

"What am I supposed to say to Elio?"

"Let me deal with him." I licked my lips, annoyed at his tone. Who did he think he was?

"I don't think that's how this will work."

"Just tell him that I have some video he will be very interested in. It's of his aunt being seen different times at the Coppola mansion. Tell him it's just a sample of how helpful I can be. I could be very useful to his family." She looked at me, and I nodded. If we could get some evidence of Noemi being at the Coppolas' home, that could work in our favor.

"Let me speak with him, and I'll get back to you."

"I'll be waiting. I really want a job."

She hung up and shook her head. "He really has some nerve, doesn't he?"

"Salvo's an opportunist. He'll do whatever he can to survive, including worming his way into the family, and between us."

"I'd like to see him try." She glanced over her shoulder and wiggled her bottom at me.

"Me too." I followed her and enjoyed the view of her sleek dress, knowing there was nothing underneath.

"Where's Vinni?" She eyed Gain as he opened the door for her.

"At the Beach House," I said quietly as we made our

way over, "more or less to keep an eye on Noemi without him even realizing it."

"Oh, okay." She smiled at Gain, but I knew she wished it was Vinni. So did I, but Noemi needed to be watched, and I didn't trust Nonna Greta's preoccupation with Sienna. "Have you spoken to Wyatt today?" She checked her phone, and I saw the last text message she'd sent had no response.

"No, but Vinni said something about how he needed to go into town to meet someone. Something about an interview."

"How do you know more about what my best friend is up to than I do?"

"That's because your best friend has an eye for my cousin, and I know where Vinni is at every moment."

"Stalker much?" She smirked, and I raised an eyebrow at her comment. "Well, could you ask Vinni to ask Wyatt to text me back."

"I'll send your message along." I kissed our entwined hands and settled in for the drive to the restaurant.

When we pulled up to the entrance of La Leggenda dei Frati we were greeted by the owner and escorted to our table out back. Normally, I'd insist we have the entire outside area to ourselves, but I knew Sienna liked having others around, so I requested only three out of the seven tables be used.

"Here we are, sir." The waiter poured the wine I had ordered earlier and waited for us to be seated. Our table was raised slightly higher than the others around us, so we had the advantage of the view of the town below.

This was the same place my papa had taken my mama on their first date after they moved to Florence years ago. It was special, and I hoped it would be for us, too.

We ordered, and once we were alone, I felt Sienna relax and settle in.

"This place is simply stunning." She looked around with admiration while I took a moment to admire her.

"You're simply stunning."

She smiled at me and licked the taste of wine from her lips, as she let her gaze slowly drift down over my suit. The pure heat in her expression made me shift to tame my urge to ravage her right there and then. My eyes burned into hers, desire totally unveiled.

"I know that look, Elio, and if you want to keep this evening on track, you better stop because a girl can only take so much." She chuckled. "I'm changing the topic. When are you going to share more details about this tour we're supposed to be going on?"

"Ah, yes, the tour. Well, now that we've announced that we're the new Don and Donna, it would be customary to show respect to the masses. We need to be seen together as a united front. Many important people need to meet you and know that I am the boss, so to speak."

"We," she corrected, and I smiled my apology.

"Yes, my *bella*, we." She set her chin at that, so I went on. "The tour will take us through a sweep of the different syndicate holdings. It's tradition that a new Don does this, plus it's my opportunity to show you off and to let them see you for who you are, and that you're willing to end the Coppola-Capri feud. It's very important to show that we are joining forces. And that you," I took her hand and held it tight to drive my point home, "are untouchable."

"A tour of Italy with great food, wine, and parties?" She sighed playfully. "I think I can handle that."

"I figured as much."

Dinner was served, and we ate, reminiscing about old times. It was nice to see that flicker of hurt that used to flinch across her face occasionally didn't show itself anymore.

"Have you spoken to Cara since that day in the park?" Her friend Cara meant something to her from all those years ago living in the Di Vaio house, but I knew that when I spoke of Cara, Renzo memories were always close by.

"No." She sipped her wine. "It was wonderful to catch up, but that part of me is closed. It felt good to connect and know we're both doing well, but I think that's where it ends."

"Did she ever tell you what happened to Renzo?" I thought back to those days. I was glad I now knew that Francesco had sent someone to watch over Sienna. There were so many times I wanted to ask what he knew, but whenever I came close to speaking of it, Francesco would steer the conversation away. I understood, but it had hurt so much being in the dark.

"Yes," the corners of her mouth rose, "he's dead."

"Oh?" That was news to me. "Any idea how?"

"Assault with a pipe."

"Pipe?" I raised a suspicious eyebrow, and her smile grew. "Is it possible to love you more than I did five minutes ago?"

She chuckled. "We have some twisted love, Elio."

"Twisted only makes things better." I winked, and she blushed.

"Hey, Casanova." A purse landed on the table, and I turned to find Carina with her hands on her hips and a sardonic smile on her face. A man I didn't recognize stood behind her, looking nervous. "Thanks for the heads up about your announcement." She looked at Sienna. "Congratulations, by the way."

"Thanks?" Sienna gave me a strange expression.

"Things happened quickly. My apologies for not calling you first." I chuckled, then turned my attention to Sienna. "*Bella*, this is Carina. She and I posed as a couple because of Nonna, even while I had you, my darling, and she had her loved one behind the scenes." I winked at her.

"Oh, the girl in Salvo's picture." Something must have clicked for Sienna as she stood and offered a hand. "Nice to meet you. I'm glad I don't have to kill you." I muffled a laugh.

"Happy to hear that. This is a new dress." She matched Sienna's dark humor. "This is Paolo." She smiled warmly and reached out her hand to him. "After you announced your engagement to the world, I decided to take a stand with my parents. It wasn't easy, but if you can break the rules, why can't I?"

I stood and shook his hand. "Nice to meet you,

Paolo."

"Same to you, sir." He nodded politely. "A thank you is in order as well. You might not see it yet, but you're paving a new way of life for our generation and those to come. We should be leading with love and not just duty."

"Look at you, changing lives," Carina joked.

"Carina, why don't you and Paolo join us for dessert?" Sienna looked at me, and I gave a nod. It wasn't quite how I wanted this night to go, but I accepted the intrusion for what it was. The best laid plans and all that.

"I'd really like to hear your story." Sienna smiled.

The sun's warmth felt wonderful on my back as I looked over the wagonload of goodies I'd had Donte prepare that morning. "Thank you for this, Donte." I took the blanket he offered and laid it over top.

"Not exactly what you had planned." He chuckled as he swept his hand to indicate my clothing.

"No, but when does life go as planned?" I smiled back at him.

"Very true, boss." He looked around. "Anything else?"

"Yes, call me immediately if Nonna Greta or Noemi decide to show up today."

"Of course."

I rolled up the sleeves on my shirt and looked down at my jeans, feeling utterly too casual, but that was what today was all about. I wasn't the Don, and she wasn't the

Donna today. We were just us.

"Good morning." Sienna met me at the bottom of the stairs in one of her sexy little sundresses and cardigan. "Wow, jeans and a shirt?" She squinted at my outfit. "What am I missing?"

"Nothing." I took her hand. "I want to take you somewhere."

"Don't we have meetings or people to hunt down?"

"That can wait until after this."

"After what?" She stepped outside and saw the little white wagon. "Oh, how sweet."

"Yes, I'm very sweet, but don't tell anyone." I took her hand while she laughed, and we walked together up to the Hill House and down into the sunflower garden. When we got to the perfect place, I rolled out the blanket and motioned for her to sit.

"You told me a long time ago that you wanted to sit in the middle of a sunflower garden and stare up at the clouds."

"I did, yes."

"Well, today we are going to do just that."

"Okay." She lay down, and I joined her, pulling her into my side. We both looked up to watch the puffy white clouds as they slowly drifted by with a little help from a light breeze. The sunflowers made a rustling noise as their leaves brushed one another. "Gosh, I've waited a lifetime to do this."

"So have I."

"What?" She strained her neck to look at me, but I just kissed her head. "Look, that one looks like an elephant. See the trunk and the ears?" She drew the outline, and I could see what she was picturing.

"There's a cupcake." I pointed.

"A bird over there."

"I see it." I began to let go of the stress each day brought and allowed it to slowly drift off with the clouds. It had been a long time since I had stopped and just enjoyed a morning. My head felt lighter than it had in a long time. "What about that one?" I pointed. "Right there, it looks like a heart."

"I don't see a heart." She giggled. "Now you're reaching."

"No, it's right there." I held up the ring so it would catch the light and, she stilled as she realized what it was. I turned onto my side and looked down at her. "You deserve to be asked this question in a place that is special for you, and it just so happens this place is special to me, too." I ran my finger down her cheek and saw her eyes gloss over. "I've loved you forever, Sienna. Maybe even in a past life I hunted for you. I will always hunt for you." I wiggled my eyebrows, and she let out a little laugh. "The boomerang always brings us back together. Let's do this right and make it official. Will you marry me and be mine forever, Sienna?" Her tears fell, and she nodded.

"Yes! Of course, I will." I slipped the ring on her finger then swooped down to kiss her. Then she pulled away and sat up to admire the shape of the stone.

"It was my nonna's on my mother's side," I explained. "She was a wonderful woman and died way too soon. Mama showed it to me and told me when I was ready to give it to you, I could have it."

"It's stunning."

"I didn't want us to go on the tour without doing this properly." I handed her a glass and filled it with her favorite prosecco. I tapped my glass to hers. "To another new beginning, and this time, we'll get it right."

Chapter

THIRTEEN

Sienna

"Where are you?" Wyatt's phone rang and rang, and I closed my eyes when his voicemail picked up. I waited for the beep and cleared my throat of emotion. "I don't know what kind of interview Georgio has you on, but you need to call me back. Elio proposed, and I need to tell my best friend every detail, but you're not picking up. Just…" I sighed heavily. "Just let me know you're all right, okay?"

"Hey." Vinni came into the kitchen and snagged a coffee cup. The guys were playing Rummoli in the other room, and I could hear their happy chatter. "You looked stressed. Is leaving for the tour bothering you?"

"No, I'm worried about Wyatt." I slumped over the

island and rested my forehead on the counter. "He isn't answering his phone."

"Still?"

"Yeah. It's been three days, and that's not how we work. We always call each other back within twenty-four hours if one of us leaves a message, even if it's just a quick 'I'm okay.' I know we're co-dependent, but it works for us."

"I wasn't thinking that." He leaned his back against the counter while he thought. "He also told me he'd check in yesterday and didn't."

"What? Why would he check in with you?" He sipped his coffee and avoided eye contact with me. "Vinni, what are you saying? You know I can shoot, and I'm mighty fine with a blade, so don't make me do something I'll regret."

The corners of his mouth fought to rise, and he licked his lips to stop the smile that begged to be let loose.

"He called to tell me he felt like he was being followed. I got him to give me the plate number and a description, but the car came back fine. He agreed he was just being paranoid. You know, now he's friends with a mafia Donna." He smiled, but his face had begun to reflect a little worry.

"Anyone can steal a car. Damn it, you know that."

"I know." He held up a hand to stop my rant. "That's why I stayed with him until he checked into his hotel. He did tell me he'd check back in the next day, but he also said he had a lot lined up with the guy he was meeting. I wasn't that concerned when he didn't call. I was going to wait until this afternoon before I called him myself."

My phone rang, and I shot up, seeing it was Salvo. Vinni called in Elio as I answered it on speaker phone.

"Exactly like we practiced," Elio whispered as the call connected.

"Hi, Salvo." I tried to keep my voice light. "Thanks for calling me back."

"I would have called sooner, but I had a one-day contract. I really need more income than I can make doing contracts here and there. Have you good news for me?"

"Well, Elio and I spoke about it, and though it took a little convincing, he saw the benefit in you joining us."

"He did?" He sounded surprised. "*Fantastico*. I knew you'd come through for me. So, what now?"

I glanced at Elio, who gave me the nod to keep going with the conversation as we planned.

"Let's meet up in town. I'll text you the address, and we can iron out all the details from there."

Silence.

"How do I know I'm not walking into an ambush?"

Elio motioned for me to mute the call, but I knew Salvo better than anyone in this room, so I shook my head and turned away as I answered.

"I guess you're going to have to trust me, Salvo." I pictured how it had been with us when I was around him to keep my voice real.

"I think, given the circumstances, you can see how that would be hard for me."

"I do, but you're the one asking for this job," I

reasoned. I waited a beat and let the silence hang. "All right, Salvo, would it help if you and I met up somewhere first? Just the two of us. Then we can go and talk to Elio together?"

"That would be better," Salvo replied, and I saw Elio nod. It was all going according to plan. "We can meet today at noon at the old church. You remember where we went that day, by the pond at the edge of city." Elio was nodding.

"I do, I'll see you there then."

I hung up and looked at Vinni. "You'll let me know if you—"

"—hear from Wyatt. You have my word."

"Thanks." I checked the time and took a breath. "I should get going."

"We," Elio corrected me. "Let me call Gain and Harris, and we'll get moving."

The wind whipped my hair around as it wafted up the cliff from the water below. I stood near a picnic table close to the edge so I could see the water. The nearby church hadn't been used in years, but people often drove out there to get away from the city and to enjoy the beautiful view of the lake.

"Careful," Salvo suddenly pulled me back with his hands on my hips, "the ground is very loose there." I hadn't seen him approach, but had heard his car pull in.

"Thanks." I tucked my wild hair behind my ear and

waited for him to remove his hands, but he didn't. "It's lovely, isn't it?"

"Yes, it's always been a favorite of mine." Salvo smiled, and I stepped away from him, knowing Elio was probably just itching to drive a bullet into his head.

"How many men?" I nodded over his shoulder, and he smirked, knowing neither of us would have come alone.

"Five, give or take."

"Mm," I thought out loud, "you came with men, yet you lead me to believe you're broke?" He looked away, and I chuckled softly. I knew Elio would have Gain and Harris keep a watchful eye on any men Salvo might have brought with him, while he kept his laser eyes on Salvo.

"Let me guess, yours are in the tree line?"

"Of course." I nodded. "How've you been?" I'd noticed he looked tired.

"Aside from losing a family I'd devoted more than half my life to, I'm holding up."

"Yes, I can understand how hard that would be for you."

"I see you're doing well." He took my hand and admired my ring. "You know, I could have given you one just as big. Well, I could have back then, anyway." He gave a shrug when I shot him a look.

"It's not about the ring size, Salvo." I pulled my hand away. "It's that I love Elio." I hated that he thought material things like a ring would be what I wanted.

"Do you love him for him or who he is? Some women just need powerful men."

"Be careful," I warned. "You obviously don't know me that well."

"Sorry," he stopped himself, "that was out of line."

"Way out of line," I corrected. "Are you sure you can do this? You pointed out that you gave a lot of your life to the Coppolas, to my family. Now I'm the Coppola Donna, but I've joined Elio, and he's the Capri Don now. I need to know where your loyalty will lie. Will you be able to take orders from us as the Capri syndicate?"

"Yes." He nodded, but I could tell he was holding back.

"Good. Now, for good measure, give me something good that I can take back to Elio to show him you can be useful to him, to us."

"Good measure?" He chuckled. "Elio wants something for good measure?" He nodded and thought for a moment. "Rosa has been staying in churches, working her way northwest toward Spain."

"Why Spain?"

"I know she has some family there."

"Where in Spain?"

"Badajoz."

"Has she left Italy yet?"

"Not the last I heard."

"Where was she when you heard from her last?" I shot him another question.

"Parma."

"Why is it you know she's in Parma, yet you told me you hadn't heard from her since the night of the fire?"

"I didn't know if I could trust you before."

"Trust goes both ways, and right now you lost a little of mine."

His lips pursed, and he swiped a hand through his hair as he thought. "You think I asked for this?"

"You think I did?" I challenged, not letting him off that easily. I wanted to keep him talking about what he might know. "Do you have anything else you can share with me? Like the name of one of the churches she stayed in? Who's helping her? Anything?"

"The minister, the one who swore you in, he's helping her."

"Okay. Let me text Elio and let him know you want to talk. He'll trust you if I tell him I do. You can give him the information you just told me." I pulled out my phone to text Elio, when suddenly Salvo stepped close.

"What about what I want?"

"I'm not following. You told me what you wanted, and that's why I'm here trying to help you."

"I gave you something. Now what do I get?"

"What do you want? I thought it was a job."

"Isn't it obvious?" He took me by the tops of my arms, and I shook my head. This wasn't good with Elio hidden close by. "I want you."

"Salvo, please let me go." We were way too close. "I'm not yours to have. I'm with—"

"I know, you're with Elio." He rolled his eyes rudely. "But you're in a world where men are gods and they take whoever they want when they want. Besides, history has a way of repeating itself, you know, with the lovers your mother had. You could do the same."

Wait, what?

"Pardon me?" I tasted tin as I moved my tongue to dampen my suddenly dry mouth.

"This is the mafia, after all." He snorted. "Your mama had a lover while she was married to Theo, Noemi had Bosco while she slept with Theo. Theo had lots of women while he was married to Elenora. Elio's a Don, so he'll have multiple women while being with you, and now you can have me while still being with Elio. See how we all win? It's the mafia way."

"You think I would cheat on Elio with you?"

"Your mama didn't seem to have a conscience on the matter. I just figured like mama like daughter."

I saw red.

I pulled the syringe from my pocket and jammed the needle into his neck, injecting the drug into his bloodstream. His eyes went wide with pain and shock.

"My mama was sold off to the Coppolas like a slave. She loved Francesco, and I love Elio!" I screamed into the wind, and my words echoed along with gunshots off the cliffs. He wavered in his step and turned away from me as the drug coursed through his veins, clouding his ability to think.

Elio suddenly appeared and snagged the syringe from my hand, tossing it aside.

"Damn, I couldn't get a safe shot. Are you okay?" I nodded and angrily turned as Salvo tried to take a swing at Elio, but Elio calmly stepped out of the way, and Salvo tripped over his own feet and fell. His head smacked hard on a rock. The sound his skull made when it impacted the rock make my stomach roll. *Yuck.*

Elio nudged him with his foot and looked at me. "What was this?" He'd picked up the syringe.

"Goodfellas." I smirked at the street name for it. "Seemed kind of poetic, don't you think?"

"Fentanyl," Elio wrapped the needle in a handkerchief, "I see." He seemed impressed. "What made you snap like that?"

I watched as Gain and Harris casually rolled Salvo off the cliff. His body landed in the lake below.

"He said my mother slept around and then implied everyone in the mafia sleeps around, and that he'd be a companion for me." I glanced up at Elio and held his stare. "If we're modernizing the syndicate rules, that will be one."

"Agreed." He pulled me in for a kiss and then walked me to the car.

During the ride home, I was lost in thought. Elio tried to get me to talk, but I let him know I needed to be alone with my thoughts. Salvo had opened a door in my head I didn't like, and I was working hard to close it.

I hardly noticed the drive, and when we arrived and he opened the door for me, I had to blink myself to the present.

"Hey," he bent down so he was at eye level with me, "I'm sorry you had to kill someone who was a friend. I know it's not easy."

"No," he'd misunderstood my silence, "his death didn't bother me, but what he said did."

"I'm sorry he said that about your mama." He

rubbed my leg. "Despite everything else about Elenora, she was still your mama, and he shouldn't've said that." I nodded, and he stood, offering me a hand, which I took. That *wasn't* what was bothering me, but I didn't want to bring it up to him right now. Today had been mentally tiring, and I just wanted to be at the Hill House without any more drama.

Elio left to go fill in Piero while I gave my play by play to Niccola, who needed to document everything. Some nearby hikers had heard the gunshots, and now we needed to provide a simple alibi to give the police, along with a pile of cash. I knew that was how things worked in this life.

After dinner, Andrea came to me in the living room. I was looking at the family crest, thinking how crazy my life had been.

"Sounds like you were pretty impressive today." She took a seat behind me while I studied their family photos. I loved Elio's smile. It never changed over the years. I loved that even in his darkest moments he could bring me to my knees with it.

"It was different," I muttered and moved my gaze to the next photo. It was one of Elio and me at the old house in Sicily. I'd never noticed until now that in almost every photo I was in, so was Francesco. He really had watched over me.

"Elio said Salvo had some pretty nasty things to say about your mother." She tried to fish as to what was bothering me.

"He wasn't wrong."

"Perhaps not, but it doesn't mean it doesn't hurt."

"I just block it out." I shrugged and heard her let out a little sigh. "But that's not what's on my mind." I kept my back turned, unsure I wanted to even touch this topic.

"You'll feel better if you talk it out."

"I'm not sure if I will." I moved to the window and watched the breeze push the blowup swan around the pool.

"Ahh." I caught her reflection in the window and saw her sit up a little straighter. "Sienna, come sit here. We should have this talk now."

I turned and immediately felt uneasy. Of course, Andrea had figured it out.

As I sat across from her, she took my hand and rubbed gently over my engagement ring. "There are two types of Dons. There are the ones who think they're gods, rule with an iron fist, and sleep around with whoever they wish until they get a son. After that, their wives take care of whoever that child came from and act like it's their own." My throat felt like sandpaper. "Then there are the Pieros and Elios, who find the person they're supposed to be with, then hold tight with every fiber of their being and rule with love and respect. Not that," she smiled, "they don't still have that iron fist when they feel they need it. When their loved ones have a son, or a daughter, they'll raise that baby together no matter what as a solid unit."

I nodded and looked down, knowing she was right, but…

"It's okay to be nervous of this life, Sienna." She

tucked my hair behind my ear. "No one is expecting you to not have doubts or fears. Just know you can talk to me about anything. Besides," she smiled, "Elio knows I would splash bleach on one of his beloved suits if he even entertained those kinds of thoughts." She winked, making me laugh.

"He does love his fashion, doesn't he?"

"He had his first Armani suit at six." She laughed harder. "I swear we had no idea what we were creating."

Elio snickered from the hallway clearly eavesdropping. "A suit speaks volumes about a man. Cheap suits are a disgrace." He shut the door behind him and joined us.

Andrea rolled her eyes and tilted her head at me. "Do you feel better now?"

"I do. Thank you." She reached out and cupped my chin tenderly.

Suddenly, the door opened and one of the house staff rushed in. We all jumped to our feet.

"What the hell happened to him?" Niccola's voice found us as he rushed by.

"He's okay," Vinni shouted as we all ran out of the room and into the hallway where we found a battered Wyatt. Andrea rushed in the opposite direction.

"Oh, my God!" I rushed to my best friend and helped him into the room and onto a chair. "What on Earth happened?"

Elio was on my heels asking the same question while Andrea returned a moment later and handed him a glass of water.

"Thank you." He took a few sips and swallowed down the pain killers she offered him.

I bent down in front of him and inspected his bruised face. I also suspected a few cracked ribs as well by the way he held his arms around himself. "Wyatt, tell me you're okay."

"I'm all right," he assured me as he glanced over at Vinni, who looked noticeably uneasy.

"What?" I looked from Wyatt to Vinni. I wanted to know what the hell was going on. "Who did this to you?"

"Mariano," Vinni said, and Elio shot up straight to his feet. "Wyatt had just gotten back to the hotel after the interview, and they jumped him there in the parking lot. He's bruised, his ribs and back, but all things considered…" He trailed off.

"What did Marino want?" Elio asked as I inspected his cut cheek.

"He wanted me to relay a message to Sienna." He lowered his voice and put a hand on my shoulder. "That if she doesn't return to him, he's going to publish some video he has of her and Anna in a hot tub." I blinked at what he'd said. I always thought I'd felt someone watching me that day, but I never imagined they were filming me. "He also said something about her father and some alliance they had with your family, Elio."

I stood quickly and started to think of a way out of this. "It had to be either Rosa Coppola or Salvo who took that video."

"What happened in the hot tub?" Niccola stepped farther into the room.

"I held her underwater until she stopped breathing." I looked at Elio, who was deep in thought. "I should've known to be more careful."

"Don't you have the police paid to look the other way?" Wyatt tried to help, but it was more complicated than that.

"If the video gets out, there's no stopping the repercussions," Vinni explained.

"Mama." Elio commanded our attention.

"I'll set it up." Andrea didn't miss a beat and raced out of the room.

"Vinni, get Wyatt checked out with the doctor."

"Yes, boss."

"Sienna, it's time to pack for our tour."

"Now?" What was I missing? "I can't leave Wyatt."

"He'll be fine, and I need you to help me finish this once and for all."

Chapter

FOURTEEN

Noemi

I fumbled with the pack of cigarettes. The stupid packaging made it impossible to break into, or maybe it was just the fact that my hands were shaking. In one last desperate attempt, I used my teeth and tore the package open. Finally, I put the filter tip between my lips and lit the end. Drawing in a deep breath, I let the sweet smoke coat my lungs and settle my nerves. It had been sixteen years since I'd given in to the white devil stick, and at that very moment I couldn't for the life of me wonder why I'd ever considered giving it up.

"I thought you said you were going to quit that shit." Niccola shook his head in disappointment as he leaned over the railing of the patio. "What's going on with you?"

"Mind your business, Nicco." I couldn't handle that he had the same annoying mannerisms of his father.

"Not until you tell me why you just blew up at Vinni," he huffed.

I rolled my eyes and took a moment until I could feel a little of the old me returning. I needed to get myself back to who I really was. I used to be so good at dealing with whatever came my way. How did I become this boring stay-at-home housewife, with a husband who lived with his mistress, while I was left to raise the boys and deal with his mother?

"He was only making sure you were all right. Are you?" Niccola's voice grated.

"Don't I look fine?" I snapped.

"No, actually. You look the way you did when we were younger, and you promised those days were long gone. So, tell me what's going on or—"

"Or what?" I turned to face my son straight on, and he shook his head at me. "You'll kick your own mother out of her house? Toss my stuff in a bag and leave me to be homeless? Or better yet, make me live with that perfect witch Andrea and gag-worthy Piero?" The words were out of my mouth before I could stop them.

"Wow." He took a step back and chuckled darkly. "Please, Mama, tell me how you really feel about our family."

"Don't," I scoffed. "You're telling me that family doesn't make you want to poke your eyes out? Elio and the girl from the wrong side of the tracks playing dress-up, going on tour like they think they can make a difference in this heinous world?" I drew in another deep breath of poison, almost wishing it would be my last.

"No, Mama, I do not feel that way." He said the words slowly as though to let them sink in. "In fact, I think Elio and Sienna are exactly what this world needs. They're good people, and up until a few minutes ago, I thought you felt the same way."

"Well…" I shrugged then saw his gaze move over my shoulder.

"You owe Vinni an apology," he muttered, "so quit being a raging bitch and be the mother you claim to be."

"Pardon me?" The nerve of him, but I kept my mouth shut as he stepped closer.

"You heard me." He plucked the cigarette from my mouth and tossed it over the edge. "Grow up and get your head on straight."

I leaned far out over the rail and let out a silent scream until I felt like all my blood had rushed to my head. I took a couple deep breaths, fixed my blouse, then went inside to do some damage control.

I found Vinni in the weight room. He was doing chin-ups, and by the looks of him, he was on his last rep. I moved to sit on the bench and waited for him to spot me. He took a few moments then carefully pulled out his earbuds as he purposely pretended not to see me.

I stood so he had to acknowledge me. "Can we talk?"

"You can," he huffed, clearly annoyed with me.

"I know I said some things before that hurt your feelings, and I'm sorry. I'm dealing with a lot right now that isn't sitting well with me, and I took it out on you."

"Yeah, you did." He started to lift some free weights. "It wasn't the first time, and I'm sure it won't be the last."

"I'm trying to apologize here, Vin."

"Yeah, I know." He acted like I was a villain. "But just like always, you lash out, then you come down here and blame your shit on everyone else and expect us to just brush it off."

"No, I don't."

"You do."

I tried to control my breathing, but it was taking a lot of will power, and then I thought about Rosa's words.

"Okay, fine. You want to know the truth of what's really bothering me?"

"I really don't care."

I was going to lose it. "I caught Sienna going through my things today, and I'm not sure how to deal with that." I watched as his eyes went to slits and wrinkled at the corners. "She didn't see me, but I watched her dig through my purse, you know, the big brown one I always use. So, maybe you can tell me why she would be doing that."

"Sienna wouldn't do that."

"No?" I folded my arms. "Ask her, then."

"Okay." He held up his ear bud as if to ask if I was finished.

I did love my boys, but we'd always had an up and down relationship. I wasn't happy what life had dealt me, but they were. I thought part of me was jealous that they'd always gotten what they wanted. Not to mention that Bosco got what he wanted, too. So, that left me here, under the watchful eye of his mother and that creepy driver of hers, Abramo, who always seemed to be watching me. Sure, Bosco had offered many times to divorce me, but I needed the security of his money, so I refused, and so I'm forced to stay here.

"Do you really know where her loyalty lies?" I said to my son, and he simply shrugged, but I hoped I'd at least planted a seed.

"Do me a favor." He dropped the weights, breathing heavily. "Keep your own insecurities away from Sienna."

"Meaning?"

"Mama," he used his teeth to peel back the Velcro from his workout gloves, "you get into these moods, where everyone annoys you, and you pick one person to be the target of your anger."

"Vinni—"

"No, Mama, just stop. Elio is happy, Sienna is happy, everyone is happy but you. Don't drag us all down with whatever the hell is bothering you this week."

"Vinni?" Bosco called from another room, and I cursed under my breath.

"Like that." He pointed at me. "What did Papa do now to get your back up?"

"Well, for starters, he never told me he was coming."

"To his own house? The nerve!" He dripped with sarcasm, which only annoyed me further. He started to walk out of the room, but I stepped in his way.

"Sienna is just like her mother, slippery, and devious when poked. Just question her, see why she's here digging around. I bet she'll deny everything."

"Maybe she'll deny it because she was never here."

"She took my notebook, the one with the leather string that ties around it. You don't believe me, so ask her about it."

"Whatever." He pushed by me, and I stayed put, waiting for him and Bosco to leave the house. Once I felt it was safe, I whisked upstairs, grabbed my purse, and headed for my car. I needed to plant the notebook.

Chapter
FIFTEEN

Wyatt watched as I zipped the last of the suitcases and ran through my list one last time.

"So, where are you going first?"

"Umm," I flipped open my notebook, "Grosseto, Rome, Sicily," I gave him a weary look, "Naples, Bari, Pesaro."

"Is that all?" he joked and opened a bottle of water to down his next round of painkillers. He gave a quick *ouch* as he lifted his arm.

"Those ribs will hurt for a while." I sympathized. "There were more, but Elio wants to have a summer wedding, so we shaved off about six other places."

"Summer wedding, huh?" He tried to play it cool,

but I could tell he wanted very much to be involved in the planning.

"I already told Andrea that you want to help," I assured him.

"Yes, that was wise of you. And what about my position in the wedding?"

"Well, that really depends on something, doesn't it?" I eyed him as I pretended to dig through my purse.

"What?"

"What really happened when Vinni found you?"

"I'm not following. You know the story."

"Yeah," I sat down next to him, "I know the story you told everyone, but I also know there's a whole chunk of time that was skimmed over. I know you well, Wyatt, so spill it."

He stood and winced in pain again as he took a seat across from me so he could prop up his sore hip. Mariano had done a number on his legs, and I felt another surge of anger and guilt that my best friend was in pain because of me.

"Vinni found me where I'd tucked myself in a small alcove to wait for help. He got me into his car, and we drove here."

"That's it?" I studied my best friend. I knew there was more to it, and it wasn't like him not to share.

"That's it." He looked away, and I wanted to pry more, but he obviously wasn't ready yet. "When do we leave?"

"What? So, you're coming?" I tossed a shirt at him.

"A chance of a lifetime to be wined and dined all

over Italy like royalty? Hell, yes, I'm totally tagging along. Besides, I quit today, so I have nothing better to do with my life right now."

"Wait, what?" This was news to me.

"It was time. I'm tired of working for Georgio, and if I'm ever going to get my name out there, it needs not to be associated with his. Besides, Elio has some friends who are going to help me launch my own company, and being my own boss sounds a whole lot better than working for Georgio. He never sends the good stuff my way, anyway."

"Well, that's great news to me." I smiled and thought how amazing it was that Elio would do that for him. "In that case, we leave for the airport tomorrow at five a.m."

"I should pack." He limped out of the bedroom.

I watched as he walked down the hall to the guest room where he was staying. I was happy for Wyatt, and more than pleased that he would have more time to spend with me.

I had just returned to my packing when I heard the front door open. I checked the time, thinking Elio's meeting with his father must have ended early. I put in another pair of shoes then went to peek over the railing only to see the door close again. *Huh, odd.*

"Si?" Wyatt poked his head out the door. "Any chance you want to help me pack?"

"No."

"Good. My bag is on the bed." His pleading face found me, and I rolled my eyes and went to help my friend pack his belongings. I was done with mine, anyway.

After we dragged our bags down the stairs and left them by the door, I started dinner, trying to mentally prepare for what this tour meant for us. I was mostly nervous about going back to Rome to plead with the people who thought I was Mikey. We not only needed them to know that I wasn't Mikey, but to join with us. Going home again wasn't something I'd ever wanted to do, but Elio insisted it would be healthy for us both to go back and spend a little time with the people there.

"Should I keep stirring?" Wyatt broke into my thoughts, and I nodded for him to keep going. I was just finishing up chopping the shallots when Vinni came in looking stressed.

"Hey, you hungry?" I brushed the onion into the sauce.

"I think so." He sat on one of the stools at the island and dropped a notebook with a leather strap on the counter then rubbed his face.

"Bad day?" Wyatt asked while I added salt to the pasta water.

"My mother is on a good one." I went still and tried not to show my discomfort with the mention of his mama. "Niccola and I have always had our problems with Mama. Sometimes we wonder if she suffers from being bi-polar because she gets in these dark moods. She often will disappear for days at a time. It's hard to take, and it's why we understood when Papa left. It just wasn't healthy for anyone."

"My aunt is bi-polar," Wyatt admitted. "I've seen her pull some nasty things, like trying to break up my sister and her now husband. Her mind games can be pretty damaging if you're not careful."

"Well, that's why I'm here." He cleared his throat. "Sienna, I know the answer to this, but I just have to ask it. Did you take this?" He held up the leather notebook, something I'd never seen before.

"No, why? Whose is it?"

"It's okay." He closed his eyes and whispered something I couldn't understand. "Thanks."

"Vinni, what's going on?"

"Let's just say I believe you're her current target."

"Me?" I wasn't shocked, and I wanted to tell Vinni the truth. I hated lying to him, but Elio and I couldn't afford her running off, not when we had too many lingering questions.

"Just be happy you're leaving for a while. Hopefully, she'll straighten herself out before you get back."

"Wait," I eyed the notebook again, "did you find that there?"

"It was on the hall table, just as you come in."

That slippery little rat must have planted that evidence just before he came over. I remembered hearing the front door. *All right, Noemi, you want to play dirty, we can play dirty.*

Elio showed up late for dinner, and when he was filling Vinni in about some dockyard news, I took the opportunity to call Francesco.

"What are you up to?" Wyatt caught me at the door just as Francesco arrived.

"I'm going to deal with Noemi," I grabbed my

purse, "and you're going to distract Vinni by whatever means necessary."

"We all have our talents, my dear, and mine is to find a way to show Vinni he's playing for the wrong team." He grinned.

"Right, so go change into a bathing suit, flex those muscles, and invite him for a long soak in the hot tub."

"I aim to please." He caught my arm. "But in all seriousness, watch your back, Si. Most sons wouldn't have put you first when second-guessing something their mother told them. She must be scary."

"You have no idea." I shrugged at his uplifted brows. I felt so bad for Vinni and Niccola. It was only a matter of time before their world exploded, too.

With a quick kiss to his cheek, I left Wyatt and shot out the front door to the car.

"You know what you're doing?" Francesco asked as we walked toward the steps of the beach villa. "Because if this goes sideways, it won't look good for you."

"She tried to play a Greta move with Vinni and maybe even with Niccola. I've worked too damn hard to prove I'm here for all the right reasons. If there's something I can do to tip this woman off her game, I'm going to do it before we leave tomorrow."

"I'm giving you fifteen minutes. If you're not out by then, I'm coming in," he warned me. "It's bad enough that Elio doesn't know you're here."

I rested a hand on his shoulder and looked him straight in the eye. "I've been through more than most in this lifetime. I promise you, Francesco, I've got this."

"Fifteen," he muttered, but I knew he heard me.

Careful not to make much noise, I slipped through the front door, down the hallway, and into the room where I'd first come face to face with dear old Nonna Greta. Goosebumps rose along my skin as I thought about that day, with her wrinkly skin and those cold eyes that burned into my soul.

When I spotted what I wanted, I tucked it into my palm as I listened for the footsteps I knew would come. I'd purposely made enough noise to draw her from wherever she was in the house.

"Vinni?" she called. "Son, is that you?" She turned on the lights as she checked each room. "Niccola?" The lights became brighter as she switched each one on, then she entered the room I was in. She clicked the light on and off, but I had unplugged it. "Greta?" she called again.

I clicked on the lamp then, and she jumped, putting her hands to her chest.

"Lord, you scared me!" She caught her breath, and the anger seeped back in. "So, now you're breaking into my house?"

"Seems fair, seeing as you did the same to me this afternoon."

"I did no such thing!"

"No? So, your notebook just happened to be at my house for Vinni to find when he arrived? Come on, Noemi." I laughed. "You failed at killing me, you failed at setting me up, and now you failed at keeping this a secret too." I waited a beat, knowing she was squirmy inside. "I know." I let those words marinate in the air. "I know everything." I was impressed at my own lie. I knew I had to sell it to her. The truth was I knew nothing about her secrets, but I was determined to figure them out before she could inflict more damage on anyone in the family. To me, that was what a great Donna would do for her people.

"And what is it that you think you know?" Her voice was unemotional and detached, robot-like. When I didn't answer, she closed her eyes and swallowed hard. "You have no idea what door you just opened."

"I do." Another lie.

"You want to hurt me?" Her eyes flickered open, and I saw I'd woken something inside of her. "Let me return the favor." *Yes, this was what I wanted, more truths, more answers!* "Rosa Coppola took your mother and me to New York one weekend. The trip seemed last-minute, and there was a cold weight that seemed to hover over the whole thing." Her voice went almost sing-song as she related the story. "I couldn't understand it until Elenora came back to the hotel one night, looking upset." She smiled, but it was almost as though she was talking to herself, her voice was so odd. "Rosa had found out why Elenora was so sick. She found out her secret." I felt my stomach tighten. *Oh no.* "She had that baby plucked from your mother so it wouldn't be in the way when she and Theo tried to have kids. Yes, Francesco's child would certainly have been a major inconvenience."

I felt sick.

"Your mother got in the way of everything." She sniffed, while I tried to mask my own reaction to what she was saying. "I've always hated her. Our lives clashed so many times, but New York was one of the worst. You claim you know the truth about this, but I call your bluff, because if you did, Francesco wouldn't just be standing outside waiting for you. He'd be right here, front and center."

I literally felt like the air was sucked from my lungs when I remembered something Mama told me a while ago about how she hated New York.

"I know you spent time at the Coppola house, Noemi, and I know you were there while you were pregnant with Niccola, yet you lied to everyone around you. How do I know you're not lying now?"

Her head quickly turned to look at me, and I saw I'd hit a nerve.

"Like I said," I shrugged and pushed aside the sadness from what I'd just learned, "I know all."

"If you don't believe me, just call Dr. Finley in New York and give him Rosa's name. The rest will fall into place."

"Your days are numbered, Noemi, and I'm sure Bosco would be very interested in your time spent at the Coppola house." I looked straight into her eyes to show I wasn't afraid of her. "The truth will come crashing down here very soon."

I didn't wait for a response. I headed outside to where Francesco was waiting, and he followed me to the car.

"Are you all right?" He put the car in reverse and spun around to leave. "Did she say something to upset you?"

I slowly exhaled and tried to choose my words. I waited until we were on the open road and a good distance away from the beach villa before I said anything.

"Your silence is making me uneasy, Sienna,"

"I know," I admitted. "I'm just processing."

"Did your plan work?"

"Yes."

"I knew you'd be able to pull it off. I'm very proud of you. It takes strength to go face to face with someone who tried to kill you." He looked at my face and continued to talk, which told me how nervous he was. He rarely said more than a few words at a time these days. "Lord knows, I've never been a fan of Noemi." He glanced at me again. "I mean, when Elenora told me who she really was and about her connection to the Coppola family and to her brother, I couldn't believe it. She's been living under our roof all these years. Sometimes I wonder if Piero knew something was up with her, and that's why Mrs. Greta moved in. *Dio santo!*" He chuckled. "I bet Greta knew who she was all this time."

I'd never heard Francesco talk this much in my life. I sat back and listened to him until we got to the Hill House. I saw Elio's car in the driveaway, and a few others. I wondered who else would be joining us on the tour.

"Did Mama ever mention a trip to New York?" came

flying out of my mouth, and Francesco's hand fell away from the door handle.

"Why are you asking about New York?"

"Did she?" I struggled with my words as he looked forward and frowned. "What did she say about it?"

"Just that she'd had to go there and would never return. I just assumed Rosa had made her witness a hit or something."

"Something bigger happened."

"Oh?"

"Apparently, she was pregnant with your baby when they first got together." I hesitated. "Rosa found out, and took her to New York to…"

"I see." He licked his lips. "Your mother was never very forthcoming with information. So, I shouldn't be shocked she didn't share this either."

"I'm so sorry, Francesco." My heart broke for him. It killed me thinking what they could have had.

"I'm sorry, too." He reached over and squeezed my hand then moved it back to his lap.

"It's strange, though." I stopped myself as I reached for the door handle. Something just hit me out of the blue. "How was it that Noemi could be at the Coppola house carrying Bosco's baby and not be kicked out by Rosa? I mean, she crossed the forbidden line, right?"

"Something tells me that Noemi was feeding them information in order to stay there."

"Seriously? How do you figure?"

"Because we'd have known about Noemi's pregnancy long before."

"Wow." I shook my head, trying to process everything, but more than anything, I was very happy I hadn't been raised in that kind of an environment. "You should know that Noemi said to look up a Dr. Finley in New York for proof. I'm not sure if you'd want to do that, but I thought it was only fair to pass it along."

"*Grazia*." He wouldn't look at me.

"The lies get tiring, don't they?" I let out a heavy sigh and wondered what hornet's nest I'd just kicked over in Noemi's world.

"They really do." He cleared his throat, and I knew he needed a moment alone to digest everything. "Sienna," his tone was chilling as he picked up his phone, then he held it up and squeezed tight as he thought, "kill who you wish, but Rosa's mine."

"Just drag it out, for all of us. I'm going to give you some space." I hooked my purse on my arm and stepped out of the car. The cool air felt good on my head, so I took an extra minute for myself to swallow back what might have been.

Elio met me at the door with a puzzled expression.

"Where were you?"

"Getting one last word in before we leave."

"With who?"

"Noemi."

"What?" His eyes widened. "Why?"

"She played a bad card, and I wanted to show her I'd come back swinging."

"What's wrong with Francesco?" He nodded toward the car.

"Just give him a moment." I motioned for him to come inside. "We both got hit with a blow, one that will take him a bit longer to accept."

"And what was that?"

"Mama was pregnant with Francesco's baby when she first arrived at the Coppola house. Apparently, Rosa found out and 'took care of it' in New York." I air quoted.

"What?" he hissed, looking back at the door, worried for Francesco. "He had no idea?"

"No. Neither of us did. Yet another thing my mama took to the grave." I saw Andrea speaking to Donte. "On a different note, I planted a lie with Noemi. She thinks I know the truth about her secrets, and I know she's about to crack. It's only a matter of time."

"Good." He pulled me in for a hug, and I buried my face into his chest, needing him right now. "Let's go home. We have to get up early tomorrow."

Chapter

SIXTEEN

Elio

Syndicate Tour
Grosseto

Sienna was just as I knew she would be, amazing with everyone who came out to meet her. I thought back over the day. My second cousins, who ran the Grosseto syndicate, were skeptical of her at first, but by the time dinner was through, they were laughing and inviting her to join them for drinks on the terrace.

"Thanks for keeping an eye on her while we're gone, Francesco. We shouldn't be more than a few hours."

"I won't let her out of my sight." He smiled, and Sienna grinned back at him.

"*Pfft*, you sure about that?"

"Are you sure you don't want to come?" I reached over and brushed a lock of her hair from her cheek. I never liked to leave her, but we had some things to take care of, and I knew she was already tired.

"If today has proven anything to me about what this trip is going to be like, I know I'm going to need sleep." She leaned forward and rested her head on my chest, and I kissed the top of her head. "Lots and lots of sleep."

"You were amazing today."

"Thanks." She looked up at me, and I could see the exhaustion on her face. She'd spent most of the day being questioned and, in some cases, almost interrogated until she passed their tests and won them over. "Your family is great, but the idea of meeting more people at a noisy bar, well, it honestly doesn't sound very appealing. I won't be good company. I'm going to have a nice glass of wine, maybe read a little, then call it a night. Besides, you should go have some fun with the guys. I think they need it whether they realize it or not, and so do you."

"You're a good person, *bella*." I kissed her lips, lingering there a moment longer, breathing in her delicious scent. "Make sure Francesco knows where you are, and don't leave the house."

"I'll be fine." She kissed me again, and I heard Wyatt's laugh coming from the other room, and I had to chuckle. Any stress I still had faded. She'd be in good hands between the two of them. "I'll text you when I'm in bed."

"Text? Or send me a photo?" I smirked playfully.

"I guess," she stepped back, holding on to my hand until she was out of reach, "you'll just have to wait to find out."

A fleeting image of her naked in bed sent a thrill through me, and when she disappeared through the door, I felt a desperate need to take her quickly before I left. But who was I kidding? I'd never leave her once I had her in my arms.

Niccola and Vinni hopped in the car, and I started the engine.

The pub was just what I expected—dark, seedy, live music, and the food nearly inedible. It was perfect for keeping a low profile.

We had arranged to meet with three friends who we had business dealings within Spain. As luck would have it, they were here on business themselves and were free to meet up for drinks.

"I hear congratulations are in order." Santiago slapped my shoulder with a huge grin. "Think of the possibilities. I see a lot more opportunities for import and export with you at the top. No more worrying about that little *ratto* Stefano Coppola. I like that it will just be a direct line from Libya to America."

"The feds are still working their way into our ports." Ian, his older brother, rolled his eyes. "They are posing as workers and burrowing into our operation. Our friends to the west just got shut down and were taken into custody. I won't lie, my friend," he leaned closer, "we could use the business."

"I'll see what I can do." I gave him a nod and put a

hand on his arm. I wanted to let him know I understood. They needed the money to put food on their tables the same as we all did.

"Niccola, bring my father up to speed on that." Niccola took out his notebook and made a note to hand this information over to Papa. He could start to make some calls to his friends there.

"I can think of a few ways to get the feds going in another direction," I whispered into Ian's ear. I knew a show of good faith that we'd have their back was needed. "One idea would be to leak Rosa Coppola's name to them. That should draw them away from you and put their focus on her."

"That would be much appreciated." He tapped my glass.

Now that the business was taken care of, we sat back and swapped old stories as we enjoyed the music. At midnight, my phone buzzed in my pocket to indicate a text message. I felt an instant jolt of heat and leaned back away from the others as I tapped the screen. Sienna had sent me a photo of herself in bed, her breasts just under the covers. She wore a very sexy, sleepy smile.

Sienna: You can see more when you get back.

I smiled, loving that she'd sent me a tease and not a nude photo. It left more to the imagination and showed she knew I wouldn't be alone.

Elio: You're beautiful. I'll be back soon.

"I know that look." Niccola drew my attention over to his knowing smirk. "I think it's best we start back. We have a busy schedule ahead of us."

"Yes, my wife has texted me several times as well." Santiago laughed. "My phone may be on silent, but the buzz in my pocket can't be ignored much longer. I don't want to irritate the boss."

"We don't want that." Vinni sighed. He'd been enjoying a little attention from a pretty young woman and made a show of regret as he handed her his card. "Thanks for the company, but we've got to get going."

"I can spend the night," she purred, and Vinni looked hopefully at me for approval. Normally, I would have agreed, but we were guests in someone's house tonight and not at a hotel.

"Sorry, not tonight."

"So, what, your father here says no?" She shot me a nasty look that transformed her pretty face, and Vinni lifted her off his lap and stood. He towered over her.

"It's time for you to leave," Vinni said as he snatched his card back with a stern expression. It made her stick her middle finger in his face. He tried everything not to laugh at how ridiculous her behavior was.

"This is why I won't ever find my wife at a bar." Niccola shook his head as he tugged his jacket off the back of his chair.

"You won't find a wife because you're too busy finding me *men* to take home." Vinni made a face at him.

We made our way through the tables and the sea of people to the front door.

"Which reminds me, by the way, Shantee was asking about you the other day."

"And how would you know?" Vinni huffed back at

him.

"I was texting with Minnie as Shantee just so happened to be at the bar, and she..."

Whack!

Something hit me between the shoulders, and I shot forward into Vinni. I whirled around and ducked at the last second as the baseball bat came at me again.

Leaning my weight on my back foot, I kicked out hard and collided with the man's ribs.

Vinni and Niccola were dealing with a few others when yet another man stepped out of the shadows. He was huge. We turned so our backs were to each other so we could face our attackers. Everyone stood ready to fight.

"So, this is Elio Capri." The big man's thick accent told me he was from Slovakia. "You're the man who's going to marry the woman who stole my business from under me."

Mikey.

"I've made it very clear that my fiancée is not Mikey." I was going to go on, but I had already made the truth public and would not repeat myself to someone who'd just attacked me.

"You lie! Your business partner told me the truth."

Mariano.

My blood heated, and I stretched my neck to relieve some tension then quickly pulled out my gun before he could reach for his. His hands went up, palms toward me.

"Vinni, record this," I ordered. Vinni slid his phone

out and started to record. The men around us all looked at the Slovakian for direction. He just stood staring at me. "Never bring a baseball bat to a gunfight." I eyed the guy who'd hit me with the bat and shot him before he could react. He slumped to the ground, and I slammed a foot on the handle of the bat. It flipped up, and I grabbed it with my left hand.

The Slovakian looked around, motioning the others to fight, but they just stood there, unsure if they wanted to die. These guys were just a bunch of brainless thugs.

"If you want to get my attention, this isn't the way to do it." I shot the guy next to the Slovakian as I spoke. Then I stepped slightly to my left to keep everyone in my line of sight. Vinni didn't stop recording as Niccola fired off a bullet into a guy's leg as he bolted for the door. The sound of the shot echoed off the walls. "Also, you should never trust the words of a man who spends more time with a straw up his nose than he does handling his business."

"You're crazy." The sweat broke out on the Slovakian's face as he took a few steps back. I closed the gap by taking a few toward him. "I was told it was her, but I can see now that I might be wrong."

"I'll not have this conversation again. My fiancée is not Mikey, nor has she ever been Mikey, do you understand? Do I make myself perfectly clear?"

"Yes," he swallowed, and a bead of sweat slid down onto his shirt, "perfectly."

"Good, because if not, you and the rest of your kind will find yourselves dead in a rat-infested sewer where you belong. Now, I'm going to send this video to my ex-partner and let him know I'm coming for him next."

"I understand, yes, yes!" His eyes went wide. "We will go peacefully now. Sorry, Sorry." Vinni handed me his phone as they noisily vacated the bar, leaving their dead and injured behind.

"You good, boss?" Vinni reached for the door handle.

"No." My rage boiled up as I wondered who would come for her next.

Once we were back at the house, Niccola headed into the office while Vinni filled Francesco in on what had happened. Wyatt was passed out in front of the TV while some old American movie played on mute.

I went upstairs, showered, and took a moment to stare at Sienna in the dimly lit room.

Her even breaths told me she was fast asleep, but I couldn't help myself. I needed her.

I quietly tossed my towel over a chair and ran my hands through my hair to remove some of the dampness. My fingers skimmed her bare hip as I crawled into the bed naked. I slid my arm under her and pulled her smooth body to mine. She immediately molded herself to me with a little sigh. My fingers slid down her stomach and in between her legs, finding her warm and snug. My lips brushed over her neck, and I stroked her with the pad of my finger then slid it inside her. She stirred but didn't wake, and I was fine with that. I just needed something to settle my head.

"Coming home to you is how I know there has to be

someone higher out there watching over us," I whispered, feeling my stomach coil with need.

Once I was wet with my desire, I slid inside her. Then I slowed and just lay there a moment. I let myself totally relax, buried my face in her neck, closed my eyes, and let sleep take over.

Chapter
SEVENTEEN

Sienna

Syndicate Tour
Rome

"How much farther?" I glanced at my phone as my breaths shortened. To say I was nervous about going back to Rome was an understatement. I could practically smell the gasoline and burning embers from my bedroom. My memories threatened to overpower me, and my fear of how we would be received this first time entering Coppola territory now under Capri rule made things even worse.

"About ten minutes." Elio continued to stare at the laptop that rested on his lap. I knew he had a lot going on, but I desperately needed his attention to settle my nerves. He'd been a bit off since his night out with his friends. He did say they'd run into some trouble, but he'd been distracted ever since, and when I questioned him, he deflected and never went into any detail. I let it go, as I knew he'd tell me when he was ready.

"Remind me again where we're staying?"

"Ah," he squinted as he read something, "a villa."

I smiled and shook my head, then I side-eyed him again.

"A villa, okay. Are we meeting up with some of your family?"

"Mhm."

"I'll have to watch for Anna."

"Good idea," he answered, a million miles away.

"Yes, well, I'm going to strip down naked so you can have your way with me."

His gaze shot over to mine, and I could see him trying to rewind what I had just said.

"All right," he laughed as he set his computer on the seat beside him and turned to look at me, "you have my attention, *bella*."

"Do I?" I teased.

"Yes, my undivided attention." He wiggled his eyebrows then dragged his gaze down the front of my dress.

"I'm feeling uneasy about this stop," I confessed. "What if there's more hate here than understanding. Rome is not the same as Florence or Grosseto. People here aren't as familiar with the Capris, and they aren't as kind."

"*Bella*," his voice warmed, "I think your memories of this place are affecting how you perceive everyone." He squeezed my knee in reassurance. "We must inspire confidence here. When you're at the top, you have to act as though you belong there. People will be cautious, yes, and there will always be those who will want to see the bad in your success. Granted, this situation is a little different than most," he smiled, "but the truth is the Coppolas never took care of their people properly."

"And we have to show them that we're different?"

"Yes, *il mio tesoro*." He loved that I was quick to grasp what needed to be done here. "That is of utmost importance. The Coppolas drained their people's businesses while providing less than adequate protection, and the money they took from them wasn't going back into their own towns. We now know it was being funneled into accounts under Mikey's name. Rosa Coppola has a lot to answer for." I nodded. He placed his hand on the back of my neck and gave it a light massage. "They might not be able to see it yet, but we're going to improve their lives and give them more freedom to make their own choices. So, when you step out of this car, straighten your back, raise your chin, and prove to them that you are the right person to do this job."

"And if that doesn't happen?" I challenged.

"Then we kill anyone who doesn't agree." He smiled, but I knew he meant it.

"All right." I shook off my nerves and listened to what he said. He was right. This was my time to prove to the people that I had what it took to be their leader. I had just as much right as anyone else, and I carried the blood of Theo Coppola. It still seemed strange to me to know that.

Elio waited for Vinni to open the door, and he slid out and offered me a hand. I watched as a few soldiers stepped out from the front door and each took a place on a step. Then, to my surprise, a young couple came out with happy smiles. The young woman held a baby, and they both looked very excited to see Elio.

"You must be Sienna!" The woman stepped forward after she thrust her baby into Elio's arms and wrapped me up in a huge hug. "We've been so excited to meet you."

"Oh!" I laughed, completely taken back by her friendliness. "You must be Tab—"

"Just call me Tabby." She smiled and took my hand. "This is my husband Andy, and the little squirt your man is holding is Andy Jr." I looked at Elio, who was holding the little guy in the air like an airplane. "Be careful, Elio. You'll be sorry if he spits up on that fancy suit you're wearing."

"How do you know Elio?" Why hadn't Elio told me how friendly these people would be? All my nerves would have vanished.

"You're a jerk," she shot over to Elio, who flashed me a killer smile. I just shook my head. "Men," she said with a laugh and motioned for me to follow her inside the house. "The three of us went to college together," she said over her shoulder. "Unfortunately, Andrew's father got a job with the Coppolas, and Andrew was summoned to join him. You know how fathers can be. They only want what's best for their kids," she said sarcastically, "even when it means they have to work for the enemy, so to speak."

"Couldn't he have said no?"

"Andrew graduated top of his class in world economics, and when a syndicate like the Coppolas comes knocking…" She shrugged and poured me a glass of cucumber water. "It all worked out for the best, anyway. Andrew stayed in contact with Elio and, well, he's one of the reasons the Capris were able to make some big business deals in the east." She waved her hand. "No more about me, though. Your story is much more interesting. So, when I heard Theo's long-lost daughter and Elio's childhood love had returned, you could only imagine how intrigued we all were."

"News travels pretty fast, I see."

"Andrea and my mother are close," she chuckled, "and when the biggest mob underboss," she threw her gaze toward Elio, "wouldn't settle down and get married like most of the others before him, people want to know why. So, tell me, what was it like? I mean, finding out everything about your past. All I know is that you've discovered you're Theo's daughter."

"Nothing like finding out your father was a mob boss." I chuckled, and she joined in.

"Have you seen this yet?" She slid over a tablet and clicked on the screen before handing it to me. It was a photo of a newspaper.

Wait, where have I seen this before? I moved closer to get a better look at the photo of a field and some police. Oh! It was the one I'd seen in my mother's hotel room. I'd wondered about it, but never got to really read it.

"Remains of two bodies found in a field." She recited the line from memory, then began to read out loud. "Authorities conclude they are the bodies of a mother and daughter who went missing recently from the Coppola manor. It is believed they are the bodies of Elenora and Alessia Coppola, wife and daughter of Theo Coppola." I shook my head, thinking if only I had read it before when I'd seen it in my mother's room maybe I'd have gotten my answers faster, instead of waiting for her to decide when to tell me. "What's it been like for you since this whole thing started?"

"Truth," I sat down on the chair she pointed at, "it's as if someone printed my entire life on a piece of cardboard, cut it into puzzle shapes, shook it up nice and good, and left me to figure out how it goes back together."

"That painted a pretty good picture." She lightly chuckled then followed my line of sight over to Elio who was now elbows deep into some kind of baby food. "He's a pretty special guy."

"He is." I smiled when he caught my eye, and he smiled back.

"So," she pulled out a notebook, "let's chat about tonight and who you're going to meet and who you really need to win over."

I was impressed with Tabby's knowledge of the people we had to meet. She had even gone so far as to host a party the previous week to make sure everyone was told the real story about me and what was going to happen. A few times Andrew would speak in a low voice to Elio, and I tried not to watch, but I could tell something was going on.

After a good rundown, Tabby suggested we go upstairs to get ready. I looked around at their modern home and was impressed with the simple beauty of it. The huge windows with their curved chocolate wooden trim allowed a view of the garden beyond. The honey-colored walls made a lovely backdrop for the subtle striped furniture. Simple and gorgeous.

"I absolutely love your home. It's beautiful." I had to complement her as we walked up the staircase lined with large stone.

"Thank you. I did put a lot of time into choosing the fabrics, but my husband loves to design, and he's the one with all the inspiration." She laughed as she left me in the doorway of our room.

"See you downstairs later." She continued down the hall with a wave, and I got to work on myself.

"I see you're almost ready." Elio entered the room and planted a kiss on the top of my head, giving my bare bottom a friendly tap. He looked thoughtfully at my blue dress that was draped over a chair then removed the green tie he'd chosen for one that matched my outfit.

"How are you feeling?"

"Better," I assured him. "You could have told me how wonderful Tabby is."

"You told me you wanted to learn this life. Well, part

of that," he came up behind me in the mirror and kissed me again, "is walking into things not knowing what to expect. We're often going to be in situations that we can't predict or control. It comes with the territory." His eyes went serious. "Sometimes you'll have only seconds to react and pivot."

"That makes sense."

"I may look for teachable moments, but I won't let anything happen to you." He kissed my neck.

"You looked pretty comfortable with that baby." I watched his gaze move to mine while his lips still lingered on my skin. "Like a natural."

"Do you want kids?" His question threw me.

"Of course I do," I answered honestly, "but should we wait until we get married—"

"I can get a priest here in five minutes."

"And," I continued through my laughter, "not until we get this situation under control."

"I have everything under control," he purred, and I heard his belt strain as he undid it.

"There are a lot of people who need to get handled."

"Everything is being handled." He leaned me over the vanity and hooked my panties with his fingers and slowly slipped his massive erection into me. "And we can get married whenever you want. I vote for now." He chuckled. "But since we have a party to attend, we can at least work on the kid part."

"Do you really think right now is a good time to start thinking of kids?" I tried to sound serious, but he was dragging himself over the good parts, and I fought to think straight.

"We can always find a million and one reasons we shouldn't have kids in the moment," he flicked his hips, and I let out a shameful moan, "but the truth is, we've known each other a lifetime, you're mine, and I want little parts of you and me running around the house. So," he picked up the pace lifting my leg to rest on the bench seat so he could come at me at a different angle, "I think we should be practicing making a baby every chance we get."

"I think I," I gasped, trying to hold on to anything that could take the force that Elio was now coming at me with, "love that idea." I closed my eyes as my stomach tightened and my throat became dry.

His arms wrapped around me as he came. His teeth bit down on my shoulder, and he cried out, pulling me right along with him. He twitched and jerked, lifting me off the floor. I fought to breathe then became putty in his arms as I floated down from that blissful moment.

"Now," he panted into my ear, "get ready and think pregnant thoughts."

"I don't think that's how it works," I huffed then cringed when he slipped out.

"Shall we go again, then?" His eyes danced with excitement, and I held up a hand.

"Not if you expect me to walk without a limp tonight."

He winked and turned to gather up his pants and boxer briefs while I headed to the bathroom to freshen up.

Just as we were about to leave the bedroom, Elio stopped me.

"Tonight, you're meeting some very important businessmen who have worked closely with the Coppola uncles in the past. They'll be testing your loyalty, as they know they've only one year left before the contracts are up for negotiation. Let them know you have no plans to change anything until then." He checked his watch. "It doesn't matter that you don't know what all the businesses are, just that you're willing to hear them out and smooth over any concerns they might have with the Capri family. Remember to remind them of who you are and how you're fighting for them too."

"True." He was right. I just needed to show them that.

"The Coppolas did a terrible job running any kind of business. We'll give them that one year, then we'll come in and run the place the way it should be."

"All right," I smiled at him, thankful for the pep talk, "I can do that."

"I know you can." He opened the door and waited for me to go first.

Tabby and Andrew met us at the bottom of the stairs a while later. They were also dressed to impress.

"Our driver is waiting outside." Andrew inclined his head. "It's only about ten minutes away, but," he pointed down, "I'm aware of just how painful those pretty shoes can be."

"He knows me well." Tabby laughed and led the way out the door.

The place was crowded. There were a lot more people than I had expected, and even Tabby was shocked at the turnout. Elio held out his arm, and with his earlier comment in mind, I entered the room with my head held high and put a big, confident smile on my face. I caught sight of Vinni and Niccola, both with happy smiles, and it instantly eased my nerves. Wyatt would have been great in this situation, but he was off chasing down a lead he couldn't give up.

We met countless people over the next hours. After many introductions and small talk, Elio gave my arm a squeeze and left me to work the room on his own. Everyone wanted a moment with me, so I gave each one of them as much time as I could. We were fairly well practiced at it by now, but it was still exhausting.

"My turn." Tabby jumped in front of one of the men I was talking to and gave him the brushoff. "This is me giving you a breather," she joked.

"Thank you." I took a deep breath and licked my lips, then massaged my temple, as I felt a headache come on.

"How's it going?"

"Shockingly well. Everyone seems nice."

"Well, all of these people run their businesses under the Coppola umbrella, so it's in their best interest to meet you. The fact that so many showed up here today shows just how important you are."

"I'm glad they were willing to come out." I shook my head. "Many of these businessmen were working directly with the uncles. I wasn't sure if they'd even show up and give me a chance."

"Yes, as you know from Elio, the Coppolas were an older run syndicate, and since Theo and his brother both died years ago, the power was put into the uncles' hands. Instead of Theo overseeing all the companies, he had his men run everything. The uncles sort of outsourced and paid the larger companies to work directly with them. It's a risky move not having your own men directly working for you, but for the most part it seemed to work smoothly."

"How do you know all of this?"

"Andrew is a lot like Elio. He doesn't keep me in the dark. When Andrew and I met in college, we fell in love, and when his father saw how good I was at moving money around, he got me a job here." She grinned like something came to her. "It also helps that I'm very observant and demand to be kept in the know."

"I like that."

"Yeah," she speared the cherry in her drink with a toothpick, "I wouldn't have it any other way."

I nodded my agreement then took a sip of my prosecco. I drew in a deep breath, happy in the knowledge that Elio looked at me like an equal as well. I'd really lucked out with him.

I scanned the room and spotted him on his phone. He looked fit to kill.

Uh oh.

"How many people are there left for me to meet?"

"Umm," she leaned in her chair and did a quick count, "ten more, maybe?"

"All right, let's get this over with," I said, and she stood and looked around. I watched her approach the man she had brushed off earlier. She invited him over, and he took a seat in the chair she had left. With her hand on his shoulder, she made some last-minute comments that had him smiling at me. I leaned in with renewed determination and began a conversation.

Ten more people turned out to be a lot more, but it didn't take me long to discover what they all wanted to hear. My gut was right; they wanted nothing to change. I reassured each one that the only thing that would be different was the person collecting the cash at the end of the month. Rather than Pippo Coppola, it was now me.

Elio and I had discussed running the Coppola territory exactly the way he ran the Capri territory, but I had my reservations about making such a huge change so quickly after the Coppola syndicate's downfall. It was my feeling that we should ease in and make small changes at first. Resistance and mistrust came with changes made too quickly. We couldn't just bore into their lives and businesses and expect them to accept the Capri way without building that trust first. I was pleased that Elio listened then stepped back and gave me the space to make some moves of my own. I made some calls and possibly some mistakes, but I knew I could learn what worked to build the relationships I needed.

I also was pleased that Elio had taken the time to explain what the night was all about. He explained the contracts that were already in place, and those we hoped to form in the future. Knowing those details really helped give me a leg up. I felt confident and positive as I talked to these men and women about what was to come. I didn't promise anything I couldn't hold up to.

My phone buzzed against my lap, and I had to peek at who it was.

Niccola: Say you have to come out outside for a breather. I need your help just for a sec. It's for Elio's birthday. Can you slip away?

I knew Vinni and Niccola had been planning something special for Elio. I was pretty sure it was a custom sports car they were importing from Britain. I'd overheard Niccola on the phone with someone saying he didn't care that there were only three made, he wanted one. Niccola had some incredibly impressive hookups all over the world. It even amazed Elio at times. It was certainly an odd request at this particular time, but, of course, I couldn't refuse him.

I scanned the crowd and saw Vinni walking toward the door with a girl. I shook my head with a smile. He never failed to have a beautiful woman on his arm.

A man approached me, but I stood with an apologetic smile.

"Forgive me, but I just need a few minutes. If you wouldn't mind waiting, I'll be right back."

"Of course." He gave a slight bow and stepped back so I could pass.

I walked in the direction of the restroom then casually snagged a drink from a tray and veered off and slipped out a back door. I sipped as I strolled along, enjoying a moment away from the crowd. I glanced at my phone as

I made my way along the path.

Niccola: We're in the side driveway near the garage.

Sienna: On my way.

I made a quick turn and rounded the house then cut through some shrubs toward a garage. I hid a chuckle when I heard Vinni's voice coming from the shadows near what looked like a pool house. His deep voice and a giggle prompted a quick look. The girl had let her dress slip down around her ankles as Vinni took her hand and helped her step out of it. Her skin gleamed under the pool lights. I sighed and silently wished him luck as I quickly looked away. I assumed they'd reappear at the party in a bit.

As I neared the garage, I looked around.

Sienna: Where are you?

Niccola: I see you. Look where the second detached garage is. See the covered car? Francesco and I are right there.

I squinted to see in the dark and tried to pinpoint them.

Suddenly, something struck me as strange.

Wait. Francesco had been speaking with Andrew when I passed by them only a moment ago. How could he get down here before me?

A cold feeling prickled up my spine, and before I could react, something was whisked over my head, and a hand grabbed me around the waist.

"No!" I screamed, but a hand clamped over my mouth. I tasted blood. I saw lights flicker and hoped the hood was being removed, but the relief was short lived as a rag was jammed into my mouth and the hood pulled tight.

There was no way I was doing this again. I would not live in fear every day of my life just because some morons thought they could make a few bucks by capturing Mikey. Fear and anger mixed and burned as I was slammed over a hard shoulder and bounced about as he ran with me. A few minutes of that, and the rag slipped from my mouth. I took advantage of the moment.

"I'm not Mikey, and I have proof!" I shouted in hopes I could get through to this person I knew had been sent by that damn witch, Rosa Coppola. I jerked quickly and threw my body weight hard to one side. He lost his grip, and I hit the ground hard and rolled like a rag doll down an incline. Sticks and rocks took their toll on my body, but anything was better than being held. I came to a hard stop and fought to keep my head straight. I ripped the material off my face and blinked to look around.

"Ahh! Bitch!" I heard a voice behind me as I was shoved forward onto my stomach. Hands were all over me trying to get me to flip over, but I curled in a tight ball to protect myself. All I could think of was I was away from people and alone with some angry man.

"Help!" I shrieked as loudly as I could. "Help me!"

"Shut up!" he hissed as he shoved my face into a puddle of muddy water. I used all my strength to keep my mouth free so I could breathe. I coughed and spat as the dirty water filled my mouth and left me gasping for breath. I choked and fought for oxygen. Suddenly, I was picked up and slammed, coughing and sputtering, onto my back. His body was like lead as he straddled my waist and held down my arms. My eyes were full of mud and dirt, and I shook my head in a desperate effort to clear my vision. Everything remained stubbornly blurry, and I couldn't put together a straight thought as my brain fired off in a hundred directions for some way out of this.

"No!" I screamed.

"You think I wouldn't find out!" I tried to place the crazy voice as I blinked furiously at the dirt in my eyes. "Where are they?" he screamed down at me as he shook my body.

"Who?" I tried to follow as the fear ebbed and my blood began to boil. It was infuriating. "Where are who?" I screamed at him. "Get the hell off me."

"Where are my parents? I know they're dead! Who killed them?" He slammed his lips to mine, and everything clicked. My anger boiled over, and my body reacted.

Mariano.

I bit down on his lip and rammed my knee up into his crotch, and he shot up and fell forward, hitting his mouth and nose against my forehead. Blood dripped from his chin onto my face, and I turned my head and gagged.

"Ah!" He recovered and used his arm to quickly wipe the blood from his lips. "Where are they?"

"I don't know!" I screamed, hoping to hell someone would hear us. "I just got back from the Coppolas. I don't know anything about your parents."

"That's a lie, and you know it! I know it was Elio!"

He reached over for a rock, and I knew it was meant for my skull. I realized this could be it, and my adrenaline spiked. I swept out my arm and felt one of my high heels under my fingers. I grabbed it and swung my arm up and drove the pointed heel as hard as I could into his ear. He screamed in pain and leapt up. He grabbed at the shoe and pulled it out as blood spurted then threw it madly away from him. He was bent over moaning with a hand pressed against his head, so I didn't waste a second and scrambled to my feet and raced off blindly, away from him.

I limped, as the forest floor wasn't forgiving of my bare feet and arms. I wasn't registering much else but that I needed to find my way out of there before Mariano caught up to me. I guessed by his almost superhuman strength that he was high on something.

I could see the glow of the house and hear the music from the party, but I didn't dare go that way, as Mariano was between me and the house. I found myself in a clearing. It was too exposed, so I ran into the trees in hopes there might be a road or a house somewhere up ahead where I could get help. I stopped short at a small pond. I didn't have a second to think as I heard his steps approach at a run, and I was tackled to the ground. Pain exploded in my knees as my head was shoved underwater. I held my breath for as long as I could as I thrashed to escape his hold, but the adrenaline pulsing through me soon had my lungs empty themselves in a whoosh of panic. I fought the instinct to suck in a breath.

I was yanked up just as I saw stars, and I took a deep

thankful gulp. My chest heaved, and water poured off me as he held me up and yanked my head back to look into my face.

"This is what you did to Anna, isn't it? How does it feel to be going out the same way!"

"She deserved it," I gasped. "You deserve each other!"

He roared as he pushed me back under, and I knew this was it. He was out of his mind, high as a kite, and blind with fury.

I wasn't going out like this. There was no way I was going to drown in the dark in the woods like an animal. I'd been through too much to give up now. If I was going to die, I was going to go out swinging. I kicked and thrashed and gouged at any part of his body I could.

Suddenly, the hold he had on me was gone, and everything went black. Had I died? I felt myself being lifted out of the water and placed on my side. Someone put their mouth on mine. *Oh, no way.* I fought to push it away as I heaved up water and opened my eyes wide.

"Are you okay, miss?" A teenage boy hovered over me, and then his eyes went wide. I knew by his outfit he was from the party. "Ms. Coppola, I didn't know it was you!"

"Where is he?" I could barely talk as I tried to search for Mariano.

"When he heard us coming, he let you go and went off that way." He pointed. "My two buddies went after him."

"Call them back." I threw up some water. "He'll kill

them."

"He's gone," another voice said behind me. "Is she okay?"

"It's Ms. Coppola." the boy beside me made it sound like I was royalty.

"Seriously?" His friend moved into my line of sight. "Oh, my God!"

"Go tell the Don." His friend looked at him like he was crazy. "Go!"

The two boys nearly tripped over themselves as they raced off.

"It's okay, *signora*," the boy whispered, trying to soothe me as I tried to sit up. I just hoped to God Mariano wouldn't circle back.

"Where is she?" I could hear Elio's voice boom through the trees, and then what could only be described as a bull moose crashing through the forest brought a welcome sigh of relief to my frazzled nerves. I was terrified that the young man who stood guard over me would be in danger if Mariano reappeared.

"She's over here, sir!" the boy called through his cupped hands, and he lifted his arms and waved.

Elio dropped in front of me, on his knees, his face a picture of fear and worry.

"Jesus, are you hurt?" His voice was tender and caring, and I wanted to curl up on his lap and just take a second to feel safe, but instead I caught his hand to grab his attention.

"Mariano," I rasped. "He ran that way." I pointed in the direction Mariano had gone. Elio's face went murderous. He started to stand, but I held on tight to his hand and shook my head. "Please."

"Shit!" He wrestled with his urge to go hunt Mariano and his need to stay with me. "Go!" he ordered, and the soldiers who had followed him spanned out and started to search. Francesco arrived and immediately began to question the kid on exactly what he'd seen. The boy was keen to help, and I managed a smile at him as he did his best to tell his story. Francesco threw me a relieved look that I was okay, and I was able to nod back to let him know I was fine. Elio draped his warm jacket over my ruined dress and helped me up. We began to make our way back toward the house with Francesco and the boy.

"He knows," I whispered quietly to Elio and Francesco, "about his parents and Anna."

"I see," Elio grunted.

"I'll make some calls," Francesco muttered, but to my surprise, Elio shook his head.

"No, I think it's time to call in a friend."

"Vinni, I've decided we're going to skip the Villa Del Cardinale. I know it was an important stop, but with recent events, the less we do in Rome, the better." He waited a beat then hung up. I was surprised to hear we weren't attending the party there, but unbelievably thankful Elio decided not to go.

"How are you feeling about everything today?" Elio tapped his finger on the steering wheel and side-eyed me.

It had been two days since Mariano had tried to kill me in the woods, and a lot of discussion had been held since. He and I, however, had not had a chance to share our private thoughts in the last day. The search for Mariano had kept everyone busy. He had managed to slip away and couldn't be found. The guys were convinced he'd been getting help from someone.

It turned out my phone had been stolen from my purse during the party. I was quite sure Mariano was the one who had taken it and had probably accessed my contacts. I felt a little foolish as I knew I'd been lax at keeping my purse secure. A member of the staff had witnessed someone who had been near our table and could have had access to my purse while I'd been busy with the guests. He described a man he'd seen near the table long enough to warrant remembering him but hadn't gotten a good look at his face. We believed it was Mariano. No one knew for sure just how he had gained access to the party. Niccola was very relieved when he realized there was an explanation as to how someone could have used his number to draw me away from the others. I reassured him that I would never have thought for a moment he was involved and apologized for my own possible part in it.

"I'm fine. Still mad that he ruined my favorite Gucci dress, though." I sipped my water, not sharing that it felt like I could still taste mud in my mouth. I knew Elio was furious that Mariano had been able to get to me despite all the safety guards he'd put in place and that he managed to slip away into the night. I knew it was a point of pride for him.

"Mmm," was all he offered as he started the car.

Tabby and Andrew still felt terrible about what happened and wanted us to stay on a bit longer, but Elio had made the decision that we had to move on. He wanted me to join him for the drive this morning, and vaguely mentioned something about a package. I was happy to join him, as I was tired of everyone fussing over me. The fact that we were off to Sicily the next day didn't help. It was the one place I never wanted to return to. Memories of my younger life there at the Di Vaio house kept me awake at night.

"I shortened our next visit." Elio fiddled with his lighter. "I know you're nervous about returning there, and I'm comfortable because it's already our territory, but that's all the more reason we can't skip it altogether. We grew up there, so it would be insulting if we didn't show our faces at all."

"I understand." I really did, but it didn't make it any easier. I had a lot of demons that still resided there and ones I had zero intention of ever facing again in this lifetime.

"You'll not leave my sight." He stared at me, and I felt the authority radiating off him. "Is that clear?" He pulled onto a side road, and we bumped along until he stopped at the edge of a field.

"Yes, sir." I smiled, and we both leaned in for a kiss.

"I'm serious." His hand moved under my dress and up my bare leg.

"How serious?" I played along but stilled as I heard

a bike engine coming closer. "Where are we, anyway?" I squinted to see the biker headed our way, and Elio opened his door and stepped out. I followed suit and joined him where he leaned on the hood of the car.

"What the heck is that?" I saw something moving up and down and realized it was another biker, and they both approached us. It looked like something was being dragged behind the lead bike.

"This is a means to an end," Elio said, and he reached for my hand as the bikers came to a stop in front of us.

"I can't imagine what you're up to this time, but he's a big guy, so I hope he's a friend. But then again, if we are going to off him, I hope you have a really big gun, because…" My voice got sucked down into my lungs as I stared up at the man that now stood in front of us removing his helmet.

If the Devil had a son, it would be him.

"You must be Sienna," he said in English and looked me up and down as I felt the blood drain to my feet. "There's no need to kill me, I promise you that." He smirked, amused with my comment. "Nah, we're just here for the entertainment."

"Good to hear." I sagged into Elio, who wrapped an arm around me.

"Sienna, this is Trigger and his wife Tess." I turned my head to take in the stunning blonde who was in the process of removing her helmet. She placed it carefully on the seat of her mean-looking bike.

"Hey!" She waved, but my gaze jolted back to the huge, tattooed man in front of me. I was frozen to the spot. "Don't mind him," she laughed, "I know he can be intimidating. Trigger, let her pass," she called. I forced myself to move and stepped toward her. As I got close, she reached over and offered me her hand.

"Where are you from?" I wasn't even sure where to begin.

"Vegas." She shrugged. "Elio and Trigger go way back. Elio let us use his villa for our honeymoon. I'm really enjoying Rome. We've been touring the city, and I'm pleased to say even Trig has found some things that interest him."

I eyed the now moving thing behind the big guy's bike and figured we were not here for a purely social visit.

"Where was he?" Elio directed his comment at Trigger. He stayed close to my side, not letting me stay more than a few feet out of his reach.

"He was spotted at a truck stop. We just happened to be eating there." Trigger grinned, and I wasn't sure if he was kidding or not, but I wasn't about to ask too many questions.

"He's not that scary," Tess whispered, "unless he's sexually frustrated, then that's a different story. That's when I really get what I want."

Trigger slowly turned his massive body to look at her, and she just shrugged while I peed a little.

"Guess he was hiding out, staying with some of the junkies." Trigger shrugged. "He started running his mouth about how you were looking for him. Junkies ain't no one's friend. Guess he didn't get the memo. Let's just say one of them took the opportunity to get some easy money. So, a few bills later, they let me know where he ate."

"I see." Elio nodded. "What do I owe you?"

"Oh," Trigger chuckled darkly, "no need for that, man. I had a lot of fun."

"Ah," I tried to find my voice, "who was it that you found?"

Trigger stepped aside, and my eyes followed the chain that ran from his bike to whoever or whatever was attached to the end of it. Elio slipped off his jacket and placed it neatly over the hood of the car, then he walked over to the bike. I followed and watched as Elio yanked on the chain and dragged the package closer.

"Oh, my God, is that…?"

"Yup," Trigger said from behind me, "the shit from the woods. Special delivery, just as I promised my friend here." His slow smile grew, then he spat at his feet.

"I appreciate you taking the time from your honeymoon to pick him up for me." Elio nodded.

"Yes, I appreciate it, too." I smiled at them. "The fact that you're visiting Rome and now are here in a field where we're about to kill someone is very much appreciated." I figured if they were friends of Elio's and had brought Mariano, they must know the plan.

"It's the cherry on top for our trip." Tess winked, but I could see she was serious.

What the hell kind of comment was that? I found myself laughing at how sadistic she was.

"He's the shit from my nightmares, so I hope I get

a part in it." I laughed, making Trigger chuckle with approval.

I stood over Mariano's battered body and nudged his shoulder with my shoe.

"He's alive. I made sure I was careful."

"Good," I nodded, and Elio stood next to me, "I want to finish what I started."

"What does that mean?" Elio raised his eyebrow.

I kicked him in the ribs, and his mouth opened to show his missing teeth. When Elio made the connection, he looked up at me.

"The teeth you sent Papa, they were his?"

"I wished it was proof of a hit," I whispered, repeating what I wrote on the note to Piero when the teeth arrived in the mail, and Elio smiled, clearly impressed.

"I've never been more attracted to you." He kissed my hand as he stood.

"We're two messed up individuals."

"No, no," Tess peered over my shoulder, "that's Trigger's and my title. Find your own." She laughed, and I joined in, thinking how easy it was to be around Tess. I didn't feel the need to curb my dark humor because she was one step ahead of me.

"How are we doing this?" I asked Elio, who had unbuttoned his dress shirt and looked relaxed.

Trigger spoke up "I have a suggestion. We've been checking out Rome, sightseeing and the like," he peered over at Tess, who just smirked, and something told me there was more to that story, "and it got me thinking… They have some cool old torture chambers down there, man. Lots of pictures of what they used to do. So, you know? When in Rome." He stepped closer to Elio and spoke quietly in his ear. "There's two bikes." I heard the last few words.

"Have you ever ridden a bike, Sienna?" Tess asked, ignoring the guys as she draped an arm around my shoulders.

"No, I haven't."

"Wanna learn?"

"Yes, I do."

Before I knew what was happening, I was sitting on a bike with Tess straddling me from behind as she taught me how to shift gears. It took about thirty minutes before I got the balance down, but when Elio removed another chain from the trunk and tied it to Mariano's arms, I suddenly lost my confidence.

"Trigger," I called as I slipped off the bike, "here," I tossed him the helmet.

"You don't want to rip him apart?"

"Call it a late wedding present." I smiled

"You sure, even after all he did to you?"

"Yeah." I looked over at Mariano, who barely moved as Elio secured the chain. "Some things are even better from the sidelines."

"If you change your mind..." He backed up and headed for the bike.

"You don't want the revenge? Despite what people say, it feels amazing, kind of an aphrodisiac, if you ask me." Tess licked her lips while watching Tigger mount up. Something told me a lot of things were an aphrodisiac for them.

I held up a hand for them to hold off as Tess handed her helmet to Elio and he got on her bike. I bent down to speak to Mariano.

"Please, please, please, Sienna," he was pathetic, "you know that wasn't me, it was the drugs. I love you. I was the one who brought you and Elio back together."

"Shhh." I leaned down close so he could hear me over the roar of the engine. "When the bikes take off and you feel your body slowly rip apart, remember this. Andrea and Piero killed your parents, and they deserved it. I killed Anna and Salvo, and they deserved it, and now Elio and I are killing you. Say hello to the Devil for me. This is going to hurt like hell, and you deserve it."

He started to cry and struggle, writhing about in the dirt, but I just smiled. It was his time to go. I nodded to Elio, and he and Trigger started their engines and jolted forward in opposite directions. Once the line was taut, they inched forward, and Mariano screamed and yelled gibberish. The sound of bones and flesh ripping at the seams was oddly stimulating. It meant one less person to worry about and one less person to have to watch for over my shoulder.

Then he tore apart, sending a spray of blood into the air, like the fireworks that ended a party.

"That was beautiful." Tess sighed, and I turned to look back at her.

"Your definition of beautiful is vastly different than mine, Tess."

"You begin to see beauty in the darkest things," she

explained. "Death can be the most beautiful thing of all." She shrugged. "When someone's tried to take your life, it warps your view of the world. You can let it swallow you up, or you can embrace it." She pointed at what was left of Mariano. "You look for the hidden gems in it all. Sure, his mangled body is gross, but it was either you or him. And it needed to be him."

"I see what you're saying." I did; she was right. It came down to one of us being killed, and the other night it was nearly me.

"Whoo!" Trigger clapped his hands with excitement. "That was one hell of a wedding present."

Chapter

EIGHTEEN

Elio

I handed Trigger the lye, and we got to work. It took some time to prep the spot and add the chemicals, but once it was ready, we wasted no time and tossed Mariano's body parts into the drum then sat back to enjoy the evening.

Tess started a bonfire a few yards away. She and Sienna had retrieved the drinks from the trunk of our car and set up the lawn chairs.

"Hey, Sienna, if you squint hard enough, you can see the evil escaping as his flesh dissolves." Trigger grinned at her, and she laughed and squinted over at the barrel. I shook my head and thought how Trigger hadn't changed much since he was a boy. Trigger had been dealt a bad hand in life, but somehow, he'd found the strength to turn things around and made it better. Although the word *better* might be subject to the beholder. "Shall we celebrate?"

"We shall."

Tess was in the middle of sharing a story with Sienna, so we both grabbed a beer and stood, listening.

"I'm tellin' ya," Tess held up a strange looking purple thing, "carry one of these in your purse and all your problems are handled."

"Do you buy that shit in bulk?" Trigger hissed.

"What is it?" I studied the thing in her hand.

She tossed it at me, but Trigger reached out and snatched it from the air. "Trigger!"

He crushed whatever the hell it was within his hand and tossed it in the fire. A double A battery dropped at his feet.

"Trust me, you're welcome." He glared at his wife, and I decided I didn't want to know.

"And that's why they invented Amazon." Tess pulled out her phone, and Trigger muttered something, making her laugh.

Trigger leaned to one side and pulled out his buzzing phone. He glanced at the ID for a moment before he answered.

"Irons, what's going on?" Trigger walked a few steps away from us, and I came up behind Sienna, lifted her chin, and kissed her.

"Thanks for including me today," she murmured against my lips.

"We're a team now." I kissed her again. "We're in this together."

"You two are really cute." Tess sighed. "Oh, Elio, I heard your cousin Vinni has some connections with the Cartels. Any chance he could dig up some info on a certain name for me?"

"Anyone in particular?" I straightened.

"Yes, actually. Brick's brother."

"His brother is part of the Cartel?" That was news to me.

"Yes, or just mixed in and maybe over his head. We're not sure. Brick is keeping things quiet, but I know it's weighing on him. I'm a bit nervous for him and Minnie."

"Really?" I had thought Brick seemed a bit off at the fight in Vegas. I wondered if it was connected to his brother. "What's his name, and what do you know about him?"

"From what I know, he's changed his name to Dave Wilson, and he used to have connections to Washington."

"Used to?"

"I don't know much. I'm thinking he's mixed up with the Cartels now since Brick seems to be spending a lot of time in Mexico." She looked at Trigger then over at me, and she seemed to make a decision. "Normally, I wouldn't ask such a favor from someone I'd just met, even if you are a friend of Trigger's." She chewed her lower lip. "I would normally call Savannah and get her to speak with Logan. It's just that lately I get the sense," she nodded in Trigger's direction, "that there's tension in the house.”

“Oh?” I looked over my shoulder and watched Trigger stroke his beard as he talked.

“Mike Irons has called him a lot lately.” She pointed her chin at Trigger.

“Who’s Mike Irons?” Sienna asked, trying to follow along.

“He’s part of a U.S. military team,” I answered. I wondered what in the world could be happening. Trigger had told me about Cole Logan and his Blackstone team a few years back. A family member of mine had gone missing on holiday in Texas. I didn’t take up Cole’s offer of help at the time, as Vinni got him back, but from what I knew, that team was run like a well-oiled machine. I hoped she was wrong about things not going well.

“I hope everything’s all right…” Sienna’s voice trailed off when Trigger came back to join us.

“All good?” Tess asked. “Did—”

“Yeah.” He cut her off with a look. Clearly, the story wasn’t meant for our ears. From his grim expression, it was easy to read that things were far from good.

“Shit,” Tess murmured with closed eyes.

“Yeah.”

“If you need anything…” I muttered next to him.

“Appreciate it.” Trigger ran a hand through his Mohawk then walked over to his bike and pulled out a bottle of whiskey and two collapsible cups. “Let’s toast this fucker to the grave.”

Once we all sat around the fire and were a couple drinks in, the earlier tension faded, and Trigger relaxed again. Tess began to share stories about their parties in the desert. She had Sienna in stitches over her escapades with her friend Minnie.

"Who knew you could wax your vajayjay to the floor?" Tess tossed her hand in the air; this kind of conversation seemed the norm for her. "But sure as shit, she did, and of course all the staff had to witness it, so we just held a," she held up her fingers and did air quotes, "vag-viewing party while Minnie sipped a glass of champagne. Everything was funny up until we had to peel the wax off the…"

I tuned her out with a shudder. I didn't need the visual.

I noticed Sienna had only had a few sips of her drink and seemed tired. Maybe Mariano's murder took a toll on her. I wrapped an arm around her shoulders, and she nuzzled in with a happy sigh. I waited for Tess to finish her story before I spoke.

"Would you like to leave?" I looked at Sienna.

"No, this is fun. I'm just a little worn out from everything that's been going on."

"So," Tess pulled our attention over to her, "when is the wedding?"

"At the end of the tour," I announced. Sienna and I had decided it was the perfect way to end the tour and start our reign as one.

"Well, that's fucking romantic." She smiled at Trigger. "Will it be a big wedding or small?"

"What mafia wedding is ever small?" Trigger chuckled. "And *she* sure as shit won't be wearing a black wedding dress."

"You wore a black dress?" Sienna's head popped up as Tess nodded. "Do you have pictures?"

"Yeah." Tess pulled out her phone, and the girls gushed over her wedding. "We're anything but traditional." She laughed at that, and Sienna joined her.

The night went on, and the girls seemed to hit it off, but when Sienna could barely keep her eyes open, I knew it was time to pack it up. I helped her to the car while Trigger and I cleaned up and disposed of what was left of Mariano in a pit. While Tess was putting on her helmet and about to mount her bike, Trigger put his hand on my arm.

"Thanks."

"For what?"

"For all of it, and for this." He nodded around.

"You're always welcome, Trigger, and Tess seems great."

"She's my fucking other half." He smirked around his joint.

"Glad you found her."

"Look," he squinted when the smoke blew back in his face, "I'm going to send you a name and photo. If you'd circulate it through your men and just keep your eyes open, that'd be great."

"Sure." I turned to leave when he called me back.

"One more thing. Does the name Agent Collins mean anything to you?" I laughed and rolled my eyes. Oh, I knew Copper Collins.

"Yeah, why?"

"He's not FBI, is he?"

"He was," I raised my eyebrows, "until he took over the family business." I held up my family ring to indicate Collins was an American mobster still working as an FBI agent. It was actually quite brilliant. Risky, but brilliant.

"Fuck."

"Why?"

"One of Irons' buddies accepted a favor from him. Didn't realize who he really was." I made a face, knowing that could backfire. "Any suggestions?"

"Your buddy," I used his American term, "shouldn't have accepted that favor."

Trigger rubbed his beard as he thought, and I could tell that some things weren't sitting well with him.

"Collins and I have crossed paths a few times. I'll make some calls, see what I can do."

"Yeah." He nodded and threw me a wave as he climbed on his bike. Tess drove up beside him and waved goodbye, then they headed off to a hotel before going back Florence.

By the time I got back to the car, Sienna was fast asleep. I pulled the extra blanket from the trunk and covered her then started the car. We had a long trip to Sicily in the morning, and I knew she'd need all the sleep she could get to help her make it through that one.

Syndicate Tour
Sicily

To say Sienna was off her game was an understatement. I'd known that leg of the journey would take a toll on her, but I didn't expect her to shut down altogether. It was the reason I sent for Mama, not because I couldn't handle it, but because I thought she needed some female strength around her before we left for the meet and greet dinner.

"Thanks for coming." I kissed Mama's cheeks when she came through the front door.

"Of course. Where is she?"

"Out there." I motioned for her to follow me. "She's honestly fine, just distant."

I opened the patio doors and found Sienna asleep on a pool lounge chair.

"*Bella*, Mama is—"

"Thank you, *figlio*." Mama turned to me and kept her back to Sienna. "I'll take it from here. You go to your dinner and let everyone know Sienna needs a night off."

"Mama, this is a really big deal. Not having her by my side will look bad."

"She needs a night to herself," she insisted. "Give her that."

"Of course." I shook my head and remembered Sienna always came first. I glanced over my shoulder as I shut the doors and saw my mama curl up next to her. I was so thankful she was able to come.

"With Mama, you got me." Papa smiled as he approached me, and I would be beyond pleased if he could tag along. "How's our Sienna holding up?"

"I think Sicily is proving to be too much for her."

"Well," he thought for a moment, "this dinner is mandatory for you. Why don't I join you, and we can win them over together?"

"Sounds like a plan. Thank you, Papa." I clapped him on the shoulder in relief. Then we both went upstairs to get ready.

Dinner was stuffy and beyond boring. If I never had to sit through another one of Cousin Diego's stories about how he killed some guy at a corner store, I'd be just fine. Papa and I did our best to answer their questions. They showed little if any interest in Sienna. What they really wanted to know was how much money we'd absorbed from the Coppola family.

"There's money coming in from many directions," I explained. "We won't really know the full picture until we've combed through it all."

"I heard a rumor they were broke." Diego whirled his wine glass around, eyeing me suspiciously, which only further pissed me off. "And that your partner, who seems to be MIA, was dating your fiancée before you?"

I licked the inside of my dry mouth and took a breath, not wanting to anger family, but he'd crossed the line with me in the past and was pushing his limits.

"Diego," I gave him a dark warning not to push me too far, "you're a smart man, yet you run your month in front of me, your Don. One would think you'd learned your lesson years ago when you crossed Niccola."

"I just feel the people have a right to know who's running the family business. A right to know if the woman you're sticking it to is really in this for all of us."

Red. I saw red.

"You dare question me and my love and loyalty to our organization? The business that my family built?" I didn't waste a beat and drove my steak knife into the table just a hair from where his hand rested. He jumped, and his mouth dropped open. "I never liked you, Diego, and to think I included you in our tour out of respect. Guess what?" I tossed my napkin on the table and pushed my chair back so hard it crashed to the floor. "You just lost it."

"Oh, *mio*!" I heard his wife cry. "What did you do, Diego!"

Papa was right behind me and let out a loud laugh once we were back in the car.

"I've wanted to tell that little shit off for years, and you do it at one dinner. *Figlio*, I'm so proud of you."

I sighed and backed out of the driveaway. "Now I don't feel so bad about trying to drown him when I was eleven."

"Who are we to get in the way of destiny?" Papa dripped with sarcasm.

Once back at the house, I made some calls and decided we should leave for Naples that night instead of waiting the few days we had originally planned. I couldn't wait to get out of here.

"Where's Sienna?" I asked Vinni, who had his face in his phone.

"Not sure. She left shortly after you. I figured Andrea and Francesco took her out for a walk or something just to clear her head.”

I pulled out my phone and called Mama. I wanted to hear what she'd found out from Sienna.

“How was dinner with Diego?” she asked.

“Interesting,” I grunted. “Where are you?”

“Well, um, we are out.”

“Out where?” I didn't like that she was being vague, and the hair on the back of my neck warned me I wouldn't like what I was about to hear.

“Sienna wanted to go visit the dockyard.”

“What?” I roared, making Vinni jump to his feet.

“No, Elio, hear us out.”

“Mama!”

“Elio Piero Capri, you will not talk over your mama,” she scolded me, and I swallowed back my next sentence out of respect to her. “Sienna needs to face her past and not let it overpower her. We came here, and she got the answers she needed. Now she and Francesco are correcting a wrong.”

Papa walked into the room and wanted to know what was going on. I held the phone away from my ear and wanted to kill someone.

“Please talk to Mama before I do something I'll regret.” I handed him the phone and walked out of the room.

Chapter
NINETEEN

Noemi

It wasn't until Niccola was six months old that Greta finally left, and we were alone in the house. She hadn't wanted to leave even then. She always hovered within earshot, never allowing me any privacy, but something big had happened in Sicily and her presence was being requested. She had no choice but to go.

"Mama and Abramo just left, and I'm about to go out as well." Bosco tucked his hands into his pockets and leaned against the pillar on the porch as he watched our son. Niccola was in the swing while his nanny made him smile with her goofy faces. "I'll be back later."

"You always are," I muttered low enough he couldn't hear me.

"Maybe you could go in town, meet up with some people. Perhaps make some friends."

Or maybe I cut the brake lines in your car, so you'd crash and burn on your way to your lover's house.

"Yeah, maybe." I kept my gaze on our son.

"It's not healthy for you to be here alone all the time."

"I'm hardly alone." I half laughed, and he sighed, annoyed I was poking at his mother's constant presence.

"It was just how the situation came about, Noemi. Mama's old fashioned, and what we did was not the traditional way to have a child. But here we are, and she only wants what's best for Niccola."

"So, making me feel unwelcome is her way of welcoming me into the family." I finally peered over at him. "You know the only person I have left is my aunt. You know how hard my mother's death was on me. Do you have any idea how difficult it's been living in this house, feeling like a prisoner?"

"Truth?" He came to sit next to me, and I envisioned my hands around his neck squeezing out what little life he had left inside his mama's-boy body. "Someone told Mama that you'd been spotted at the Coppola house not long before you arrived here. Needless to say, it made her nervous to leave you alone here."

What?

"Who said that?" I swore to all the demons that walked this Earth if it was Elenora, I would hunt down her daughter and remove each of her bones right in front of her.

"I don't know who it was. I think it was an anonymous call."

"I thought it was your house," I snapped.

"It is," he stumbled like the coward he was when it came to his mother, "but she was only being vigilant, and it's protocol to watch over those we're unsure of."

"Let me ask you this." I turned to face him straight on. "Do you trust me?"

"I'm leaving you alone here today, aren't I?"

Yes, to leave and have sex with Amara. Your not-so-secret lover.

I nodded and went back to watching Niccola while I waited for him to leave. We didn't kiss each other goodbye, and we hardly ever used any terms of endearment. I was saving that for when I needed to have another child. I wanted a stronger hook into this family. I still worried I'd be kicked to the curb when our boy was of age. I needed to make sure this was my forever home.

I waited a good thirty minutes before I told the nanny that I needed to go to town and that I would leave Niccola with her, as he had so much fun with her. That made her smile, and I matched it. I was desperate for a break from this Capri prison.

I emptied my enormous beach bag on the table and started to fill it with food, a set of clean sheets, a warm blanket, and the little cash I'd been able to put together. I swiped a little from our joint account every week.

I put the bulky bag in the car and left for the city. I turned onto a short side street and parked next to the local pub. I could hear music coming from inside.

The bakery below her apartment smelled delicious as I awkwardly carried the bag up the stairs and knocked on the door.

"Cuoricino!" My mama opened the door wide and hurried me inside. I knew I shouldn't have come here. Everyone thought she was dead, and I wanted it to stay that way, but I needed it. "Where's my Niccola?"

"It wasn't the time to bring him, Mama. Next time." I started to unload the things I'd brought and put it away in her tiny apartment. She'd only moved in about a month before. She wanted to be closer, and living above the bakery was cheaper than most of the places in the area.

"Did you see my new rocking chair?" She pointed to a wooden rocker that squeaked when she sat down on it. "The seat needs to be reupholstered, but that's for another day."

"It's lovely, Mama."

"It's where I do my knitting." She pointed to her basket of colorful wool.

"Very nice. Now, look, I don't have a lot of time, so come sit here." I patted the bed.

She came across and joined me. The apartment only consisted of one room, and the bed was directly across from her TV. I sighed in the knowledge that she only had two channels on that old thing, but at least her bookshelf was well stocked.

"If anyone asks, who do you say you are friends with?" Sometimes I wondered how well my mama's head was and I couldn't have her muttering anything about

the Coppolas. Ever.

"The Capris." She took my hand in hers. "I know you don't think I'll remember, but listen, mia figlia, *I was there when you and Rosa Coppola made your agreement. We're in this lie together. So, you do your part and live your life with Bosco, and I'll be just fine right here."*

"Has she called on you?" I was referring to Rosa and how part of our deal was we'd keep each other's secrets. I gave her information on the Capris, and she promised never to tell that I'd dated Theo.

"No." She stopped to think. "But there was that woman, you know, with the jet-black hair, she came by asking where you were." My stomach sank.

"What was she asking about me?"

"She wanted to know if you had a son or a daughter," she held up a hand, "no I didn't say a thing, but it wouldn't take much for her to figure it out."

"That's odd, her coming here and asking you that. How did she even find you?"

"I don't know, maybe Rosa?"

I stood, feeling uneasy. I thought it was her way of letting me know she could get to anyone I loved, including my mother whose death I'd faked. I gathered my bag and keys.

"Her son was adorable."

"She had a boy with her?"

"Yes, sweet little cheeks, too. I believe she said his name was Hector."

The loud ring of my phone jolted me out of my memory and nearly out my skin. I glanced at the ID and shot straight to my feet. I must have been half asleep.

"I told you I needed time!"

"And you promised me they'd be at the Villa del Cardinale!" Hector yelled angrily. I felt like the wind had just been knocked out of me.

"That was the plan. I'm not there, so I don't know what's going on. Did you ask Vinni or Niccola?"

"No! Because that was your thing to handle. The deal's off, Noemi. I'm tired of your games!"

The call disconnected, and I stood there in the kitchen feeling as though the floor was about to open up and swallow me whole. I reached out for the counter and let out an Earth-shattering scream.

Chapter
TWENTY

Sienna

"This is where you grew up?" Wyatt shifted to see out the window better. "Suddenly, everything all makes sense now."

"See over there," Andrea pointed past his nose, "that takes you to the path that leads to our old house." She moved her finger. "It also leads to the pond where Sienna and Elio used to meet." She gave my arm a warm little pat, but I couldn't take my eyes from the decrepit house where I'd once suffered so much physical and emotional pain.

"Ah, yes, the famous pond. I'd like to say something about how romantic that is, but I think I caught something just from being in this driveway," he joked darkly and followed my gaze, while I pressed my knees together to stop the shakes. Andrea answered a call and spoke quietly as Wyatt reached over and gave my shoulder a loving squeeze. "I'm really proud of you for having the strength to come back here and do this, Sienna."

I nodded and tried to smile. I knew he knew about all the horrors of this place and understood the depth of my emotion.

"Are you sure?" Francesco asked me for the hundredth time. I knew he was worried, but this was something I needed to do.

"Try to understand, Francesco. These kids are just living paychecks." I swallowed down the emotion that crept up my throat. "Nothing but slaves, worked to the bone. There's not a birthday or a Christmas recognized for any of them, ever. No child should live like that." I dashed a tear away. I wasn't sad for me; I was sad for those kids. It wasn't long ago that I was one of them, hopeless, hungry, and exhausted.

I looked once more at the children who sat in various spots outside the decrepit old Di Vaio house. I knew the drill. You stayed outside as much as possible to keep out of the way, but you were too exhausted to even think of play. You had to stay within the borders of the yard, and if you strayed, you were granted quite the beating. Andrew and Julie Di Vaio worked the system and made a lot of money "fostering" kids. A prison camp would have been an improvement. At least they'd get a hot meal every day.

"Sienna, I'm so incredibly sorry to know you lived

this way. I honestly had no idea." Francesco's voice carried a deep tremor of sorrow. It reached me on such a personal level I felt I had to console him.

"Don't be sad. You couldn't have known. Besides," I shrugged; the past was the past, "it only made me stronger."

"They're on the way." Andrea tucked away her phone as she spoke. "I let them know the urgency of the situation and who I was. I don't think they'll be long." She reached forward to squeeze my shoulder.

We settled in to wait in the car across from the house. I thought back to our visit at the dockyard earlier in the day, where I discovered the Di Vaios were still very much in control of things. Though Elio and Francesco had stripped them of their positions there years ago, somehow, some way, they'd been quietly reinstated. I tucked that knowledge away. I'd make sure Elio looked into just how that could have happened.

A short time later, the four of us watched as several cars arrived. The police, along with a representative of the foster care agency, stormed onto the property. Children scattered then gathered in groups to watch. Andrea's conversation with the powers that be obviously had the desired effect. She had told them everything about the neglect and illegal operations that happened at that house. She'd also shared the location of Andrew's second house where he always kept teenage girls. I had no doubt he was still up to his neck in that operation.

"They found the stash." Francesco chuckled as one officer knocked over some rain barrels in the intense search that followed. The cocaine baggies were tagged and put in one of the patrol cars. "Compliments of Mariano." He laughed.

"How much did you plant?" I asked, not taking my eyes off what was going on outside the car window. The whole time, I kept thinking if only I'd come back years ago, I might have saved so many more kids.

"Enough to make them do a careful search, but the scales and other tools I tossed in the field should ensure a lifetime behind bars."

"It's like we're part of a reality TV show," Wyatt breathed.

I bit my lip while the kids were rounded up and loaded into a van then whisked away. I knew they'd be looked after now. I only hoped they'd be given a second chance at a better life. I couldn't imagine it would be any worse than this place.

Once Andrew and Julie were arrested and taken back inside for some questioning, Francesco revved the car and we pulled into the driveway.

"All right, kid, you're up."

I opened the door, stepped out, and ran my hands down my skirt to smooth it for something to do then took a deep breath.

Be strong. This is the moment you've waited a lifetime for.

The female officer approached and addressed us. She nodded to Andrea and said she was the one she had spoken to earlier. She looked over at me and gave a polite nod, and Andrea introduced me. When I told her what

I wanted, she walked with me to the house and stood aside while I entered. I was glad she followed me, as the memories of this place had my stomach heaving. I forced myself to take a disinterested tone as I spoke.

"Do you recognize me?" I directed my words at Andrew, who looked me up and down then spat at my feet from the couch where he sat. His face was old and weathered. He looked twice his age, but alcohol and drugs would do that to a person.

"Should I?" he grunted, and Julie leaned forward to get a good look at me.

"No!" she gasped, and I saw half her teeth were missing. Yikes, she must have moved up to some harder drugs for that to happen. Now I knew why Francesco had chosen to plant cocaine for the officers to find. "It's that girl who ran away. Our obligation. Seena or something, isn't it? I remember that necklace." She nodded toward my pendants.

The officer who was standing near me answered her radio and stepped a few feet away. I smiled at the opportunity I'd been given.

"You little bitch." Andrew glared at me. "You cost me some clients and—"

"A son?" I couldn't help myself and relished their reactions of pure shock. "If it counts, Renzo felt all kinds of pain when I beat him to death with a pipe and left his body in an alley."

"You're a sick girl!" Julie tried to wiggle over to me, and I laughed at the comedy of how stupid she looked in handcuffs. "I'm going to kill you!"

"No, actually, you aren't, because I just made sure you both are going to prison for a very long time. I'll guess neither of you will last long, but at least I'll know you're getting what you deserve."

"You did this?" Andrew hissed. "You bitch. Who the hell do you think you are?"

"Ah," I smirked, "that's a really good question. I'm very happy to answer that for you, Andrew. I happen to be Donna to the Coppola syndicate and am about to marry the new Don of the Capri syndicate, and your worst nightmare." I grinned happily at them. "I can promise you two monsters this…" I bent down and spoke slowly, so they didn't miss a word. "I control everything in this country, including the prisons, so if you think you're in for a vacation, think again." I stood and slammed the front door on their stunned faces.

Gosh, that felt amazing. Maybe even better than Mariano's death.

On my way back to the car, I felt all the stress of my childhood lift from my shoulders, and I knew I could finally let this go and start living again. With each step, I became lighter and felt more in control. *Yes, that was just what needed to happen.*

"You look happy." Andrea smiled at me as I got in the car.

"Happy doesn't even begin to describe this feeling." Wyatt put his arm around me and hugged me tight but didn't speak.

"Good." Francesco nodded and started down the driveway.

When we arrived back at the house, the sun had just set, and the crickets were starting their evening warm-up.

"Apparently, the dinner didn't go as well as we'd hoped," Andrea explained as we unfolded from the vehicle. "I'm not sure what they were up to just now, but…" She stopped me as Vinni came out and handed her a bag. "I was hoping you'd join me on a little walk."

"Of course." She took my arm and directed me toward a massive rose garden that opened into a grassy field. Once we were a way from the house, she stopped then closed her eyes and took a deep breath.

"Oh, *mio*, I just love the smell of roses and sweet grass."

"I love the sound the grass makes when the wind travels through it," I added, joining her enjoyment of the sights and sounds around us.

"Life can be so simple at times, while other times it confuses us and makes it almost impossible to navigate." She smiled warmly at me. "Sienna, I want you to know that a while ago, Elio shared one of your journals with me." She shifted like she wasn't sure if I would be upset by her reading them. "I would never presume to take the place of your mama, but I wanted to do something for you. Something you should have had when you were younger."

"Okay." I tilted my head and waited.

"You had so many questions, but no one to answer them." She reached in the bag and pulled out a heavy package wrapped in brown butcher paper and tied with string. She placed it in my hands. "I know it's too late, but if I'd been your mother, these would be my answers. Only I would have given you them when you asked."

I shook my head as emotions prickled. Carefully, I undid the bow and ripped the corner open then lowered to the ground as I recognized my journals. She joined me and made herself comfortable, not saying anything. I opened the first cover and flipped immediately to the middle of the journal. I knew where my questions were, and I skimmed through my childhood words.

Questions for Mom:

Is it strange that when he's near me, I feel warm and my head gets foggy?

Instead of a blank space after the question, Andrea had written an answer in her familiar small, neat script.

No, it's not strange, my dear Sienna. The warmth is because he makes you feel good and safe inside, and the foggy head is because you're attracted to how he looks and smells. This is all completely normal to have these feelings toward a boy. Especially a special boy.

I smiled at her answer as a tear raced down my cheek. I skipped down to the last one, the one answer I'd wanted the most.

How do I know I'm in love with Elio?

Love is when you're spinning so fast that everything blurs around you. Butterflies take home in your tummy, you feel giddy whenever he's around, and most of all, he makes you laugh. Being in love should bring you joy. Staying in love takes patience and compromise, yes, but most of all love is about living life to the fullest together as one and making each other laugh. Life is too glorious not to laugh at the good, the bad, and the ugly.

I used the back of my hand and did a poor job of clearing my tears.

"I hope I didn't overstep in answering your questions, Sienna, but no little girl should go through life without some kind of guidance."

"The fact that you did this…" I tried to pull myself together, but it was no use. I was a weeping mess. "It's like you've gone back in time and soothed a heartache I never thought was possible." I threw myself in her arms and hugged her tight. "Thank you, Andrea, for the kindest gift a mother could give."

"You're very welcome, my *bambina*." She sniffed as she stroked my hair the way a mother would a child. "I just adore you, Sienna, and I can't express how excited I am that you're going to be my daughter-in-law."

I laughed happily back at her because I'd dreamed of being Elio's wife my entire life, and it was finally going to happen.

"Do you feel better than you did this morning?" She dried my tear-streaked cheeks.

"Yes. I think I needed today more than I ever realized."

"Good. Would you be up to eating something?"

"Yes, I would." I thought for a moment as I felt my stomach grumble. "I'm starving."

I was pleased the cook prepared simple food tonight and nothing too rich in flavor. I was hungry, but with all the rich food we'd been eating throughout our trip, it was hard on the stomach. I just wanted good old bread and cheese and seasonal vegetables. I was delighted when that was exactly what was served. We all ate at the table and talked over the plan for the next day.

"We leave at five a.m. and take this route here to the airport." Elio pointed at a map and ran his finger along a back road that he knew of from when he was young. "Once we board, it's roughly a three-hour flight to Naples. From there, we'll meet Marco, Vinni's friend, who'll drive us to Pozzuoli, where we'll spend the night, and then we travel to our next destination, Castello Aragonese."

"Wouldn't it make more sense to go to Bari first then Naples?" I asked, looking at the map and trying to understand why we'd backtrack to Bari after we went to Naples.

Elio looked at his father then at me. "There's been some unrest in Bari. We're holding our visit a bit to see how the city fares."

"Unrest?"

"Let's just say our friends to the east of Bari are upset with the sudden changes with the Coppola downfall. They too were victims of Rosa Coppola and aren't happy, and now that she's gone into hiding, emotions are high. As soon as things settle, and we feel they're ready to talk, we can go and pay our respects. They are already under Capri control, so we aren't too worried. Naples, on the other hand, is the last remaining Milani syndicate. Though we know Pauly quite well, Mariano's been close with him. That stop is more important."

"Naples is merely a speck on the map. You'd think

they'd just roll over and hand you the keys," Wyatt joked.

"Us the keys," Elio corrected, and I smiled over at him. "There's the Coppola way of getting land, and then there's ours. We will visit, explain the situation, and come to an agreement that will benefit them and their people."

"And if they don't comply?" Wyatt sipped his water.

"Then we'll take over and the deal is off the table. We pride ourselves in our ability to perform in a more refined manner with our clients. Steamrolling over people was never how we wanted to do business, nor will it ever be. If you are to be a leader, then be a good one. It's how you maintain power the longest. Respect goes a long way, and it's an underestimated tool that a lot of people lack. It's why we are now the strongest syndicate to date."

"Refined, but dark, if I may say so." Wyatt smiled. "I'm impressed."

"Well said," Andrea chimed in. "Now, who's up for dessert?"

Just like that, the work talk ended, and Elio soon had everyone delighted with his tale of how we'd disposed of Mariano.

Chapter
TWENTY-ONE

Elio

Syndicate Tour
Naples

"Deal with it!" I boomed through the phone then picked up a clay lamp and threw it across the room. It didn't help, so I grabbed the other and did the same. Niccola ducked as he came in the room, narrowly escaping a concussion. I faced him and put my hand to my head. It felt like it was going to split in two.

"Whatever you want, boss, just say the word."

I leaned on a table and looked out at the view. The water from the top of the Castello Aragonese was beautiful, but it barely registered. We'd only arrived the day before, and things were quickly getting out of control back home at our dockyard. I knew the news had spread that I was away traveling, and some men tried to attack my port. Was it Rosa or someone else trying to take advantage of my being away? I hated not knowing.

"Boss?" The urgency in his voice needed action.

"Kill them all."

Silence.

I hung up quickly to make my point. Not that my people would ever question my decisions. I wanted to set a precedent here that anyone who came with the intent to harm would automatically be killed.

"What do you need from me?" Niccola knew just what to ask.

"Find out what's going on at the dockyard. And where is—"

"The last time I saw her, she was in the marble pool downstairs." He smiled then sat down at his desk and got right to work.

I headed down the stone stairs, powering off my phone as I went. I saw a few staff members, but they scurried away when they spotted me, which was a good thing because I was in a mood to snap. The shower room was empty, so I stripped down to nothing and headed out to the marble pool. Three women were in a corner of the pool. When they saw me, their gazes dropped to the massive erection that only came when I thought of my fiancée.

"Out," I ordered, and they darted out of the pool in a blink. I looked around for her and spotted the red light was on in the sports sauna. I made my way over and looked inside to see Sienna draped naked on her towel. She lay on her back, and I took a moment to enjoy her through the steamy little window.

When I opened the door, she lazily looked up, and when she saw it was me, her lips stretched into a sexy smile.

"Anyone could find you this way." I scowled at the thought.

"I paid one of the staff members to discourage the men from coming down for a bit." She eyed my heavy excitement. I was moments away from erupting. "I see you got past them." She giggled.

"No one says no to me." I felt some of the earlier tension ease away just from being near her.

"Is that so?" She lifted an eyebrow as she rolled onto her side, making a show of admiring the view. "What happened?" She read me all too well.

"How do you know something happened?"

"Oh, please, Elio. You have several different tells, and when you're pissed about work, you get rock solid like a hammer." She dragged her gaze down my stomach, and her nipples hardened. "So, what's happened?"

"Let's just say the grass won't be green when we get home." I shut the door to put her between me and the exit, then I moved toward her. She strained her neck to look up at me as I fingered one of her nipples, then she moved closer and let out a happy sigh. "Did you know these benches are made to swivel?" I unlocked the bench she was on and rotated it, so her head was right below my erection. "Fighters would come here from all over Italy, and after their fight they'd get a massage in the sauna to ease their aching muscles." I kept my tone conversational even as my eyes burned into her.

"Oh, so, each day would have a happy ending?" She smiled up at me, her eyes dancing with all kinds of dirty thoughts.

I leaned over and used my hands to hover over her body and placed a kiss right below her belly button.

"I'm not sure." I kissed her side. "I've never experienced one." I kissed her pelvic bone, breathing in her arousal. I was addicted to her scent and felt my mouth water.

"You've been missing out." She stretched up to reach my back and pressed her fingers into my ass and gently messaged it. Her soft, warm breasts pressed against me and felt amazing on my stomach.

Then I moaned. I hardly recognized the primal sound that came from deep within me. Her tongue licked the length of my shaft and urged me forward, slipping me between her hot lips. I stilled, begging my head to let me last, and once I gathered myself, I pulled out of her mouth, pushed my weight back on my hands, and lifted my legs to rest on my knees by her head. I leaned forward again and pushed myself back into her mouth as I reached between her legs to split her folds.

"Mm." Her vibrations had my eyes roll back in my head.

She was wet and ready. I fed on her, trying to balance my desire to take with my need to go slow and give her what she needed as well. It was always a head trip with Sienna in these moments. I never knew if I was coming or going, nor did I care. I licked and lapped and caressed her with my free hand. All the while, she sucked hard then soft and used her tongue in unimaginable ways to apply different pressures that drove me wild.

She cried out in a muffled voice when I nibbled on the inside of her leg, and she gently bushed her teeth over my tip.

"Again!" I ordered, loving the new feeling she'd just brought to the table. She did it again, and I fought to breathe. Every muscle in my neck popped, and I held back the blow that was coming her way. "I need to be in you!"

I hopped off and nearly cried at the sudden loss of her sweet, plump lips. Her breasts and stomach were heaving, and I needed more. So much more.

"Ready?" I barely waited for her to respond as I hooked her legs and slid straight inside her.

"Ahh!" she cried out in bliss, and I started to rock at a painfully slow pace. We were both slick with sweat, and our bodies slapped with a sweet sound as we connected. My head was in pure utopia. It was amazing how one small person could make an army of stress evaporate with just a simple connection.

She hooked her legs over my shoulders and lifted her hands, so I'd take them. Her slick body on the smooth bench met each of my thrusts, twisting so I hit different angles. It was unreal. My vison started to spot, and I knew I was close. She suddenly bucked and screamed, and I let her hands go to wrap my arms around her back so I could bury my face in her breasts. I came to an enormous peak. I lost track of how long I left my body, but when I floated down, all I cared about was the woman under me and that she was safe, sound, and full of me.

We showered, changed, and met downstairs, ready to continue our tour. The day's meeting was to be held on a boat, and I was glad it was a good day for it. A tour along the coast would be a nice change.

Niccola met me by the door and motioned for me to step aside.

"The men at the dock," he pulled up a photo on his tablet, "they were sent by Mariano. Apparently, Pauly Milani had orders from him to send in some men if he didn't call last night, and since we know Mariano couldn't have showed, the order was sent out. I wonder if he had a hunch his end might come."

"Pauly. Makes sense." I slowly nodded and thought about how I'd handle it. "Good work. Let's go, or we'll be late. First business, then I'll deal with that traitor." We got in the car with Vinni.

It was a short trip down to the boat where everyone was waiting for us. Sienna was in a white dress and a big floppy hat, and I matched in white cotton pants and a loose shirt. Though I felt extremely underdressed, I reassessed when I saw the way Sienna eyed me from across the deck. Wyatt, on the other hand, looked like he just stepped out of some American commercial with his tight striped shirt and even tighter light pink shorts. Neither left anything to the imagination. I swore if he crossed his leg any higher his mouse would be loose.

"Don't try to hide it, Elio." Wyatt leaned back to soak up the sun. "I'd be looking at my thighs too."

I hid my laugh. I wasn't normally comfortable with a personality like Wyatt's. I actually didn't know anyone quite like him, but he was incredibly refreshing and quite funny at times. He had a type of finesse about him that was oddly endearing. He exuded confidence, and I admired that. He knew who he was and embraced it; not many could say they did the same. He reminded me of Vinni at times. Not that I'd ever point that out. Vinni took pride in being a ladies' man. But I could see why Sienna was so protective of him. He wore his heart on his sleeve, and he loved her without conditions.

"It's not your thighs people are looking at," Sienna scoffed. "I can practically see your berries."

"Practically?" Niccola laughed out loud. "I can determine the circumference of each berry from here."

"I knew you were doing the math." Wyatt grinned, and I shook my head, thinking how different my conversation had been the last time I visited Naples.

"Ready to meet our company?" I nodded to the dock where four men stood ready to be won over by us. One of them was Domenico Milani. The Don of the Naples syndicate and Pauly's father. Domenico knew this day would come. The Milani family were being killed off systematically by the Coppolas, and the only reason the killings had stopped was because of the Capris. His debt was about to be called, and he needed to answer.

"After this morning's workout, I'm ready for

anything," she whispered as the men were welcomed aboard. The sea breeze and open water set a beautiful stage for our meeting.

Sienna was extraordinary to watch. She sold them on us within the first twenty minutes. She had them laughing and agreeing to things I'd never have thought to bring up so soon. A few times, she'd reach over and touch one of them on the forearm, and that little interaction made them feel connected and special. She was very good, and they now were only too happy to be part of our new movement. We could expect them to cooperate with whatever we asked of them.

"So, Sienna should be at all of our meetings." Niccola chuckled softly in my ear from where we stood on the deck watching the magic unfold. "It's like she's cast a spell over them."

"She's something, isn't she? She used to amaze me when she worked the bar." Wyatt sucked on an orange slice he'd snagged from the table next to us. "She'd double the business whenever she'd work. Needless to say, she got her choice of all the best shifts, six days a week."

"What's impressive is they're not even looking at her chest," Vinni pointed out. "They're looking in her eyes. That's talent."

I secretly smiled inside at my cousin's comment, but he was right. None of the men took any opportunity to look at her body. They kept their eyes on hers as they talked. They were being respectful of her, and therefore, of me.

"Nice." I sipped my drink as I thought. "I like these guys. Maybe I *can* work something out with them."

"Smart move, boss." Vinni nodded as he watched Wyatt pop a grape in his mouth.

I snapped a quick photo of Sienna and sent it to Papa.

Elio: Making magic.

Papa: Wave that wand, little lady! Mama and I will meet you after dinner. Looking forward to hearing all about it.

I was pleased Papa had convinced Mama to stay on for the rest of the tour. I knew how much Sienna needed her here. They were both enjoying the girl time. I made a mental note to remember that she would, at least most of the time, be surrounded by men—and, well, Wyatt—so a little estrogen would be needed now and then.

Domenico excused himself from the group and made his way over to where we sat.

"Mr. Capri," he stood and waited for me to acknowledge him, which I did with a simple nod, "I must say your fiancée is very special."

"She is."

"You're a lucky man."

"I am."

"I must admit I wasn't looking forward to this meeting."

"I wouldn't think so." I pointed to the bench across from me, so he'd sit. "We've been very generous in helping with your family's difficulties. Wouldn't you agree? Now, I'm sure you won't mind what I'm requesting in return."

"You have been." He nodded. I knew it was hard to swallow his pride. It was hard work to run a syndicate, no matter the size. "Of course, I knew this time would come. I must say I thought this was going to be a very stuffy meeting with the usual rum and cigars. I was expecting sly remarks about my imminent downfall, but I see now you conduct business very differently than those in the past."

"I'm not in the business to degrade or tear down others where it isn't necessary. But this merge is happening, and I respect that you came to meet and listen to what I have to say."

"I don't want to lose my position overseeing my," he caught himself, "your Naples ports."

"I'm not asking for that. I think you do a fine job here, and the idea of moving someone else into the position sounds like more work than I'd like to think about."

"Happy to hear it." He glanced over at Sienna and the others. "I think this change will be a good thing." I could see him relax a little.

"I'm glad you feel that way, Domenico, because I have a favor to ask of you."

"Oh?" He suddenly tightened up again.

"I know your son has a drug problem," I lifted my glass to the waiter, indicating I wanted another, "and I know he sent a group of men to attack my dockyard in Tuscany at Mariano's request."

His shock was genuine, and I knew I was speaking to a man who had no clue this happened.

"I swear, Mr. Capri, I had no idea."

"I believe you, but if Pauly steps out of line again, in any way, he'll meet the same fate as our recently departed Mariano. I have the bikes and chains ready to go at a moment's notice."

His throat contracted, and sweat broke out on his forehead. I smiled, knowing I got through to him.

"Understood." He stood so quickly he knocked a fork, and the loud clatter brought eyes our way. "I should make some calls."

"That's a wise idea, Domenico."

Niccola chuckled and took a seat next to Wyatt just as Vinni emerged from below deck. Everyone took some time to enjoy the rest of the cruise. Sienna soon had everyone together, and even Domenico began to relax a little with her easy conversation. We all sipped some top-shelf rum and kept the conversation away from business for the rest of the trip.

I wanted to be alone with Sienna when we got back to the castle, but she went off looking for some headache tablets, mentioning something about the bright sun. Mama, of course, followed her, concerned as always. I heard Sienna laugh at something she said, and knowing she was in good hands, I headed out back to fill Papa in on the details of the day. I knew he'd appreciate the good news.

Chapter
TWENTY-TWO

Sienna

I was awakened by a loud crack of thunder then a flash of lightning that lit up the whole room like fireworks in the night sky. The power flickered and then went out, and I was left in a dark room high up in the castle. As my imagination soared, I immediately reached out and swept a hand across the bed, only to feel a cool, empty spot where I'd hoped Elio would be. I wasn't sure if he'd even come to bed yet. After Andrea and I had a talk, I'd taken a couple painkillers and gone to bed early. I needed to close my eyes. I knew he needed time with Piero, so I told Andrea to let him know to come to bed when he was done. I wasn't sure of the time, so I just lay there and enjoyed the coziness of the blankets and let myself drift.

Rain began to tap the stones of the windowsill, and I rolled over to listen. It sounded like pearls dropping on a marble floor, then every few seconds the rain music would go to a higher or lower pitch depending on where it hit the stones. It was quite pretty, and I was glad I'd cracked the window a little when I went to bed.

Suddenly, the wind picked up and the white sheers billowed out and began to blow around violently. We were so close to the ocean I could smell the salt in the air as I climbed over the bed to shut the window. I looked outside as another giant bolt of lightning lit up the stormy sky. I was mesmerized by how mad the sea looked as the waves crashed against the rocks that protected the castle walls from their destructive force. As each wave hit, a massive explosion of white spray and foam would fly high into the air in wild shapes. *Sea art.*

My phone lit up the corner of the room, and I raced over to grab it.

Wyatt: It's lost, Sienna, I can't believe I lost it! Can you see me from your window?

I raced back to the window, wondering what in the world he was talking about.

When the next bolt of lightning came, I saw a figure below on the roof moving about as though looking for something. I squinted to see, and sure enough, it was Wyatt.

"Wyatt!" I cupped my mouth and screamed into the wicked wind. "Wyatt!"

I realized it would be impossible for him to hear me. I sent off a quick text.

Sienna: What are you doing? Are you crazy!

He suddenly turned, looked like he was talking to someone, then flung backward, losing his footing.

"Wyatt! No!" I wasted no time and raced out the door, using my phone like a flashlight. I tore down the stairs to the next floor and out onto a private patio. "Wyatt!" I screamed, but my voice was immediately carried away on the wild wind.

I searched the roof below me but was blinded by the rain. It was huge and flat, and the few chairs and tables scattered around told me people must use it from time to time. Surely, it was safe enough to walk around on. A wave of recklessness came over me. I couldn't lose my best friend. I hooked my leg over the edge, hoisted myself up and over and dropped down the few feet to the roof below. I landed gracefully, to my surprise, and quickly tested out just how slippery the rain-soaked stones were. My knees wobbled at the thought of not having any safety rails along the edge. I wasn't a fan of heights, and my heart pounded. I extended my arms in front of me and calculated exactly how much room I had to work with before I came too close to the edge. Taking a deep breath, I moved along the uneven roof, aware that my bare feet had nothing to grip. My nightgown was slicked to my body, and my hair was heavy and drenched. I shivered in cold and fear in my desperate search to find Wyatt. Where had he gone?

Lightning lit my way as I moved along the castle walls. The clouds rolled in waves and seemed to fold under as they met the sea below, its angry roar mixed with the sound that erupted from the sky. I felt the vibration in the stone under my feet as it sent a warning that this was no place for me.

I felt it before I saw it. It was as if someone took an icy finger and drew it up my spine to warn me. I wasn't alone. Slowly, in the heart of the storm, I turned to find Greta Capri standing in front of me. For a moment, I wondered if I'd imagined it, but then I saw her rosary beads dangling from her neck. They swung in the wind as she bent slightly to clear her wet dress away from her legs, and I knew she was real. The knife in her hand glinted in the light.

As my lips parted, the wind changed direction, and the air was forced back in my mouth. It forced me to swallow back my scream.

Then with a horrific battle cry, I saw him emerge from the shadows. Abramo stood tall in his suit, looking just as terrifying as the day I met him. I knew then I wouldn't have a chance.

"I can't let this happen," Greta called to me. "He's blinded by you."

I shook my head, trying to understand how we got here. How they got here.

"I need to keep our bloodline clean." Rain flew from her weathered lips. "You're a cancer that must be stopped."

"I love him." It slipped from my lips, then I shared my secret with her and watched as each word sank painfully in.

"It's not enough," she screamed, and looked like a

nightmare hag as the wind and rain swirled around her. "You'll never be enough for him."

Abramo started to walk toward me, and I held up my hands as if to ward him off and moved in the only direction open to me, toward the edge of the roof. My heart pounded, as I knew I didn't have far to go. A wave crashed below, and the smell of the salty air shot up my nose. I whirled around, arms flapping like a bird to keep my balance in the wind. Abramo was now on one side of me and Greta just a few feet away.

"You think your loyalty will save you, but it won't. You're nothing if you're not Capri blood. She has to die!" Greta screamed again.

Abramo looked between the two of us, his face a mask, and I knew that was it. A million thoughts bombarded my head. I was going to be swallowed by the sea, and Elio would never know what happened or who was behind my disappearance. Or worse, would he think I couldn't handle this life and had left him?

Suddenly, Abramo leapt forward and shoved Greta off the side of the roof. It all happened so quickly that I stood there stunned, unsure of what I'd just witnessed. His chest heaved as he looked over the edge, and then he slowly turned back to me.

"She said the same thing to Pauly Milani before she killed him this morning."

I blinked at him in slow motion, trying to process everything, but it was too much to take in.

"My days were numbered. I'm not a Capri." He ran a hand over his face to clear the rain.

"Please, Abramo, give me the truth." I hoped he saw it was time I knew. "How did she know who I was, before everyone else knew?"

He looked up at the sky and let the rain run down his face as if contemplating his answer. Then he turned and took a few steps toward me. It took everything in me not to take a few steps back. Instead, I fisted my hands and pressed them to my sides and rooted myself in place.

"Greta was always suspicious of Francesco." His eyes were black, and he spoke slowly. "She had him followed and discovered that his longtime girlfriend, Elenora, was about to marry Theodore Coppola. She left him alone for a while." He looked around as if checking that we were still alone on the rooftop. "But after you and Elenora disappeared years later, Greta wondered if Francesco had anything to do with it. I was sent there to find him, to watch him. On a few occasions, I noticed he'd visit the Di Vaio house. Then one day, after a particularly long visit, he stopped going altogether. I dug harder and discovered he was hiding *you* there. It didn't take me long to backtrack and connect the dots that you were Theo's daughter and Elenora had gone into hiding. You don't just disappear unless there's a reason, and Theo had a reputation of beating on his women. I didn't say anything to her until Elio started bringing you around. You were just a child." He cleared his throat, and it was the first time I'd ever seen Abramo display any kind of emotion. "I had no choice but to share what I found when she asked. But I didn't know she'd—" His face hardened then; he was done with the storytelling.

He took a few steps back then and looked at me with a strange expression. "You have more blood around you than you think, Sienna," he shouted then turned and jumped to join Greta in death.

I looked over the edge and covered my mouth as I saw him hit a rock, spin, and disappear into the ocean.

My foot crunched on something, and I looked down to see a strand of Nonna Greta's rosary beads caught in a crevice. I hooked them with my finger and held them up in the wind. I squinted to see the marks left by her fingers. Years of manipulation and control pressed into grooves. All her hidden secrets were scored into those beads. How could something so holy hold such cruelty and deceit? A deep chill raced through me along with a fleeting thought that I should return them to Piero. Perhaps they would bring him some mild comfort. But the truth was they belonged with Greta. It was time for her to answer for all her sins, and I wasn't about to have her skip a single one. I flung those dreaded things out over the edge as far and as hard as I could. I hoped they'd find her beneath the sea and tangle themselves around her neck to ensure she might have a most painful death.

Squeezing my eyes shut, I let out a cry, not for them, but for myself. How did I keep managing to cheat death? How much longer could I keep that up? How many people were out to kill me? What did he mean? I emptied my lungs then stepped carefully away from the edge and over to the stone wall and leaned back to feel it solid behind my back. The rain washed away my tears and—*Wyatt!*

As I turned to run, I jumped as the lights flickered back on along the castle walls, and I saw a dark figure standing not far from me. He stood out stark against the rain-streaked wall. The Finder stood there with a gun in his hand. He gave me a sad smile and a nod, and in that moment, I knew he was there for me. Had he been watching over me, ready to step in if needed?

I didn't know why I shared my secret with him, but I did. My hand went to my stomach and rubbed a small circle. I fought the urge to break down and cry again. It wasn't just about me and Elio anymore. It was about *us*.

I took a few shaky steps toward him, incredibly happy he'd been a witness to what happened. When we were shoulder to shoulder, I cleared my throat of pain.

"Name your price. I want to know what Abramo meant by the blood comment." My teeth chattered as I spoke.

"No payment necessary, Miss Sienna." He gave me a nod. "I'll get right on it. The door Greta used is that way." He pointed but made no move to go with me.

My mind flew back to Wyatt. I had to find him. But first I needed Elio. I followed the wall until I found the door she and Abramo must have used.

Once inside, I was swallowed up in a hug from a very upset Elio.

"Oh, thank God!" He squeezed me tight then held me at arm's length. "One of the house staff said they saw someone fall past their window, and when I went to check on you, you weren't there. And—"

"Where were you?" Wyatt came racing up the stairs

with a towel over his shoulders and blood dripping down his arm. He threw the towel around my shoulders, and Elio led us downstairs and into a den with heavenly heat pouring from a fireplace.

I stepped out of Elio's hold and wiped my face with the towel as I tried to keep up with what was coming at me. Before I had a chance to speak, Niccola and Piero burst through the door with Andrea hard on their heels.

"What's going on? What happened?" Andrea yelled with a death grip on her robe. "I heard a scream."

"It was Margo who screamed," Niccola told her. "She saw someone fall past her window."

"What?" Andrea shook her head as she looked at me.

My eyes were on Wyatt. "How did you get here? What happened to you?"

Suddenly, everyone was talking at once, and I put my hands over my ears and turned away from them and took a deep breath. It all came back in a flood. How was I going to tell them? What did it mean that Greta was gone? I decided to start from the beginning so I could make sense of everything, too.

"I saw Wyatt outside in the storm, and he fell. Wyatt, what were you were looking for?"

"How did you know?" He looked at me oddly. "Did you see me out there?"

"Yes, I saw you, and I got your text, and I saw you slip."

"But I never texted you." He held up his hands to show me his phone wasn't on him. "I left it in the kitchen to charge.”

“Yes, you did. You texted me that you lost something. Then I saw you slip, and I panicked and ran…wow, okay.” It hit me then. Just like with Mariano, I’d been tricked into doing something by someone using a phone. I held up my hand to them.

“Sienna,” Elio wrapped a blanket around me and studied my face, “what just happened?”

“I,” I stumbled, “was out there looking for Wyatt when… Oh, my, there’s so much to tell. So much has happened.” I shivered.

“You’re cold!” Andrea admonished. “Are you all right?” She looked at me in concern. “Elio, she must—”

Elio instantly began to throw out orders. “Let’s let her get changed. She’s shivering. Mama, would you arrange a space and some drinks for us? Niccola and Vinni, check on Margo and the rest of the staff. Let them know everything is okay, and then meet us in the…” He looked at Andrea.

“The living room,” she replied as she squeezed my arm and hurried out.

“Wyatt, you have some explaining to do as well, so let’s all meet in twenty minutes in the living room, and you both can tell us everything that happened.”

When Wyatt and I finished recounting our stories, there was dead silence in the room. There had been a few interruptions and some gasps of horror when I hesitantly described the death of Piero's mother and what she had done, but I hadn't expected this silence. I suddenly felt unsure of myself. No one moved. All that could be heard was the suddenly too loud crackling of the fire. I took a deep drink of the hot tea Elio had given me and glanced briefly at Francesco, who sat off to one side, and waited.

"This's a lot to absorb," Vinni said and ran a hand through his hair as he looked at Elio. Elio had taken a seat next to me on the sofa, and his grip on my leg had never once wavered while I told my story.

Andrea got up and held her hand out to Piero. "Are you all right, my love? I know how hard it must be for you. She was your mother, after all."

"You say she killed Pauly Milano?" was all Piero said as he looked at me.

"That's what Abramo said," I replied gently. All this had to be difficult for him to hear.

"I'm not sure what that means for our deal with Domenico." Piero directed his comment to Elio.

"Francesco?" I spoke up and they all looked at me. I was sure they wondered what more Earth-shattering news I might have. I'd decided everything had been shared, so this should be too. "Greta had Abramo following you since my mother's wedding with Theo." His face fell. "That's how she knew who I was before all of you did. He found out you had placed me in that house but never told Greta until Elio brought me to the house." I turned to Piero. "She's been watching from the very beginning."

"That's insane." Niccola shook his head. "No wonder she barely left the house. She had Abramo doing all her watching for her."

"No one in this room will breathe a word about what happened here tonight, particularly that Nonna has been killed," Elio finally said. "I'll talk to The Finder tomorrow and see what else he might know about all this." He stood and took me by the hand. "Right now, it's late. Let's all get some sleep." He pulled me to him and placed a kiss on my forehead.

"Come with me, Wyatt, so I can clean up that cut." Andrea had her no-nonsense voice on, and it made Elio smile at Wyatt.

"Thank you, Andrea, but I, ahh, wonder if I could have a word, Elio?" Wyatt gave her a side hug. "Just a brief moment alone?"

"Of course." Elio kissed me again and encouraged me to go upstairs. I wanted to know what Wyatt had on his mind, but the call of our cozy mattress was strong and overcame my curiosity.

I showered, and by the time I got into bed, Elio was back. Soon I was snuggled in his arms. I was so happy he was here and not at the bottom of the sea with his wicked old nonna. I imagined her becoming fish food for some happy sharks—at least, I hoped.

"Is Wyatt all right?" I yawned as I spoke and let my heavy eyes close.

"Yes."

"You want to share what he told you?"

"Yes, but later." He caught my yawns and gave a deep one of his own.

The rain continued to pour, the wind beat the

windows, and the thunder still shouted. I shivered and buried myself in his chest. It was so delicious being safe here with him, and it made me think.

"Will it always be like this?" I asked into the darkness "Someone always behind me wanting me dead?" He didn't answer right away but stroked the side of my arm tenderly. "I can deal with it. I just want to know," I whispered.

"You shouldn't have to deal with it." He sighed heavily. "Don't you see? It's why I made the hardest decision of my life back then. I wanted to keep you away from all this."

"That wasn't your call to make." I yawned again. Even the thought of rehashing that conversation made me tired. I decided this was the time. "Elio, I have something to tell you."

"I'm listening." I reached over and pulled his hand to me and let it rest on my stomach. His fingers flexed then stilled. He shot up in bed and stared down at me.

"Are you?"

"Yes." I blinked back happy tears.

"When did you find out?"

"When we got off the boat and Andrea met me in the house. She bought me a few tests to rule out tiredness and lack of appetite. I was going to tell you, but you never came to bed, and I was so tired."

"Oh, my God," he leaned down and kissed my stomach then kissed me softly on the lips. "We're going to have a baby?"

"Yes."

"And to think that tonight," his voice dropped, "you could have," he paused. "I think this is the first time I ever appreciated that Abramo was there."

"I still can't believe he let me live."

He closed his eyes, and I knew he was digesting all that could have happened.

"Hey," I touched his face, "I'm here. No, we're here." I smiled. "That's where your focus needs to be."

"A baby." He gently stroked my belly again then moved to rest his head on my chest. He began to draw circles around my belly button. I felt so much better now that he knew. Then the exhaustion set in, and I closed my eyes and relaxed, loving Elio being so close.

Just as I drifted off, I heard him whisper, "I'm going to love you just as much as I love your mommy, and no one can top that kind of love."

A tear slipped out, and I fell sleep with his sweet words warming my heart.

Morning came and brought with it the warm sun and blue sky. There was a sense of lightness as I got ready for the day, knowing that Greta was finally gone. I smiled as I chose a brightly colored dress and flat shoes. The sheer number of steps in this castle would deter any woman from choosing heels. I heard a commotion at bottom of the stairs and hurried the rest of the way down to find a massive number of suitcases being pushed toward the front door.

"What in the world!" There was Elio a phone tucked under his chin as he barked out orders and took a bite of a slice of toast in his other hand. When he spotted me, he tossed his phone and raced to my side.

"What's going on? Why are there a mountain of suitcases in the hallway?"

"We're going home." He urged me toward a chair and snapped his fingers at the cook, who placed a bowl of fruit in front of me.

"Home? But we still aren't finished here, and then we have to go to Pesaro."

"No," he pulled up a seat next to me, "I can't have anything else happen to you. Now that I know you're pregnant, I'm not taking any more risks."

"Oh, please, Elio!" I waved him off. "There'll be no less danger between today and when this little one decides to arrive. Life needs to go on."

"And it will at home, behind our iron gates, where I can protect you. Both of you." His phone rang, and he held out a hand. Niccola handed it to him.

"Morning, Mama." He grinned as he sat in Elio's spot. "Congratulations!"

"So, you all know already?" I laughed.

"Yes, we literally woke to the news and then were told we were cutting the trip short." He poured some espresso.

"I can't believe he'd cut the trip sh—"

"Sienna," he shifted over a chair, so his back was turned to Elio, and leaned in, "last night, our own nonna tried to kill you. We had no idea she was even here.

Somehow, she and Abramo slipped by us and lured you out alone on a rooftop, in the middle of a storm, no less. No one would ever have known what happened to you. I've seen Elio through some really dark stuff, but I never want to see him the way he was last night ever again. He's not just worried about you, he's worried about the baby now too. Every leg of this trip, something's happened. I don't blame him for going home. He needs you where he has control of the surroundings. Give him this one, please."

I studied Elio for a few minutes and watched him as he spoke on the phone. He wouldn't sit, and as he kept moving, the staff were hustling around trying to avoid him. He seemed relatively calm, but I knew his signs, and I could see he was stressed by the clenching and unclenching of his fists.

"All right," I nodded, looking back at Niccola, "I hear what you're saying."

"Good." He let out relieved breath. "I thought we might have to tie you up and toss you in the car."

"No." I pushed the fruit away, only to have Elio lean over and slide it back in front of me a few seconds later. He pointed at me to eat it, and I rolled my eyes. "I'm not the one who should be tied up." I sighed.

"Come on, you." Wyatt appeared and tugged my arm to stand. "I'm gonna help you pack because you went and got pregnant," he joked, kissing my cheek.

"Wait." I tugged on his arm. "What did you tell Elio last night that you couldn't say in front of the others?"

His gaze went to the floor, but he slowly reached out

over and rolled up his sleeve to show me his bandage. "You don't need any more stress in your life, but I didn't fall by accident. Oscar pushed me when I was on the roof, but thankfully there was a small ledge that stopped my fall."

"What?" I couldn't believe what I heard.

"I never liked the guy, and now with Elenora gone, I think he's about to snap. I mean, the guy has literally nothing left."

"Where is he now?"

"He's gone. Elio said he'd deal with it."

"I'm sorry, Wy. I wished you'd told me. You know I can handle a lot."

He looked over my head and rolled his eyes. "You can, but you have a lot going on, and I didn't need to add to it."

"Hey!" Elio called and handed me the bowl of fruit. "You can choose to eat it, or I'll feed it to you, but either way, you're eating this."

"It is wrong that I'm turned on right now?" Wyatt whispered.

"Yes," Elio and Niccola answered at the same time, making us laugh.

"Yes, my love, I'll eat the fruit." I took the bowl and headed up the stairs to get packed.

Wyatt chuckled behind me. "These next nine months are gonna be so much fun."

Elio

I leaned on the windowsill and watched Gain and Harris as they piled the luggage into the cars to prepare for our departure. My mind spun with all the horrible possibilities that could have happened to Sienna last night. My gut told me not to leave her alone in the room that night, but so many things needed my attention I'd ignored my own instincts. I wouldn't make that mistake ever again. My need to protect her, especially now that she carried our child, was becoming all-consuming, and I knew I wasn't always being rational, but I couldn't seem to fight it.

"Whatever you need me to put into place back home, just tell me." Niccola sat forward in his chair, and

I knew he felt the same way as I did. Our family was too exposed here. We needed to leave, but we needed to up the protection at home as well.

"I want more soldiers. Triple the count we have now."

"All right." He nodded, and I knew from his look he expected more.

"All cars coming and going from the property are to be searched, scanned for explosives, with thorough ID checks. That goes without saying. Also, Sienna isn't to leave the property without you, Francesco, Vinni, or me. No exceptions."

"Understood."

"Same goes for Wyatt," I tossed at him. "He needs just as much protection as the rest of us. He's Sienna's family, and God forbid anything was to happen to him."

"Okay."

A knock at the door put us both on edge.

"Come in," I ordered as Niccola stood and tucked away his phone. He could finish his notes elsewhere.

"You wanted to see me?" The Finder asked as he gave a polite nod to Niccola.

"I did, yes." I glanced at Niccola, and he left us alone to talk. "Shut the door and take a seat." I nodded at a couple of chairs in the corner, and we both sat. I brushed my hands over the suede armrests and thought of my comfortable office at home. This wasn't a chair I would have chosen, but it wasn't my home.

"My apologies for not announcing my arrival in Naples," he said to start the conversation off. "I arrived last night after I heard Greta and Abramo had been spotted in the area. I stopped chasing the leads I had for Rosa and came here instead. I'd intended to talk to you first, but to cut it short, I saw Abramo go out on the roof. When I got up there, he was with Greta. I wondered what they were up to."

He paused in case I would give him some sort of explanation. When I said nothing, he shrugged and continued.

"Well, when Sienna showed, I had my gun drawn. So, you know, I was ready to step in if needed. I wouldn't have let them hurt her."

"I appreciate that." I nodded and waved him to go on.

"Again, I just couldn't understand what they were all doing on the damn roof in a storm. It made no sense to me, and it was impossible to make out their words. Then when Abramo pushed Greta off the side and started talking to Sienna, I decided it was best to wait and see. Lethal force was never on the agenda there. Unless warranted, of course."

"Understood." I rubbed the scruff on my chin while I digested his story. It was exactly how Sienna had described it. I shifted gears. "How are the leads going with Rosa?"

"Dead ends on all of them, but she'll slip up at some point. They always do."

"All right."

"I did find out something, though." He rubbed a hand over his bald head, and I could tell it was important.

The Finder never hesitated when he gave the facts, so my nerves were on high alert.

"I'm listening."

He leaned forward and handed me a piece of paper. It contained a number and a name. "I've never trusted him." He held my gaze for a moment. "But he's willing to talk for his life."

"Quit stalling."

"There's just something about how you both met. He had all those big ideas to take down the Rosario syndicate. It never sat well with me."

I swallowed hard as the realization hit me as to who he meant. It was like cold water being poured down my back.

"Tullio." I said and puffed out a breath. Tullio, otherwise known as Tieri.

"Yes." He nodded. "Over the years, I've kept my eye on him. He often went quiet, did some jobs here and there for people while he worked his side business with you. But when Sienna showed up, I noticed his bank account started to climb." He paused when he realized what he'd said. "My loyalty has always been to you, Elio. If I suspect something's off, I'll take great measures to discover what's happening."

"I'm not judging. It's why I hired you."

"Very well." He seemed to like my answer. "I traced the money to that account, and that name is who oversees the money transfers." He indicated the paper he'd given me. "He may need a little convincing," he gave a dark smile, "but he'll confirm my story and provide you with any other information you wish."

"And who is funneling him the money?"

"Rosa Coppola."

My blood roared in my ears as it suddenly came into my head that Tieri had insisted on me taking the lead when we killed the Rosarios.

"Sir, I think all of it was carefully thought out and planned by the two of them. I mean no disrespect, Mr. Capri, but I need you to hear this next part." I nodded and tried to push back the rage. "I've talked to Tieri several times over the years, and I think his grudge for you dates back to your initiation for your family ring. You killed his cousin."

"Marcello Angelo was Tieri's cousin?" I was floored by that.

"Indeed, and they were quite close growing up. Rosa Coppola was in the right place at the right time, and she saw the opportunity and took it. She offered him money, fueled his anger, and convinced him he needed to avenge his cousin's death."

"Damn, I can't believe they played me like that." The depth of their deceit had me totally stunned.

The Finder looked at me with sympathy. "Tieri embedded himself into your life. I know you thought he was a friend." He shook his head. "The thing is, sir, when you took out the Rosarios, he filmed and snapped photos through the whole thing. Now he's got evidence that could put you behind bars for life. I think he would have moved on all this earlier, but once Sienna came into play, he, Stefano, and Mariano were all like dogs chasing meat on the end of a stick. She was a great distraction, and it bought me time to figure it all out."

"And where is this evidence now?" I could barely speak, knowing that once again my enemies circled.

"Ah, you do know me, don't you? You are right, of course. I'd never leave any threads untied." He leaned back and crossed his legs. "He was holding the original copies in the same bank as he funneled the money. He has a safety deposit box there." He rolled his eyes as he held up a key. "Such an amateur," he scoffed. "The digital copies have been erased from his hard drive."

"You don't think there could be more copies?"

"There was one, but thanks to Niccola poking around on Rosa Coppola's computer, he brought a file to my attention. I took care of it. If there are any more copies, I'd be surprised."

"And if there are?" I challenged.

"In the unlikely event that something pops up, I'll deal with it personally. Also, thanks to some software and your biker friends in California, you were attending a fight at the time of the Rosario murders. Multiple witnesses will remember you winning against Taylor the Tank from Arizona."

A smile broke through my madness, and I remembered how all those years ago I'd seen something in The Finder and had looked after him like family since. His true value now showed itself.

"I'm sorry about Tieri, Mr. Capri, but better to know who your enemies are before they can strike at something that's yours." He nodded at the door to Sienna, who was watching us. I hadn't heard the door open.

"Everything all right?" she asked cautiously.

"I brought good news," The Finder said as he stood and buttoned his jacket. He tilted his head in respect to her. "Mariano had no such tape of you and Anna in the hot tub. It was merely another lie he told."

"Really?" Her face lit up, along with mine. I hadn't heard that yet.

"Yes, I coaxed that information from one of Rosa's soldiers." He winked. "He'd been there that day and assured me Rosa had watched but there was no filming involved. It was a lie."

"Well, thank God for that one." She beamed over at me, and I smiled, thinking it was one less thing to worry about.

"Perhaps, *amore mio*, in the future you'll save your kills for when you're in our own territory." I smiled at her.

"I'll try to remember that." She laughed, then offered her hand to The Finder and whispered something in his ear.

"I'm still working on that," he softly replied as he gave me a wink and a smile. I raised an eyebrow at him and briefly wondered what that was about, but my mind was already on how I was going to kill Tieri.

"Thank you." She stepped back.

"As always, I appreciate what you bring to me. Please continue to chase the Rosa leads, and when Tieri surfaces…"

"You'll be the first to know." He shook my hand and

left.

"Tieri?" Sienna looked up at me as she wrapped her arms around my midsection.

"Yes. I have a story for you, but first we need to catch a plane."

Noemi

I cut the power and listened for any house staff who might still be inside. All was clear. They normally left by ten when no one was home, anyway. I used Bosco's spare key to open the side door and quickly entered the sixteen-digit code. Elio's house had at least twelve outside cameras and one of the best security systems one could buy. Thankfully, I'd seen him enter it enough times to remember it was both Andrea and Piero's full birth dates. The system disarmed, and I was free to roam about.

I set the keys on the table and made my way upstairs to the master bedroom. Elio was extremely meticulous with his things, especially with his beloved suits. He spent more on those damn things than most people made in a year. I slid aside the door to his walk-in closet and rolled my eyes at how everything was color coded and sorted by size.

One match and these would go up in flames. Tempting.

I remembered my purpose and moved on into the bedroom to the second closet. I opened the door and found the little snake's belongings. I felt all around the high shelves, along the sides, hunted through her bags and drawers, but found nothing.

"Where are your journals or anything personal from Elenora?" I complained out loud and slammed the drawers closed as my frustration built. I hated not knowing. Did she know my secrets, or could I just keep my head down and continue moving through this horrible life?

I checked under the bed, the bedside tables, her vanity, his cufflink box. Anywhere that something could be hidden, I checked. I was frantic and stopped caring if things were put back properly. The staff could have made this mess, for all he knew.

Then a noise came from outside. I rushed to the window. A line of cars was coming up the road, and I felt my blood run cold. *Is that them?* Impossible, they had another week of their stupid tour!

I turned on my heel and flung myself toward the door but tripped over a chair and fell to the floor with a heavy thud.

"Ouch!" I cried but went silent when I caught sight of

a small file taped under the bed. Pulling it free, I quickly broke the seal and dumped the contents on the floor. I sorted through the papers in a mad rush and sucked in a sharp breath when I saw it.

"No!"

Car doors slamming had me in a panic. I hastily tried to stuff most of the items back into the folder. I knew I'd made a poor job of fastening the tape, as it had lost most of its adhesive. I rushed to the guest bedroom at the back, breathed a sigh of relief when I got the window open, then shimmied out onto the patio roof and down the lattice. I ignored the various bumps and bangs I got in my desperate attempt to get out of there. Finally on the ground, I crouched and ran to hide in the bushes for a moment, and when all was clear, I raced to where my car was hidden. Once inside, I fought to catch my breath then banged on the dash, screaming silently into the steering wheel. Frustrated at the cards life just continued to deal, my blood was at full boil.

My phone rang, and I checked the caller ID.

He always had such perfect timing.

"What?" I tried to calm myself.

"There's been a change of plans."

"No shit, Hector," I huffed.

"Where are you?"

"About thirty feet from you all," I informed him. "Why are they back?"

"They didn't say, but Elio was adamant we had to get back right away. He seemed to want to keep it quiet, though."

"Do you think they know?"

"No."

"How?"

"Because I wouldn't be here standing by the main gates if they did." His voice dripped sarcasm. "Just get out of there and wait for my call." He hung up.

How dare he! Angry at his tone, I tossed my phone and took a moment to think. Things were spinning faster and faster, and the blur was taking its toll.

I pulled out the crinkled papers and stared at them, and my eyes blurred as I slipped into a memory.

Niccola cooed from his stroller as he enjoyed the Neptune water fountain in front of him. I sipped an espresso and finished reading my book, happy for a moment to relax. We'd just had a lovely walk through the gardens and then around the city. Niccola loved the penguins, and we stayed until his eyes grew heavy and he finally fell asleep. Of course, the moment I moved the stroller, his eyes popped open, and his ten-minute catnap had given him a second wave of energy.

I decided to park his little bum in front of the fountain so I could get some reading in. Our walks were the only time I could relax. Back at the house, I always felt the old bat watching me. I not only felt her beady-black eyes on me, they scorched my skin. Her ever-present rosary beads made the most annoying noise when she threaded them through her fingers.

"Miss Noemi?" A familiar voice sent a chill through me. "I thought that was you." Her jet-black hair brushed her shoulders as she bounced a baby in her arms.

"What are you doing here?" I shifted uneasily. "You shouldn't be here." My mind immediately went back to the time when we were both about seven months pregnant. I'd tried, unsuccessfully, to push her down the stairs. Now she was a thorn buried deep in my side, a devil I had to continue to pay.

She smiled like a crazy person as we stood there like two moms watching a fountain with our babies. "I just wonder if you've forgotten our agreement. I've kept your secret. I've kept my mouth shut, and everyone still thinks you're a good little mama. So, imagine my surprise when you missed your payment yesterday morning." Her voice went low and soft, but I knew this woman was anything but meek.

"I did." I closed my book casually. "I left it in the same spot as before."

"It was short by almost half."

"I didn't have it all this time, but I can make up for it next month."

"That wasn't the agreement," she said as she jiggled her baby.

"I heard you visited my mama the other day."

"I did."

"Was that some kind of threat?" I dreamt of pushing her into the fountain and holding her head under the water. I wished once again I'd been successful in pushing her to her death when I had the chance.

"It can be whatever you want it to be. Either way, you have a week to make up what you owe me, or I'll make the call."

I stood and took a moment to tuck my book into my bag. She leaned over and held her son close to Niccola. "Hello." She mimicked a sweet baby voice. "We wouldn't want anything to happen to you, now, would we?" She looked up at me with another of her crazy smiles. "That would be a shame, wouldn't it?" As she straightened, I got a good look at her son, Hector, and looked away, feeling sick and trapped all at once. "It was real nice running into you today, Mrs. Capri. I hope you both enjoy the sunshine as much as we are." She turned and walked away, and I dropped back onto the bench with a thud.

I pressed my hand to my chest to try to relieve some of the pressure. How was I going to come up with that money without Bosco or Greta noticing?

Chapter
TWENTY-FIVE

Elio

Florence, Italy

"I've made the calls, and everyone's been—" Vinni stopped short when he unlocked the front door. I was helping Sienna out of the car but slowly eased her back inside at the tone of Vinni's voice. A strange feeling had us all on edge. Wyatt had also stepped out of the car but popped back inside.

"What?" I shot at Vinni.

"Your alarm isn't on." He stepped back, and I looked through the door at the disabled system.

"Permission to clear the perimeter?" Officer Hector pulled his weapon, and I nodded. He motioned for a few of his men to search the grounds, and then he and another man went inside the house. My two soldiers, Gain and Harris, took the outside as well while I pulled up the camera footage on my phone.

"The power was shut off," I muttered then switched over to a different app. "Forty seconds later, the alarm was deactivated from inside."

"Which code did they use?" Vinni asked. He knew I used different ones depending on the situation.

"It's not important." I tucked my phone away and glanced at Sienna, who was watching me carefully from the car window. Ten minutes later, the place was clear. "Thank you, Hector. You're relieved of your duties."

"I don't mind sticking around if you'd like."

"No, that'll be all. I'll wire your payment in the morning."

He turned and nodded at Sienna then rounded up his men and left.

Sienna got out of the car, and Wyatt took the things she held in her arms as I hurried them inside. She laughed quietly.

"What?"

"You're acting like I'm nine months pregnant, ready to deliver. I'm not made of glass, Elio." Her expression changed. "What do you think happened here?"

"I'm not sure, but I don't like it. The guys cleared the area, but something still feels off. The fact that you're pregnant does change things for me, I'll admit. I can't have anything happening to the two of you. So, sit," I ordered, pointing to the couch. "Humor me, please. Also,

I'm going to call our doctor to start a chart on you and the little heartbeat." She smiled, and I was thankful she didn't argue.

"Little heartbeat?" She questioned my nickname for the baby.

"Yes."

"That's cute."

"Feet up." I ignored her and placed my hand on her tummy once she was stretched out right where she should be. "You two stay put."

When I left the room, I heard Wyatt whisper if he could get in on the pampering, and her laugh made me smile.

The doctor arrived within the hour and checked Sienna over twice at my request. She could glare at me all she wanted, but I knew she'd been through entirely too much the past few days, and I needed to know they were both in good health.

"Well?" I asked as the doctor stepped away from a sleepy Sienna, who wanted nothing more than to close her eyes. She'd already reassured her that both she and the baby were exactly where she expected them to be at this point in the pregnancy and had urged Sienna to go upstairs and get some sleep, as she had yawned her way through the checkup. I, on the other hand, wanted more information.

"I promise you, Mr. Capri, mama and baby are just fine. It's too early to know much more, but in a few weeks, I'll come back and do a more thorough checkup. For now, just make sure she eats, drinks plenty of water, gets lots of sleep, and stays away from stress." She closed her bag. "I left her with a daily folic acid prescription, and if you have any concerns at all, you have my number. I'll come right over."

"Thank you." I felt I should ask more questions, but I couldn't think of any, so I walked her to the door where she turned around with a smile.

"Congratulations, Mr. Capri. Be sure you two enjoy this time together, because it's short, and before you know it, this part will be over, and a whole new adventure will have begun." She gave a me look that said she knew what she was talking about.

I thanked her then closed the door and locked it. After a brief check on Sienna to make sure she was asleep in our bed, I took a breath and decided I needed to work off some steam. I made a quick call to my trainer, but he wasn't available, so I took a chance and called my old sparring partner in hopes he hadn't left yet.

"Your secrecy is impressive." Trigger ran a hand through his Mohawk as a joint dangled from his mouth.

"Given the events of the last year, it no longer feels that way."

"Shit happens." He took a deep pull, then suddenly pulled the joint away from his lips. "Shit, man, you said your old lady is pregnant?" He held up his joint and seemed to swallow the smoke.

"It's okay. The basement has its own filtration

system," I assured him, or I would have asked him to put it out earlier. "It also acts as a bunker," I added with a grin.

"Still," he coughed then snuffed out the tip and went back to stretching, "I wouldn't want to risk it."

"I was glad you were still here. How are things going with your army buddies? Brick mentioned something about one of them being in Vegas."

"I can't really say." He shook his head. "Some shit's going down, and I don't think it's good."

"Sorry to hear that." I stretched my fingers and thought that as much as Trigger gave off the vibe of someone who didn't give a damn, he really cared about the people close to him. It just took time to gain his trust enough to see what was inside. It was why his people were so loyal.

"Guess they have a lot of rules and shit getting broken, or at least the boundaries are being pushed, so, yeah, that kind of stuff doesn't go over well with Cole." He shrugged. "You get a chance to call Collins?"

"I left a message." I checked the time on my phone to make sure no one needed me before we started. "I haven't heard back yet, but if I don't hear from him, I'll call a buddy of his. Take a different route."

"Appreciated."

"Where's Tess?" I decided to change the topic.

"We're headin' out tomorrow. Rail's probably ready for the grave by now from chasin' Fin. You remember my tattoo artist, Mud?" I nodded and stepped into the ring. "He's got a buddy here, and Tess wanted to get her sleeve tweaked before we go. Special memory of the trip, she said."

"You really did find your match." I chuckled, happy we'd both found something positive in our lives.

"Yeah." He held up his hands and started to practice throwing punches. "It helps she thinks the same way and doesn't want any kids." He eyed me, and I knew it wasn't merely his opinion. Trigger had never wanted to reproduce in fear he'd screw them up. "Fin and Denton are enough for both of us."

"How are they handling you being here?"

"Denton's fine, he just misses us practicing in the ring. He's gonna be a fighter."

"Oh, yeah?" I put my hands up and we started to spar.

"Yeah, he's a little shit, so he'll be fine. An' he's got a girl, so he's keeping busy." I smirked at that and ducked as his fist blew by my ear. "Fin is more attached to Tess. He calls her all the time." He slammed my shoulder, and I jabbed his ribs. "Been a few Stripe Backs sniffin' around. They got a new pres, and they're slowly tryin' to build back up what we tore down." He chuckled darkly, and I knew he would let them encroach until he was ready to make his move. "That name you mention—" His last word was cut short by my fist hitting his jaw. I blocked his kick and spun around, only to get a jab in the back.

"Yes, he goes by Tieri, but his real name is Tullio Banchi. He was last seen at our announcement party. He has some connections in the States."

"And if I find him?"

"Let me be the one to rip his heart out."

Trigger smiled, understanding the need to be the one to end someone's life.

We sparred for another hour, then Tess called, wanting to meet him for a late dinner. I felt better as I leaned over the ropes to take a breather. My muscle screamed for a break.

Francesco appeared. "You look worn out. I can't remember the last time you two were in a ring together."

"We had a good session. I needed it."

"I'm sure you did." He sat down on the bench and crossed his arms.

I snagged my water from the corner and smiled to myself at the memory of the last time I was in that chair and who was between my legs. She really was incredible.

"You don't have to ask for it." I downed my water. I knew by now he'd be itching for permission to take out Oscar.

"How does Sienna feel on the matter?"

"He tried to hurt her best friend. He might have lost Elenora and is losing it, but I'd say it's a race to the finish line."

"Well, I guess it's good she's pregnant, then." He got to his feet and left me. I needed to shower and change.

Once cleaned up, I headed to the bar to pour myself a stiff one. I found Wyatt there with his laptop. He'd set up shop in a corner of the room.

"What are you working on?" I asked as I made myself a drink.

"Your wedding." He shrugged like it was nothing.

"Your mother and I were thinking springtime, early afternoon for the ceremony, and a dusk reception."

"I see." I gave him a lopsided grin. I should've known Mama and Wyatt would have started planning as soon as I'd even entertained the idea of asking Sienna to marry me. But who were we kidding? Everyone knew the end game. It was written in the stars for us to be together. I was just so happy that everything was finally settled, and we were here together and now had a little heartbeat on the way.

"So, I'll take it you won't budge from your classic black and white suits?" He held the tip of the pen between his teeth, and I shot him a shocked look. "Yeah, I didn't think so. Fine," he sighed, but I could tell he loved getting a rise out of me. "Your mother already made up a guest list of about a hundred and fifty of, as she calls it, *must haves*, but who do you want to invite?"

"Vinni and Niccola." I smirked into my glass and watched him roll his eyes. "I'll get you a list," I promised as I glanced at my watch. It was getting late, and I was beat after the stress of getting everyone home in one piece.

"I'm tired, so I'm going to turn in. We'll talk in the morning?" Wyatt asked as he scooped up his computer and stuffed a notepad into a briefcase.

"See you in the morning." I waved and downed the rest of my drink and went upstairs.

It was still dark when something woke me, I glanced at the clock. Three a.m. I reached for her and realized the bed was empty. A sliver of light came from the doorway, so I pulled on some pajama pants, skipped the top, and quietly went downstairs to find her in the kitchen.

"Hey," I ran my hands over shoulders and gave her a neck rub, "what are you doing up?"

"I couldn't sleep." She rubbed her head. "Something's bothering me."

"What's that?" I moved to the seat next to her, and she slid over an envelope. I emptied the contents of it on the table and sifted through the papers.

"It was some things I found in Rosa's office before the house burned down."

"Is that you?" I studied the photo and smiled at her as a child. The soft smile on her small face was the picture of the one she turned on me now. Then her face turned serious.

"Yes, *this* one is of me." The way she said it made me glace up at her. "But there were two photos in that folder. This one," she pointed, "and another one that was dated two years after I was born."

"You don't think it was you as well? Who do you think it was?"

"I'm not sure, and now I might never know, because it's gone. I know someone was in our room, and I think they went through my things. This was taped up, and I know someone opened it, and now I'm sure I know who was in the house yesterday."

"Noemi?" I asked, and she nodded. Once again, I stared at the papers.

"Have you ever," she paused like she was trying to find the right words, "had a strong feeling about someone, yet you never really knew them? She came into my life and seemed to know more about me than I ever knew about her. She certainly had strong enough feelings about me to want me dead, and burned, no less."

"We certainly need to find out what is going on with her."

"That's for certain. It was on the day of the fire she set that I found this stuff." She pointed to the papers. "But there's something else I just remembered. I think it's what's bothering me. After my encounter with Noemi, I remember it was pure chaos. People were running in all directions. Anyway, I almost bumped into this woman. She had a bag filled with valuables from the house. She looked like she saw a ghost when she locked eyes with me and even called me by my birthname." She rubbed her fingers over her mouth as she thought. "At the time, it didn't mean much to me. I just figured she was someone who worked there or something, but when we announced our engagement at the castle, I saw the same woman outside on the phone just before Mariano showed up. The way she looked at me. I don't know, but I feel like she might know something about this whole thing. Something we don't. My gut is telling me to find her."

My inclination was to sweep her worries aside. She didn't need anything else to add to her stress. But I also knew Sienna, and if I didn't help her figure this out, she'd find a way to discover who this woman was without me.

"All right," I said thoughtfully, "why don't you write down her description, and I'll get Vinni to see what he can find out? But until then," I leaned over and kissed her forehead, "promise me you'll just focus on you and the little heartbeat."

"Okay, I will. Did you know Wyatt's already got websites lined up for me to pick a wedding dress?"

"Good." Perfect. I hoped Wyatt's over-the-top planning would be just the distraction she needed. "Can we go back to bed now?"

"Yes, but what do we do about Noemi?" she whispered as I pulled her to her feet.

"We need more proof of what she's about before we flip Niccola's and Vinni's lives upside down. It's not something I look forward to." I shook my head with worry for my cousins. "So, for now, we stay as is. I'll have Gain tail her for a while. The fact that she's a danger to you and for our little heartbeat here is my main concern. I'll make sure Gain doesn't let her out of his sight."

"And let me guess, Harris is my shadow?"

"If not him, then me." I winked. "Now, let's get you to bed."

Sienna

Three months later

"Yes!" Eddy K the dress designer breathed. I'd insisted he attend our wedding after he designed this magnificent dress for me, and he not only agreed, he'd become part of the occasion. He stepped back and kissed his fingers with approval. "It's not too tight, no?"

"No, you did a fabulous job, Eddy, especially around the belly. It's very comfortable, and I feel incredible in it." I beamed in the mirror as he fussed with something in the back. He made sure the dress was perfect. I was sixteen weeks along and just starting to show.

"I'm not jealous, because I'll be borrowing this later

when no one's looking." Wyatt held a piece of the soft fabric between his fingers and moaned as he pressed it to his cheek. "It's like butter."

The long, soft gown had an organza skirt which gave it a soft shimmer when the light graced it. Despite being a wedding dress, it was lightweight and perfectly suited for the warm spring afternoon, and that helped ease the stress of an outdoor ceremony. The modern bodice was elegant and embellished in a leafy lace design, and the silhouette was timeless and very trendy.

My hair was swept up into a loose low gathered style that allowed it to be let go so it would tumble freely when the reception was in full swing. It was cute that Piero thought I should wear flats because I was pregnant, but Andrea and I assured him that I was just fine in my stunning new heels. I wouldn't be caught dead in flats at my wedding, especially not when I'd fallen in love with some Saeda 100s, Jimmy Choo's crystal embellished ivory satin pumps. I didn't care if my feet ached; I was having a love affair on the side with those shoes.

Wyatt stepped in front of me, looking ridiculously sexy in his light pink and ivory suit. "Everything is perfect. Now, don't worry about a thing. You're going to love it all. I adore the tables. They're positively glorious, and the—"

"Wyatt, whatever would I do without you?" I interrupted his nervous tirade. "You've exhausted yourself with all this planning to make my day wonderful. You're my best friend. You know that, right?" I hugged him, and he tutted with worry over messing up my dress.

"I don't have any idea what I'm going to do now that the day has come." He sighed with pretend worry. "Oh, wait, Andrea and I have a christening to plan!" He positively glowed, and I could see the wheels already turning as he wiggled his brows at me. "Before I forget, I got you a little something-something." He pulled out a duffle bag from the closet, then after a quick glance, looked around. He pulled out a little black box with a gold lock hanging on the side.

"Oh, Wyatt, you shouldn't have. Why don't you add it to the gift table downstairs?"

"It's not really something you'd want to open in front of the family."

I lifted an eyebrow at him. Then he gave a little laugh and pulled the key from where it hung beside the lock. He used his body to shield the contents from the others in the room.

"Remember that underground shop we found years ago that had everything in every size you could imagine?" His eyebrows did a dance, and one of the toys wiggled hilariously with his movement. The sex toys were artfully arranged in the box so they looked that much funnier. "Well, you know me, I like a gift that keeps on giving."

I slapped a hand over my mouth to stop the laughter. "Wait." I tried to breathe and worked a particularly odd-looking one free. Curious, I moved it all around, trying to understand what made it *black-box worthy*. It was slimy and slipped around like a wet pickle trying to slip out of my hold. "What does this one do?"

"Oh, that's one of my favorites. So, this attaches together and suctions here," he pointed to the window, "while vibrating here, and then you insert it—"

"Yup, okay, got it."

"It's really more for you than him, but I can tell you the lovers love to watch the show."

I quickly tossed the silicon toy back inside and snapped the lid closed then made sure the lock was secure.

"I will accept this—"

"I know you will." He let out a snort.

"Under one condition." I moved closer. "If I die first, you need to remove it from my closet. I don't need our children to think their father and I are into kink."

"Trust me," he dropped his voice to a serious tone, "you'd be surprised as to just what kids already know. I'm mentally scarred."

I laughed and tucked the box away, then I straightened my dress, thankful for Wyatt's dirty humor to help shake off the nerves.

"Ready?" He puffed out his chest.

"Almost!" I reached for my journal and flipped it open to the marked page and re-read, for the tenth time, Andrea's words.

Mama, will you be there for my wedding?

In her perfect handwriting she responded. *I may not be your blood, but I will always be there for you. I wouldn't miss your wedding for anything in this world. I will be there to help pick your dress, dry your tears, or stand in the front row to watch you marry the man who loves you more than life itself. You have found your Piero, and I can't wait to be your mother-in-law.*

"Okay," I closed the book and smiled, "I'm ready." Wyatt took my arm, and we walked together to the top landing of the stunning Villa Medicea la Ferdinanda where three hundred guests waited in the gentle warmth of the afternoon sun.

Our theme was mid-summer night garden, and our colors were light pink, earthy greens, light yellow, and golds. I'd given free rein of decorating to Andrea, and with Wyatt's help, I knew the place would be magical. As we descended the stone stairs, I gasped at the view in front of me. The backdrop of rolling vineyards and the heavy sun first captured my attention, then it was the satin fabric that glided ahead of me to lead me to the man I would spend the rest of my life with. Once on ground level, Wyatt, tears glinting in his eyes, gracefully handed me off to Francesco, who looked as dashing as ever.

"You look," he pressed his lips together and shook his head slowly, "perfect."

"Thank you." I felt my eyes prickle and looked away so I wouldn't be overcome and ruin my makeup.

"See those two men there on the end of the aisle?" I followed where he was pointing and saw two nice looking men who looked just like… "My sons." He smiled warmly. "I wanted them to finally meet you."

"Really, that's them?" I couldn't believe they were here. Francesco was usually so private about his family that I tended to forget he had a whole other life once upon a time. "It would be an honor to meet them." I smiled, thinking how much love was packed into this wedding.

"Shall we?" He offered his arm, and I slid mine through his as we waited for the violin to start. Andrea's idea to drape the thin layer of sheer fabric along the ground soon proved how smart she was. My heels didn't get stuck in the grass as I walked in my gorgeous shoes. I smiled at the thought of the last time my shoes had sunk into the earth and how we'd ended up spending the night in a crypt. *Oh, yes, that's an appropriate thought to have right now, Sienna.* I shook the memory away and focused on all that was around me.

My goodness, nothing was spared. Gold glitter dusted the petals of the roses that adorned each chair, pink paper fans were placed as gifts for each guest in case it became too warm, and in front of me was a white arch where Elio stood on a raised platform next to Niccola and then Vinni. As we reached the front and turned, I saw that Piero and Andrea were both in tears in the front row, holding on to each other with such happiness that it nearly made me cry with them.

I blew them both a kiss then turned to Francesco. He held both of my hands.

"To watch you grow, fall in love, and now marry has fulfilled so many of my dreams. I love you, *la mia ragazza*. Now it's time to hand you off." He winked and kissed my cheek.

"I love you, Francesco," I whispered, and his smile widened. He stepped aside when Elio reached for my hand and helped me up on the platform.

"Hi." I looked up at him and was in awe at how

handsome he looked in his perfectly cut, classic black tux.

"Wow," he let out a big breath, "if you weren't already pregnant…" He made me laugh, and he smiled with pride at what he'd already done.

The minister began to speak, but I hardly heard his words, as I was so caught up with the man in front of me. He smiled and squeezed my hands at all the sweet spots in the sermon. I snapped out of my daze only when we had to repeat our vows. Then Elio slid a diamond and silver band over my finger, and I slid a silver band over his. I didn't think we waited for the minister to tell us it was time as we dove into each other's arms and sealed our marriage ourselves. I vaguely noticed the crowd cheering as I lost myself in my husband's arms, safe and sound. Exactly where I needed to be.

Later, after a whirlwind of photos and people wanting to congratulate us, we were finally whisked inside a room and told to stay there until they announced us for dinner.

"I have something for you." Elio smiled his love as he removed a gold box from his coat pocket. He opened the lid and held it out to me. "I hope you like it."

A ring? I removed it from the box to study it. It had a black oval stone much like his family ring, but when tilted in the light, I saw what he'd done. I looked up at his face, and my eyes misted.

"Yes, my love. You may officially be a Capri, but you've had a lifetime of hurt trying to find out who you really are. I'd never want to take that away from you. So," he stepped near, and we looked at the ring together, "see that little bear there sitting on the crown with the crow? That's where you belong." I studied the tiny gold inset in the smooth black stone, and my heart swelled. I couldn't believe he'd changed his family crest and blended it with mine. "We're changing history, *bella*." He slipped it on my right hand then let his hand fall gently to my belly. "One step at a time."

"I can't believe you did this." I knew what this crest meant to the Capri family, and any tiny shred of doubt that he saw us as equals in this fight to stay on top disappeared forever. "Thank you. That was incredibly thoughtful." I wrapped my arms around him and smiled at him, my husband. "I have a gift for you, too."

"Oh?" He checked the time then pulled at his tie. "I think we can be late."

"Not that." I rolled my eyes playfully. "You might want to tell your mama to buy two cribs."

His perplexed expression switched to one of surprise as it dawned on him what I'd said. The most beautiful smile stretched across his handsome face.

"Twins?" he nearly shouted. "As in two little heartbeats are swimming around?"

"Yes." I was suddenly lifted into the air and spun around as he buried his face in my neck and laughed.

"When did you…when…" He shook his head, trying to get his thoughts straight. "When did you find out?"

"A week ago."

"A whole week? I can't believe you didn't tell me until now."

"Well, that was for two reasons. First, I wanted today to be extra special," I beamed, "and second, I have more security around me than the Queen of England, and I was nervous of what might come next if you found out before today."

"Oh, there's no doubt I'm tripling our security," he solidified my fears, "but, Sienna, twins!"

I laughed even as I knew I was about to lose the small shred of privacy I had managed to keep, but it was just who he was, and I couldn't knock him for loving us that much.

"Are you two ready?" Andrea poked her head through the door and then looked a question when she saw the two of beaming like we'd found a mountain of gold.

"Yes, Mama," Elio took my hand, "the *four* of us are ready."

Her face twisted in confusion, and just as we walked by, I patted my tummy, and she connected the dots with a gasp.

Yes, the news was about to spread like wildfire, but Elio knew first, and that was all that mattered.

The tables were, as expected, spectacular. Light pink, yellow, and white roses with soft greenery burst from pear-shaped vases. Vintage pink candlesticks held white tapered candles, gold cutlery complemented the gold-trimmed fancy plates, and elegant place cards with a gold crown seal directed each guest to their appointed seat. Tiny salt and pepper shakers sat delicately next to the welcome card that rested on the center plate.

Welcome to Elio and Sienna's wedding. We are so pleased you were able to join them in their celebration of two hearts joining as one.

These two met when they were just children, and against all odds they were able to break the rules and rewrite history. They've overcome many challenges and have tested one another on countless occasions, and still managed to hold on to each other through it all.

They call it the boomerang effect, but we call it true love.

Please turn this card over and write them something special to let them know you believe in true love, too.

Much love, Andrea and Piero Capri

A tear slipped down my cheek as I glanced over at Andrea. I held the card to my chest, and she blew me a kiss.

"Hello, everyone, and thank you for coming." Piero stood tall at the end of our table and commanded the room for all to listen. "We're sorry my Mama wasn't well enough to join us, but we'll make sure she sees all the pictures." I pictured her body as she spun in the wind. I wondered if she had time to think of what went wrong with Abramo before she belly-flopped into the water. I pictured her bones as they shattered against the rocks, her soul slowly sucked down through the gates of hell.

I tuned back just in time to see Piero give a wink as he held the guests under his spell. "So, please sit back, take those photos, and enjoy the evening like we all will."

"Should we be nervous at how smooth he is at lying about his own mother's death?" Wyatt said with a pretend scared face. "That was some straight up mafia shit, right there."

"I think we should be concerned about the fact I was reliving her death with glee during his speech." I winked, and he nodded with approval.

"Lord, this life suits you."

"It really does, doesn't it?"

He tapped his wine glass to my water glass and nodded at the table diagonally across from us.

"Stage four crazy hasn't looked over here once." He referred to Noemi, who had been a wallflower during the ceremony and now dinner. "Maybe we should poke the beast some?"

"Maybe for dessert."

I let myself take in the moment, and my heart swelled to see all those who had come to celebrate our big day. When I caught Ugo's gaze, he gave me a slight nod and made the motion of money by rubbing his fingers.

I smiled, as I knew he'd been working on settling some of the Coppola debt. I let go another level of stress that had been weighing me down as Donna. For months, Elio and I had been working hard to clear up the debts Rosa had incurred as Mikey. Thankfully, Niccola was about to gain access to some money Pippo had stashed away, and we could use it to begin the process of cleaning up Mikey's mess. A lot of very powerful people wanted their money back, and they didn't really care who paid it.

Vinni had been a huge help with one Cartel deal.

The Castillo family were not someone I wanted to deal with, especially after receiving some not-so-nice photo threats if I didn't pay up. As the Coppola Donna, I was responsible for it all, and I accepted that responsibility. With Elio's help, a lot of connections had been smoothed over and deals made. Things were going to be all right.

"Is this on?" Niccola's voice boomed over the speakers. "Yes." He cringed at the volume then laughed with the crowd while he took a tight grip on the sides of the glass podium, "I felt it was only appropriate to come up here and say a few words about the happy couple. I remember when Elio first moved here. He was quiet and brooding, and of course that attracted woman from all over Italy." He chuckled and rolled his eyes. "Naturally, he barely registered them, as his heart belonged to another." He swooned at me, and I had to laugh. "Which, in turn, worked out well for Vinni and me." He wiggled his eyebrows.

"Yeah, it did," Vinni called out, making the place laugh harder.

I noticed Gain lean over Piero's shoulder and whisper something that put a frown on his face.

"What's going on?" I nudged Elio to look over at his father and saw something pass through the two of them.

"Nothing." He squeezed my hand, but I stared him down. "It's time to eat," was all he'd say.

I let it go, but I did keep an eye on them while the waitstaff served our meal.

I glanced at Wyatt, who was watching Vinni, and it made my mind go.

"Hey, Wy, so, you know how it's my wedding day?"

"Yes, I've already tucked away some memories of the day."

"Well, so the best gift you can give me is to tell me what exactly happened between you and Vinni when you were taken by Mariano."

He dropped his head like the subject exhausted him. "If something happened, don't you think you'd be the first to know?"

"No, because I think you'd think I'd tell Elio, which I wouldn't."

"Wouldn't you?"

"Tell me what?" Elio heard his name and was now tuned in.

"No, I wouldn't tell him." I ignored Elio, trying to prove to my best friend that nothing had changed between us.

"What's going on?" Elio leaned over to be in the conversation.

"Okay, well, that's good to know." Wyatt nodded.

"It is, so…" I waited while Elio grunted, and I knew he felt out of the loop.

"Nothing."

"Something happened!" I hissed, and a few guests looked over. I smiled politely and pretended to listen to Niccola.

"What are you two talking about?" Elio's frustration was perfect, and I turned to him with a knowing look. I had him in checkmate.

"What's going on with you and Piero?" I waited for

him to share.

He looked between Wyatt and me and contemplated if what he knew was worth finding out what we were talking about.

"The Finder's found something and is on his way over to talk."

"Really?" That was huge.

"Yes, so, what are you two talking about?"

"How sexy Vinni is." Wyatt shrugged, and Elio rolled his eyes and cursed under his breath. I grinned at my best friend.

"All right. He saved me. He carried me out of the place. I might have faked being passed out." He grinned and jiggled his head. "I was pretending to be one of those sexy book cover models being rescued by a gorgeous fireman or something. My mom reads books like that, and I know you do, too, my lovely. I mean, the covers are very sexy."

"I wish I had witnessed that." I smirked and moved my attention over to Niccola, who was wrapping up his speech.

"To a wonderful addition to our family and to the happy couple and their future. Now, let's enjoy this wonderful feast."

We clapped, and it became loud as everyone started to chat and enjoy themselves while an army of servers brought out silver-covered trays and placed them before us.

Vinni cleared his throat, and I glanced at him. He was slowly cleaning off his knife on a napkin. I followed his gaze and saw he was eyeing up Trigger and Tess, who were talking to Piero. It was pure entertainment to me that he was so terrified of Trigger. Vinni had a lot of connections with the Cartels and some other pretty scary people in Chicago, but that biker dude really spooked him. I noticed he had actually gone pale.

Dinner was unbelievably tasty, the music was perfect, and the dessert was moan-worthy.

"Have you ever known me to share my fruit?" Wyatt's eyebrows went high, and I grinned, reading into his comment. "You eye up my last raspberry one more time and I'll—"

"Here, my *bella*," Elio slid over his dish of fruit. I made a face at Wyatt and didn't waste any time as I cleaned the plate.

"You're married, you won." Wyatt rolled his eyes at Elio. "Enough with the sweetness." He pretended to gag as he picked up his plate and left. I accepted Elio's kiss with a dramatic flourish.

"Thank you." I let my lips linger for a moment. "The heartbeats love fruit."

Elio snapped his fingers and called a waiter over and requested a heaping plate of fruit for me. I kissed him again, then suddenly felt all the water I had consumed.

"Excuse me. I've got to visit the toilette." He went to stand, but I pressed a hand down on his shoulder.

"I'll walk you." He smiled up at me.

"I assure you, *amore mio*, I can walk out the door and down the hallway all on my own."

"I'll go." Andrea patted her son's arm. "You might

need some help with your dress." She smiled at me.

I figured it wasn't important to remind her that Eddy K had made the greatest invention of all, a hidden slit in the back for moments like this. I decided to let it go and accepted her help graciously.

I stopped walking as I caught sight of a familiar face. She was on the arm of one of Piero's friends.

"Andrea, who is that woman?" It was her again, the one I'd seen at the Coppola house during the fire, then again on the night of our announcement party.

"I'm not sure who that is," she urged me to keep moving, "but nothing would surprise me with him. He always has someone new on his arm. He's quite the catch in town."

"Would you mind finding out for me?"

"Of course. What's going on?" She tugged my arm.

"I just find it strange that I ran into her at the Coppola mansion during the fire and again at our announcement party, and now she's at my wedding. An uncomfortable coincidence, I'm thinking. Something seems off about her."

Her face twisted, and I knew she understood that my gut was normally right.

"I'll find out." She glanced back at the woman in question.

After I freshened up and stretched my legs, I stood outside the door with Andrea and thought how happy everyone looked.

"Andrea," I took her hand, "thank you for being my mother when I needed one so badly. I couldn't have done this without you."

"Oh, dear, you have no idea what that means to me." She dabbed her eyes and gave me a chuckle. "You've always been special to me, and now look where you are." We turned to watch the guests.

"This has got to be the most beautiful wedding I've ever seen, or even read about," I breathed at her. I took in all the small things she'd done, right down to the slideshow and the photobooth. She'd even had a backdrop made up of the pond where Elio and I had first met, and it stood next to the photobooth.

"Anything for you two." She seemed miles away as she spoke then patted my arm. "Stay here, Sienna. I'll be right back."

Was I really being left alone? I smiled at the thought and enjoyed the moment to let my eyes wander around the room, taking in all the faces and happy laughter. Never did I think I would have a wedding, let alone one like this, and I could only dream it would be with a man like Elio.

I locked eyes with that strange woman again. Her jet-black, shoulder length hair swung as she looked at me, and I felt something strange pass through us. She seemed nervous I'd spotted her and looked away. A group of younger guests who had obviously been enjoying the open bar passed between us, laughing and carrying on. When they were gone, she had disappeared. I scanned the room but didn't find her again. I pushed the discomfort back and refused to let it worry me anymore. Andrea said she would investigate it, so I told myself to relax and enjoy my special day.

My stomach grumbled, and I looked over at our table to see that Elio had disappeared. My stomach grumbled again, and I patted my belly. "Yes, yes, I hear you two." I chuckled and started toward the kitchen to see if I could scrounge up some more of that delicious fresh fruit. I opened the doors and came to a complete stop when I heard a familiar voice.

"Why can't you just admit it? You feel something," Wyatt huffed, but not in anger. It was more like passion. I pressed myself against the door and listened. "I felt all of you when you carried me that day."

"What you felt," Vinni pushed Wyatt against the wall and hovered over him much like Elio did to me, "was a friend saving another friend."

"Yeah?" Wyatt challenged and straightened his spine.

"Yeah." Not even a beat later, Vinni grabbed his chin and slammed his lips to Wyatt's. Yes, I was that asshole friend who watched like it was live TV because I knew this was the singlehanded greatest moment in my best friend's life, and I sure as hell wasn't going to miss it.

The kiss was passionate and loving, but as I took in Vinni's expression after the kiss, there was a huge part of me that knew this was Vinni saying *no more*. He might be attracted to Wyatt, but he was straight. My heart broke but then repaired itself all in that short moment. Wyatt got closure, and I thought that was what he needed more than anything else.

I carefully slipped out then. I didn't want to end

their moment. It could go wherever, but I didn't need to be a part of it.

Noemi

I glanced around the room and was both bothered and concerned that Greta and her ever-present Abramo weren't at this event. I felt the doubt creep up my back for the hundredth time today. I knew something was going on with all the whispered conversations.

Fear zoomed around in my head, and I started to feel as though all the lies I'd told over the years were multiplying into the thousands and each one hovered on the edge of my tongue ready to slip out if I wasn't careful. It was exhausting. I wondered where Rosa was and if she was just waiting for me to slip up as well. Was I marked for death the day I'd met Theo?

Theo…I slipped into the happiest memory I had of

him, just one last time, before I closed the chapter on us.

I sniffed and dried my eyes on the long sleeve of my sweater. It had been a hard day. Theo had to spend the day with Elenora on a family outing, one of those mandatory public things, while I had to stay home like the closet girlfriend I was. I hated her so much that merely thinking her name drove me to the brink of hateful, despicable things.

Speaking of which, I snagged a pocketknife from the bedside table then went into the hallway. I quietly moved down the hall pushed Elenora's bedroom door open and walked inside. It was spotless, cold, and dull. She had a few stuffed animals on the bed. Such a child. Her slippers sat neatly by her vanity, and I kicked them as I got close. Perfect Elenora and her need to dress like she was royalty. I tipped over her perfectly aligned perfumes bottles then popped the top off her lipstick in hopes it would dry out.

I slumped my heavy body down onto the bench and stared into the mirror and allowed myself to imagine for a second that I was her. I snarled at her hairbrush and knocked it into the trash can, hoping something caustic would leak onto it. Maybe her hair would fall out the next time she used it. Then I spotted her jewelry box and flipped up the lid to peer inside.

My breath caught in my lungs when I spotted the signature teddy bear pendant. I knew it was the one the mothers got when they were about to have their babies. The mothers were supposed to hang on to them until the child was old enough to wear it. I wondered where the lapel pin was. Generally, they were given both at that time. Did Theo take it back when her gender was revealed as a girl?

"What are you doing in here?" Theo snapped, closing the door behind him.

"You're back?" I turned to see the clock and realized I had completely lost track of the time. "I was just," I was too tired to lie, "seeing what it was like to be her."

"So, you want to feel like her? She's a bitch and could only produce a daughter." He sighed and knelt in front of me. "You know I'm in love with you." He took my hand and held it tight and pressed the other to my belly. "You're not a bitch, and you will give me a boy. Right?" It was almost more of an order than a loving moment, but I nodded at him with a big smile as I hoped to hell this baby was a boy because I wasn't sure what it would mean for me if it wasn't.

"I see you stuck with tradition." I motioned with my chin toward the teddy bear. He moved closer to see what I was looking at, and his brows pinched.

"I never gave her that." He stood and used two fingers to pick it up. "Where in the world did she get this?" he said more to himself.

"You didn't? I wondered if you'd taken back the lapel pin since she had a girl." I was digging, but I didn't care. I wanted to know everything.

"I've no idea where she got it. Maybe it was Nonna trying to win her over." He scoffed in disapproval then moved his gaze to me. "I don't have a lapel pin for our son yet, so why don't you take this one? I'll get you the

right one, the lapel pin, as soon as I can." My stomach clenched at his undying need to have a boy. "Noemi, my love, you deserve one more than anyone, so as someone who is carrying my son, take this as proof that I will always love him."

The way he said "my son" carried with it such dark promises. I snatched it from his hand in my desperate need to have something from him.

"Do we have a plan for Bosco?"

"I'll take him out myself," he waved me off, "once I know what's going on in there." He tapped my belly, and my gaze dropped right along with my stomach. Wow, I felt like my baby was the only thing anyone cared about. I twisted the teddy bear between my fingers.

"Won't she notice it's missing?"

"No." He shrugged as he stood. "I'll just toss another one in there later, and she'll never know the difference." He disappeared into the restroom, and I knew our moment was over. I hurried from the room, clutching the little bear tightly.

I would never get that lapel pin because the bitch would kill him not that long after.

My chest pained as I remembered tucking the little bear into a planter in my favorite room at the Capris' summer villa months later. It was the only tangible thing I had left of Theo except for my memories of our secrets and lies.

Stop! I squeezed my eyes to push back the panic that always came with those memories. *Get it together.* I was losing it, and I needed to stay focused on the present.

When I heard laughter, something changed inside me. My thoughts firmed up, and I took a breath, opened my eyes, and started my plan.

I pressed my phone to my ear when Bosco sat down with Amara. I had to smile at his pretense that she was just a colleague. I forced a worried expression on my face and glanced at him then away quickly. I knew I had his attention.

"Is that so?" I nodded to the imaginary someone on the other end. "I'll be sure to pass that along. Thank you."

"Is everything all right?" he asked in a tone that showed he cared, when I knew he would be pleased if I got hit by a bus. We were in front of family, and he played his part well, just like I was about to.

"Seems Rosa was just spotted in Rome and is now on her way back here."

"What?" He stood, and his chair scraped the floor, drawing a few people's attention our way.

I smiled at them and lowered my voice. "Please, Bosco, keep it down. This is not a day to ruin."

"If she's on her way, we need to get ready."

"I understand that, and that's why I'm telling you now."

He looked at Amara, who waved him off with a smile. She turned and watched him hurry across the room, and I slipped a few drops of poison in her drink. Rosa was, after all, on her *way over.* Who knew what else might just come from this chaos? I smirked and watched as my lie about Rosa was about to spread as quickly as

Amara's legs had with my husband.

I knew my lie would send Bosco over to speak to Piero. A possible sighting of Rosa Coppola would also be shared with Andrea, but she'd never involve the bride on her big day. Andrea was sickeningly thoughtful that way. God, I hated that woman.

I saw Sienna as she appeared across the room. She placed a hand to her precious belly then headed toward the kitchen. I'd nearly gagged when I overheard they were having twins. Of course, they were. What else wonderful was going to be shoved their way?

Now it was my turn. I smiled and twisted in my seat to tuck my phone and vial away, but when I turned back, Sienna's friend Wyatt slid into the chair next to me. Why was he still here? He should have gone back to America ages ago. He was like a leech sucking onto Sienna and all that she'd just gained.

"What?" I snapped, not wanting to play nice with him. I was surprised he wasn't hovering around Sienna like a fly in a cow field. He never let me get close to her.

"I wanted to know if you'd like to dance."

"Why?" I tried to curb my annoyance and looked about as I wondered what he was supposed to be distracting me from. Vinni hurried by, and I noticed Wyatt gave him a quick glance. Was he up to something with my son? Did Vinni know something about me? Dammit. I needed to think quickly here.

"Why not?"

I rolled my eyes and took a sip of my drink, and he chuckled. Suddenly, I looked at Amara's glass then at my own and spat my drink back out and coughed up any that might have gone down. The little ass switched the glasses!

"She's okay." I felt Wyatt pat my back while he addressed the guests around me. "She's just had a little too much."

My face heated in embarrassment, and I shook him off as I slid out of my seat. I quickly walked away, avoiding eye contact with the old hags around me.

"Where are you going?" Hector stepped in front of me just as I reached the other side of the room. He now blocked my path to Sienna. Clearly, he was planning on making a move tonight as well.

"Did you see what that woman's friend just did to me?"

"You mean what you just did to Amara?" He sighed, unamused, and tapped the radio on his uniform. "You're slipping, Noemi, and I can tell you're about to do something stupid right now. Don't you realize they're always watching?"

A door opened in my head, one I'd been desperately trying to keep locked. My dark thoughts flowed out and swam around freely. My blood heated and my heartbeat pounded dangerously in my throat, and I knew I was about to lose control. I was certainly finished with answering to this kid. He'd held my secret over my head for far too long. Not to mention my bank account. I bit my cheek until I tasted blood.

"Go back to your seat and stick to the plan," he said as his eyes bored into mine.

"No." I stood firm, and I knew we were both at our breaking point.

Out of the corner of my eye, I saw Niccola hurrying toward us.

"Where's Vinni?" he called in a rush. He clearly knew what was going on, but I needed to sell why I was talking with Hector.

I quickly put a hand to my chest like Hector had just given me the same terrible news. "Rosa Coppola and a few of her soldiers are on their way here!" I reached out for Hector and touched his shoulder for support to give my son a grand performance. "He has more to share, but you two have to go warn the others."

"We know, but we need more information. Officer." Niccola addressed Hector and motioned for him to follow. He had no choice but to comply as Niccola was a Capri and Hector had to follow orders. They headed over toward Piero and Elio.

Hector had shot me a warning to stay put, so I waited for them to get out of sight then hurried in the opposite direction. I spotted the bride sipping some water, all on her own.

It felt almost too easy.

I didn't wait for her to see me. I hurried by and grabbed her arm as I went, quickly opening a door to a small room, then shoved her in before she could react. I blocked her path to the door as she recovered her balance against a table.

"What the hell, Noemi?" She instinctively held her stomach, protecting her twins. *Oh, spare me the melodramatics.*

"Enough with the games!" I shouted, seeing black spots. "Where's Greta?" I demanded to know everything.

"In case you've been living under a rock for the past few months, that lady despises me. All this," she waved her hands, "well, let's just say it's been a blessing not to have her here."

"You're avoiding my question!"

"No, I'm saying I don't care to know where that nasty, old, rosary bead rubbing mongrel is, nor do I care." Her hands went to her hips. "Now, move, or I'll move you."

"Who do think you're talking to?"

"Oh," she smiled, and I saw it, something in her eyes, "I've very aware of who I'm speaking to, Noemi."

"Tell me where you got the photo." I changed my tone.

"Rosa's office." *What?* The way she just tossed that answer at me made me stop caring. "You want to tell me who it is? Or do I have to keep digging?" Sienna asked.

"You're playing with something that will undoubtably destroy everything you've worked so hard to gain."

Sienna shook her head slowly like she was tired of me, and it only made me see red.

"How about this?" She took hold of her long white gown with her perfectly manicured hands and readjusted the skirt. "Despite you trying to kill me, I'll give you an opportunity to fill in a blank for me. Then perhaps I'll fill in what I can for you."

"I'm listening." I folded my arms.

"You should…" She inclined her head. She looked so damn confident I wanted to punch her in the face, but I knew I had to hear her out. "Tell me the rest of the sentence. I saw the indents from something written on the photo. What does it mean?"

Then like the sun returning after an angry storm, it hit me…*she doesn't know.*

Don't smile. You've got this.

"All right, Sienna." I lowered my eyes and tried to calm myself so it would sound convincing. It was time to play the last card I had. "I can't keep running from my past, so let's do this. But you must promise me, if I tell you the truth, Elio can only know a part of it."

"I'll decide that after I hear it."

If only I had my dinner knife, I could do so much damage right now.

"Fine." I sagged against the door. "I was and will always be in love with your father." I watched her face fall, but she cleared her expression of emotion quickly. "When your mother married Theo, I hated her for it. I still do, so I did the one thing I could think of to hurt them both. I dated and got pregnant by Bosco. He was one of Theo's biggest rivals. It was a kick in the gut to Elenora that now I'd forever be linked to the Capris when she couldn't. It worked. Theo took me back, which, of course, upset Elenora and made me beyond happy." I gave her a sickeningly sweet smile to drive my hate for all things Elenora home to her daughter.

"Nice," she snickered.

"We kept our secret from Rosa Coppola. I knew she'd carve it out of me much like she did Francesco's baby."

Sienna looked away from me, twisting her mouth. Then she finally spoke. "And my father was okay with raising a Capri as his own?"

"Francesco did it with you. What's the difference?" I jabbed at her past. "I never said your father was a good man, Sienna. Theo felt the pressure and needed to have a son before his brother did. It was a race to the finish line. Which brings me to this…" I pulled out the baby photo and tossed it on the table. "Let's back up here for a moment. When Elenora had you, a girl, the pressure was on him again. Theo was beside himself, which was why when I got pregnant, we hatched a plan with Rosa. I'd provide information on the Capris and, if I had a boy, we'd secretly raise my son as a Coppola."

"Sienna!" Wyatt burst through the door, and I jumped to my feet.

"No!" Sienna shook her head, holding a hand up to both of us to stay put. "Wyatt, just give me a moment alone with her." Wyatt's face fell then he looked at me.

"Then let me just…" He made a motion, and I lifted my arms a little. He patted me down for weapons, then indicated my purse, and I saw Sienna nod. *Damn.* He found it and held up the vial for Sienna to see. "Don't drink or eat anything around her."

Sienna closed her eyes and cursed under her breath but stayed calm and said nothing.

"I'll be right out here." He shot me a nasty look as

he left, and I sank back down in my seat. I knew my time was limited.

"Wow," Sienna shook her head in disgust as he shut the door, leaving us alone, "the way you play with people's lives is revolting."

"It's war out there, Sienna. It's either them or you." I brushed off her pissy-face look. "Where was I? Oh, yes, but Theo, being the man he was, took it one step further. He took another woman to bed just to ensure he got what he needed."

"Stellar father I had."

"Well, we agree on one thing." I broke eye contact as the hurt spread through me. Theo could have at least waited a few months to see what I was having before he took someone else to bed. When I looked back to Sienna, I saw her mother looking through her eyes, and I felt fire lick at my insides. "You never lived in that house then. You couldn't understand the darkness that lives in them all. Even you." I jabbed again, but it didn't seem to affect her. "That baby in the picture," I paused to drag out the moment, needing it to hurt more than anything else, "is your half-brother."

"What?" She snatched the photo up and studied it then looked at me. "Where is he now?"

I let her stew on that for a long, hard moment, and just when I thought she'd burst, I went on. "Before I tell you, you have to understand something. His mother's been blackmailing me for years over this. Threating to tell Bosco, telling him where I was staying, what I was doing. That went on all through my pregnancy, too.

She's drained my bank account. If that gets out, Sienna, it'll destroy everything!"

"Noemi, stop." She tried to stem the flow.

"I'm already on the outside of that family. Bosco loves Amara, and I'm stuck in limbo. I know Greta moved in years ago because she always suspected me of playing both sides, but she couldn't prove it. Do you know what that was like? Living under the eye of that old bat? What could I do? She's a syndicate elder." I shook off the coldness that came with that thought.

"Am I supposed to have sympathy for you?" Sienna looked skeptical as she shook her head. "You played games. You were a traitor to the family that took you in. You were given a life that should never had been yours in the first place. Now, years later, you tried to kill me in a fire!"

"Please, you must understand, I was brainwashed into thinking you were going to tell Bosco my secret! I was out of my mind thinking that if you knew, then my sons would be without a mother! God, the money I took from the family just to keep her quiet…" I started to cry, and her face finally softened, so I went for it. "Bosco's just looking for a reason to kick me out so he can bring Amara in. Please have mercy on someone who's just been trying to keep her family together."

"Noemi." She just stood there, and I wasn't sure what was going through her mind. She closed her eyes and muttered something I couldn't hear. "His name."

"If I tell, he might try to kill you again."

"Again?"

"Yes," I sniffed and went for a look of distress, "it was him." I leaned forward and pointed at the photo. "He wants you dead! He told me where you were at the Coppola house. He was the one who spread most of the gasoline. He even helped me get that woman onto your bed. I didn't know he was going to stab her! It just got so out of control."

"His name," she repeated.

I needed to sell he was the true villain here.

"The bomb!" I blurted to get her to remember. Stefano had used that blast to separate Sienna from her new driver, but then Hector got her and took her to my mama's house and kept her hidden. Mama used her as leverage to make a deal with Stefano, and everything would have worked if Sienna hadn't escaped. I moved toward her. "He wants you dead, Sienna, and he won't stop until he does."

"I'm not asking again." This time her tone struck a chord, and I knew now was the time.

"Officer Hector, the policeman who's working with Elio."

"Oh, my God!" She looked shocked and suddenly paled. I wondered if she might faint, but I knew her well enough now to know she'd keep it together.

She raced past me and flung the door open, and her dress swirled around her legs as she ran. I supposed it was too much to hope she'd trip. I gathered my purse and hurried outside. I needed to get home and pack. My shoes wobbled on the cobblestones as I dashed through the sea of cars to my own and fell into the driver's seat with a crash.

As I started the engine, movement caught my eye, and I saw Hector's confused face as I spun off.

It was time for him to go.

Chapter
TWENTY-EIGHT

Elio

"Where is she?" I boomed through the private room, making Mama and Papa jump to their feet. "Is she with Wyatt? Because he's missing, too!"

Vinni returned, looking pale and worried with the phone to his ear. "No sign of Wyatt," he whispered.

I rushed through the patio doors to the outside and scanned the parking lot.

Where are you, bella? I bit my tongue to keep from lashing at everyone. This was the one night that needed to go smoothly. She deserved it!

"Elio, we have company on the way." Niccola came outside with Officer Hector on his heels.

"Why do you think I'm looking for my wife?" I

snapped.

"Sorry for coming uninvited, sir," Hector looked around at all of us, "but Rosa Coppola and a few soldiers were spotted heading in this direction. There could be more. I'm not sure who she has left working with her."

"He's right." Bosco came rushing up behind them. "Noemi got a call that someone spotted them."

I looked over at The Finder, and he shook his head. "I wouldn't risk staying, on the off chance she really is coming, but I haven't heard this from any of my people, and they're all on high alert."

"Bosco," Papa came to my side, "who did Noemi hear it from?"

"I'm unsure. Someone called her, and I didn't wait around to ask." Bosco rubbed his hand over his head as he tried to call Noemi. I glanced at Papa, and his mouth twisted.

"Papa," I pulled him away from the others, "did she just separate me from my wife?" A chill blanketed the air around us, and my head spun. "If I was going to make one last effort to figure out what Sienna knew, the wedding would be a good place to try it. There's so much going on, and we are about to leave for a three-week vacation."

"I agree." He nodded, and I knew he was thinking the same thing.

"We're concerned for Noemi's safety." I looked at Papa, and he knew I'd taken that angle to spin the story to the cousins. I was still trying to protect them for a long as possible.

"Vinni! Niccola!" Papa started to gather the guys to form a search party for Noemi, Wyatt, and Sienna.

"Sir?" The Finder cautiously approached us, and Papa raised a hand to stop everyone from moving. "One of your guests just confirmed that she saw Noemi heading into an empty room—"

"Elio!" Sienna yelled as she raced around the side of the building, her heels and gown glowing in the garden lights. She threw herself into my arms as she gasped for breath. "I need to…" She tried to catch her breath, but her face was as white as her dress. Wyatt was a few yards behind her.

"Take a breath. It's all right." I couldn't imagine her elevated heartrate was good for her or the babies. She'd probably heard about Rosa coming.

"The gasoline," she panted and squeezed her eyes shut, trying to speak, "the bomb." The hair on the back of my neck rose, and something cold passed through me.

"What are you talking about?"

"Noemi—" Her body suddenly went stiff in my arms, and her gaze moved over my shoulder to someone behind me.

"Let's give them some space," Hector ordered like he owned the place.

"Who are you to speak like that to—" Niccola's words were cut off by Sienna's cold voice.

"No!" The venom in her words took everyone by surprise, and I felt her fight response surge through her arms and into mine. "How could you?"

"Miss Sienna, what's wrong?" Hector licked his lips

while he looked around as though weighing his options.

"What's going on here? I demand to know." I stared at Hector as Sienna disentangled herself from my arms.

"Elio," she said in that cold voice, "Hector tried to kill me."

"Is that what Noemi told you?" Hector laughed in disbelief. "The lies that woman spreads!"

I saw her hesitate. She and I both knew how Noemi could twist things.

"So, you're not my half-brother?" she hissed. I vibrated at that, and my face snapped back to her as I registered her words. "This isn't you?" She held up the photo I knew Noemi had stolen from our home. "She told me we share the same father, and she told me all about the money you were stealing from the Capris."

Papa and Bosco stepped toward Hector at the same time as I tugged Sienna behind me. With a snarl, Hector pulled a gun on them. Sounds of weapons being drawn was all that could be heard in the room.

"Your mother ruined everything!" he spat. "She killed our father! Killed any chance of me having the life I deserve!" His suddenly wild eyes widened, and saliva flew from his lips. "Then you returned, and everyone just moved aside. Noemi should have kept her mouth shut. I'll take care of her later. But let me tell you, Sienna, I've gotten close to you many times before, and I'll do it again."

"Only a stupid man threatens what's mine." I chuckled. "How do you anticipate doing anything while multiple guns are pointed at you."

"It only takes one shot to kill your…"

It was as if something snapped in Niccola. Before I could even react, he charged Hector and slammed the two big rocks he held against either side of his head. Hector blinked at us, stunned, then Niccola got him in a head lock, knocked him to the ground, and began to choke him. I glanced at Sienna and saw her ball up the baby picture and toss it away from her.

"Stop it!" a woman screamed as she ran toward us. "Just stop!"

"That's her," Sienna stepped closer to me, "the woman I was telling you about. She was stealing from the Coppolas during the fire." Sienna looked at Mama, and she gave her a nod. They must have spoken about this woman earlier.

"You're killing him!" Her purse went flying as Niccola leaned back on his knees and snapped Hector's neck just as she dropped to the ground in front of him. "No!" Her face turned white, and tears streamed as she felt all around his neck, desperately looking for signs of life. "What did you do? My poor son!" Her voiced echoed off the stone wall as we all just stood there looking at each other.

"You're Hector's mama?" Sienna whispered, and her hand moved to her stomach. The woman looked over at her with such hate and sorrow. I was worried she might attack Sienna.

We were all caught up in another moment of lies, half-truths, and confusion.

"He tried to kill the Donna." Niccola, still on his

knees, spat at Hector's feet in disgust. "I'm tired of this shit! I'm tired of letting the wolves in our house."

"Wolves?" she cried as she lifted Hector's limp head onto her lap. She stroked his hair and rocked in her emotion.

"He was her half-brother, and he tried to kill his own blood," I growled, tired of whatever the hell was going on.

"Wolves?" she said again as she looked up at me with hate. "He wasn't just *her* half-brother," she spewed her words at me and flung her head toward Niccola, "he was *his* too."

Papa reached for Bosco, who fumbled in his step. "You better explain yourself now, woman, or you're about to meet the same fate as your son."

She gently placed her son's head down on the ground and stood on wobbly legs. "Why don't you ask your wife, Bosco Capri?" She dripped hate, then opened her arms as if to say go ahead and shoot.

Vinni's voice cut through. "You're not worth a bullet." His face spoke a volume of emotion, but the main one was concern for his brother, who still knelt beside Hector's body. "You'd better leave now, or I'll do horrific things to your son's body."

That did the trick. She sobbed as she looked down at the body, then turned and ran. I hoped she'd go back to wherever the hell she came from.

"Gain," I addressed my soldier who stood waiting for my command, "spread the word we left for our honeymoon and keep the celebration going. Harris?"

"I'm here, sir."

"Deal with this." I kicked Hector's leg and turned my attention back to my family. "Let's go pay a visit to the summer house."

Sienna and Niccola both looked shellshocked.

"Come on, you two," I helped Niccola to his feet and led the way to the car. A very quiet Wyatt put an arm around Sienna and followed.

The hum of the motor calmed my wild head. Though this was the life I'd chosen, it didn't make it easier when blood, lies, and secrets spilled out and threatened harm to the ones I loved and protected. I knew Noemi's past would come back and affect us all, but the news that Niccola was a Coppola had really thrown me. It would never change the way I'd look at, respect, or love him, but I knew it would be a blow that would do a tremendous amount of damage if not handled correctly. I glanced at the headlights in my mirror to confirm the family were following us. They had a lot to think about. We all did.

"I can't believe this all happened on your wedding day," Wyatt whispered over my shoulder from where he sat in the back with his arm around Sienna. I knew he was just as concerned as I was that our big day had ended with such a shock. I glanced at Niccola, who sat in silence beside me. I didn't say a word, I just shook my head in the mirror at Wyatt. What could I say?

When we pulled up to the front door, Noemi's car was parked in the driveway. I opened my mouth to tell them to wait in the car, but Niccola was fast and flew out the door and into the house before I got my words out.

I yelled at Sienna and Wyatt to stay put and ran inside after him.

Niccola's shoulders were high, and his arms were rigid at his sides as he stalked down the hallway, looking in every room as he went. He gave a hiss when he found each one empty. Suddenly, he turned to the wall and slammed his fist through the plaster. His chest heaved as he took a breath and rested his forehead on the wall. Papa and I kept our distance, as we knew his world had just been flipped upside down. I could only imagine what was racing through his mind. He removed his hand and looked down at his fingers, then he flexed them and muttered something and continued to search. He went into the living room, and we knew he'd found her when his footsteps suddenly stopped.

We slowly approached to make sure we didn't draw Niccola's focus away from what he needed to do.

Noemi sat on a chair with her packed bags beside her. She held a glass of wine in her hand. Niccola, his face furious, was facing her down.

The family, including Wyatt and Sienna, who clearly don't follow orders, quickly joined us, and we formed a horseshoe around them. We all knew this night would end.

"Am I?" Niccola stuck a finger in her face. "Am I a *Coppola*?" He said the last word with acid on his tongue.

Noemi's face fell as she looked over at Sienna.

"I don't know wh—"

"Tell me!" Niccola boomed and made her jump, and her glass tipped over.

"I had—"

"I'm sick of your lies, Mama!" He interrupted her again, rocking back and forth on his feet.

"Yes, Mama," Vinni tried to help, "now would be the time to do the right thing for once."

"Vinni, you know me. You—"

"No! Don't you even look at *my* brother," Niccola snapped and held out a protective arm as if to shield Vinni from her. "This is between us right now."

Noemi had the gall to look at me for help in that moment, then her eyes went to Mama, who offered nothing except to place a hand on Vinni's shoulder.

"I had no choice but to raise you as a Capri." Her sharp voice cut this time, and everyone stilled. "Theo was dead, and Rosa would have taken you from me. I would have been left with nothing."

It was as if the air was sucked from the room, and we all fought to breathe.

"That was it? That was your secret?" Sienna's incredulous words filled the room. "That's the reason you set fire to the Coppolas' house and tried to kill me?"

"What?" Niccola's eyes widened on Sienna then flew back to his mama. "You were behind that?" If I ever thought my cousin would lose all sense of his sanity, it would have been in that moment.

"It's not what you think. I thought she knew. I mean, if Rosa ever found out—"

"Tell Bosco the truth!" Sienna cut her off and stepped forward. "Let's get it all out. Tell him how you spent most of your pregnancy at the Coppola house, not at your aunt's. Tell him you did and will always love Theo Coppola. What was the plan, Noemi, keep Bosco on ice until you knew what you were having? I mean, you'd kept your pregnancy a secret from the Capri family right up until the very end, right up until my father was murdered."

"Yes. I was pregnant. I needed a home. I didn't care who was the father was!" She slammed her empty wine glass on the table, and when it shattered, she lifted the stem with its broken end and held it out at Sienna. I stepped out and pulled Sienna tight to me.

"Your hate has spewed itself onto my family for long enough," I boomed. "The only good thing about you walking this Earth was you gave me them." I nodded at my cousins.

"You, of all people, Elio, know what it's like to love someone you can't have!" she wailed. "I was supposed to have this great life, with the man I loved, with our children, and then that wretched mother of hers ruined everything!" she screamed in a horrific voice that seemed to snap her out of her rage. She suddenly dropped the glass like she couldn't believe what she was doing. "I'm sorry," her hand flew to her chest, "I-I—"

"You want to be with your lover?" Bosco roared.

Bang!

Noemi's white blouse spread outward in a red merlot. The sound of the gun shook us all, and the relief it brought was like a window opening, letting in the much-needed air to live again.

"That's a hell of a lot cheaper than a divorce." Bosco

tossed his gun on the table while his wife slumped to the floor. He stepped in front of Niccola and placed his hands on his shoulders.

"Look at me, Niccola." Niccola's face lifted to his father's, and a tear rolled down his cheek. "You are my son. Do you hear me?" He reached out a wiped the tear from Niccola's cheek. "You are mine."

Niccola nodded, and Vinni came over and wrapped his brother in a hug.

"I will not apologize for that." He pointed at Noemi's body. "We'll get through this," Bosco's voice had a hitch in it, "together as a family."

"We're no different than we were three hours ago." Vinni hugged him tighter, and Niccola clung to him, his face white as a ghost.

"How could she do such a thing?" Niccola's gaze cast over to me, and I held his steady to show him nothing would ever change between us.

"Sometimes people become bitter, and they just can't accept the things life brings. They simply lose their way." Mama spoke softly while she rubbed his back. I knew she wanted to give him some sort of motherly love.

"I'm sorry, Bosco," Sienna addressed him carefully.

"I'm not." He let out a long breath. "I never loved her. I can't believe the lies she's lived with all these years. She was always in the way of the life I wanted with Amara. The only thing she gave me were my sons. It needed to end this way. It all needs to end tonight."

Silence fell over everyone as we absorbed the night's events. Bosco needed time with his sons to come to terms with their mother's death, and they huddled in the corner and talked quietly near the fire. Mama and Papa made everyone drinks. Sienna sat and sipped her water, and we clung to one another both in need of an anchor.

Sienna suddenly looked up at me. "I'll be right back. I just thought of something." She left the room and returned a moment later with something in her hand. She walked over to Niccola. "This always bothered me." She reached out to him and placed something in his hand. "I found this in the garden room months ago. I found it so strange that it was here in this house. It's a teddy pendant similar to mine. The Coppolas give one to the mother when a girl baby is born. I'm guessing Theo gave it to Noemi since she was still pregnant. Why he didn't give a pin, I'm not sure. It was probably the only thing she kept when she came to live here." She moved closer to Niccola but looked at Bosco briefly as she spoke. "I know it's too soon and a lot to take in, but it's something we both share." She smiled softly at Niccola, and his chin quivered as he looked down at the tiny bear. "I've always wanted a brother, Niccola. I'm sorry for how this happened, but I'm glad it's you."

"Shit, that didn't sting," Wyatt joked, breaking the tension and bringing laughter to the room.

Niccola stood up and wrapped her in his arms and hugged her tightly.

"We're going to get through this. Okay, we may have Coppola blood, but we are Capris to the end," she whispered.

"I know we will," he said as his father and brother

joined in the hug.

Later, back at our house, Sienna and I showered and changed without saying much. Neither of us were concerned about the loss of Noemi. Relief mixed with sadness for the boys was all we shared as we chatted about the events of the night. We enjoyed a few laughs over our wedding. It would go down in the books as a typical mafia rollercoaster ride.

"Ready?" I helped her down the stairs. We drove back up to the Hill House to meet with the family. Once we got inside, we could both feel that the atmosphere had changed. It was like we were all back to our old selves again.

"Elio," Papa said as we came into the living room hand in hand, "the car is waiting to take you both to the airport. Your honeymoon will not be delayed."

"Papa." I shook my head, unsure of how to navigate this evening.

"Look here, you two, I personally shopped for this trip," Wyatt chimed in, holding a glass of rum. I smiled at his confidence of his place in our family. He was definitely family now. "Those dresses, heels, and bikinis will not go to waste and with what's happening in there," he patted Sienna's belly. "You won't be wearing those little numbers again for a long while." Mama grinned, and I could see they had this pre-planned. "Everything's in the car. Off you go." Wyatt waved dramatically.

I caught sight of Niccola out on the patio.

"I'll be right back." I headed outside, closing the door behind me. I wanted a moment alone with my best friend, who just so happened to be my cousin. He was sitting on the table, his feet on the chair, looking out over the vineyard.

"I know, everything will be fine," he said over his shoulder. "I just need time to comprehend what the hell just happened."

I sat next to him. We both took a moment to share the night with the crickets and a hooty owl.

"Do you look at me differently now?" he whispered, and the pain in his voice told me he questioned my role for him now.

"I see a boy who grew up beside me as my best friend. We chased frogs and hogs in the woods together, you helped me beat up those little shits behind the church when we were thirteen—"

"God, that was a good day."

"It was." I smirked. "Niccola, you were right there with me through so much, including when we moved here, and I lost her." I lowered my head and felt once again the pain from the hole in my heart that had never healed until that day we locked eyes at the party. "You got me through the hardest time of my life. If someone had told me then that you were a Coppola, I can honestly say that nothing would've changed." I turned to look at him. "Ever." He nodded once and pressed his lips together. "I'm sorry we are leaving at such a difficult time for you, but—"

"No, you both deserve this. You and Sienna."

"And I know I'm about to leave you to deal with the aftermath of fighting our way through this hell, but you're the under boss. You're in charge while I'm gone, and I know you've got this."

We stood and hugged. He needed to hear from me that nothing would change, and I would continue to remind him of it until he got back on track.

"Have a great trip." He smiled at me and slapped my shoulder.

"Thanks." I hopped off the table and went inside, happy we'd had the chance to clear the air.

In a whirlwind, we said our goodbyes, slipped into the car, and headed for Bora Bora. We were to spend the next few weeks in a hut overlooking the crystal blue waters.

Once we were settled in our roomy seats on our private jet, I threaded my fingers through hers and thought how our wedding felt so long ago, even though it was still the day of.

"Ready for some relaxation and a little less blood?" I chuckled and kissed her full lips.

She laughed as she breathlessly pulled away, her eyes sparkling with mischief and promises to come. She snuggled in close and gave a happy sigh. "I'm ready for anything, as long as we're together. But yes, a little less action would be a nice change."

La Fine

Epilogue

Three Years Later

Sienna

"Elio?" I called from the driveway, "I know you two are out here somewhere." Before I moved on, I took a moment to watch Vinni. I had to roll my eyes at what was going on. He was trying to convince a woman about twice his age to get into her car and leave. But as always, Vinni had that charm with the ladies—*and men, apparently*—and they always wanted more from him than just a one-night stand. So, Vinni had enlisted the help of Gain. Poor Gain had been busy training a new group of soldiers. Vinni didn't date, I laughed to myself, he just entertained. His escapades sometimes led to events such as this. *Yes, great use of our men, Vinni.*

Since the twins were born, Elio had hired several new men for security on the property. He was so protective of us that I had a hard time even going to a shop these days. It was smothering at times, but I understood.

Normally, I'd tell him he was being overwhelming, but truth be told, we had lived with a magnitude of people who wanted to hurt us for so long that I welcomed the protection.

"Where's your papa?" I bounced Marabella on my hip until she wiggled to get down.

"Papa there!" She pointed her tiny finger at the sunflower field.

"That's my good girl." I laughed, thinking how great it was that his little daughter constantly kept tabs on him. "Should we go find them?" Her sprig of a ponytail bobbed as she raced ahead, happy as could be, toward the brightly colored field.

"Po gain' frogs, Mama." She outed her brother in her jumbled speech.

"Yes, Filippo loves his frogs." I chuckled, but it soon faded when I spotted the boys. "Elio! Seriously?"

"Mama!" Filippo squealed from the pond. He was covered from head to toe in mud as he held up a poor little frog. It dangled unhappily from his grabby mitt. "Frog!"

"Elio, we have guests coming in less than thirty minutes."

Elio laughed. "Wyatt isn't a guest, *bella*, he's family." With his jeans rolled up to his knees and his white t-shirt stretched over his lean body, he looked just like he did when he was eighteen and caught me bathing in the pond in Sicily.

"His friend is a guest."

"Well, his friend will just have to be all right with a little mess, won't he?" He scooped up our son and flew him in the sky, sending mud and water everywhere.

"Eww!" Marabella ran for my legs and hid her face. I found it funny because she was normally the one getting into a mess. I guessed mud was different. It was usually Chef Donte's flour that was the victim of her shenanigans.

Elio laughed, coming up to us, and I held up my hands to stop him.

"I swear I'll leave you for another man if you get this dress dirty."

"Oh, is that so?" A twinkle in his eye told me that I should run very fast, but I wasn't about to leave our daughter with her muddy brother.

"Don't," I laughed when he tried to grab me, "you dare."

"Elio Capri!" Andrea came to my rescue, and I beamed with pride at my little family as she approached. I knew she doted on being a nonna. "Wyatt's on his way, and you two boys look like you were just hunting for frogs."

Like the typical mama's boy he was, Elio played up to her. "Mama, Filippo was just asking if you'd give him a bath." He was shameless.

"Anything for my little guy." Her tone rose, and she smiled at her grandson. Then Piero appeared and scooped up Marabella, and just like that, our children were gone, and I was left with a playful Elio.

"What?" He smiled wide. "It's not my fault they love to be needed."

"What am I going to do with you?"

"Well," he reached over his head and pulled off his shirt, and I felt my pulse quicken as I gawked at my husband's fighter physique, "I have a few ideas."

"No way." I backed up, but he closed the distance between us, stalking me like a hungry lion. My back hit a tree, and he instantly curled around my body, hooking his arm at my waist.

"I want more babies." He kissed my neck.

I laughed. "I gave you one of each. That should keep you busy for a while."

"But I enjoy the art of making babies." He didn't miss a beat as pinned me against the tree.

"I did not take a nine-hour flight to find my best friend making out under a damn tree," Wyatt called from the driveway. "Get up here and show me how much you missed me."

"I want to say I missed you..." Elio dripped with sarcasm.

"Don't you be muttering hateful things, Elio. I know you missed me the most," Wyatt called.

I kissed Elio quickly, chuckling under my breath as I pulled him up toward the driveway.

"Missed?" Elio grunted.

"Plan your lovin' around my visits." Wyatt laughed as he took a cocktail from a staff member then hastily put it on the roof of the car as I approached at a trot and leapt into his arms.

"I thought you were never coming back!" I'd missed him so much over the past sixteen months. He'd landed a job at *The New York Times* with the help of Elio, and though he'd still be able to live here for most of the year, he was required to train in the States first.

"I have someone I want you to meet." He stepped back and reached out an arm, then gave a warm smile as he drew his friend in close. He was quite a good-looking man, dressed in a nice suit…wait. I studied him a moment and pressed my lips together in fear I'd blurt out my feelings. Sweet Lord, he was Vinni. Wyatt had found an American Vinni. I pulled myself together then, as I noticed the poor fellow looked extremely uneasy. "Scott Hanes, please meet my female other half." Wyatt chuckled as he spoke in English.

"It's a pleasure to meet you, Sienna. I've heard so much, but you know now I'm here, it's a little—"

"Terrifying?" I finished for him. "I understand, I really do, but I promise we're good people."

"You should see her with a blade." Wyatt smirked.

"That helps. Thanks, babe," he said in his American accent.

"Come," I waved for us to go inside, "I want to hear all about your new job, your new friend, and New York, and your sister, and, well, everything." I laughed and led the way but not before hooking my best friend's arm and giving him a huge, knowing grin.

"I know," he whispered in Italian, "I have a type."

"Yup, Vinni." I laughed.

Wyatt grinned back and jumped immediately into a conversation as Scott looked over at us. "I have something really big to share with you later when we have a moment."

"Oh? Sounds very intriguing." I smiled at him. We both were delighted to be back together.

After I gave Scott a mini tour of the house and they dropped their bags in their room, Elio returned wearing a fresh shirt with the twins. They ran in clean and freshly dressed. I knew it would only last for about five minutes, but at least their first impression would be good.

Elio cleared his throat, and the children both stood still and smiled politely at our guests.

"Wow, they're like little people now." Wyatt pulled two stuffed animals from a bag and held them out. "I know you don't remember me but I'm your Uncle Wyatt, and I thought you might like these."

Their eyes widened with excitement, but they waited for their father to give them a nod before they took them.

"Canks u," they both said, and I was relieved I didn't have to prompt them. Then they raced off down the hallway to, no doubt, show Francesco. I knew he'd be joining us shortly.

"I've been gone far too long." Wyatt sighed and shook his head as he sipped his drink, then took a seat.

"I won't argue with that." I reached for Elio's hand. "Scott, this is my husband, Elio. Elio, this is Wyatt's co-worker and boyfriend, Scott Hanes."

"Nice to meet you, Scott," Elio said in perfect

English, taking his cue from me.

"You too, Mr. Capri." Scott tested his Italian and didn't do half bad. "Thank you for inviting us to stay at your home." I thought Scott was going to pee himself, he looked so nervous.

"Please, use English." Elio gave the poor guy a break and made sure he continued in English himself. "Wyatt's family." Elio poured me a drink as he spoke. "Anyone who's important to him is welcome here."

I smiled my thanks at Elio as I sipped the cool cucumber water. It was a hot day, and I suddenly understood why Filippo had been so drawn to the cool mud.

"So?" Wyatt lifted an eyebrow at me.

"So what?" I asked.

"Will you tell me now?"

"No." I caught on immediately and crossed my legs as I thanked the staff member who had brought in some light snacks.

"What?" Scott looked between the two of us.

Elio stood back and watched the play-by-play. He also knew what Wyatt was asking.

"You see, Scott," I explained, "in a mafia family, whoever has a son first became the next Don. Now, we had twins, a Don and a Donna, if you will." I smiled at him, and he smiled back with interest. He was enjoying my story, so I drew it out. "Well, you can imagine the question. Our children have been born into a whole new syndicate now under Capri rule, so the question is, who came out first?" I winked at him. "Would it be the boy or the girl who will be the next head of the family? And here's the kicker. Elio and I are the only ones who were in that delivery room. The birth team were sworn to secrecy, and we had them seal the birth documents so no one but Elio and I would know who came out first."

"May I ask why you won't share it?" Scott asked politely.

"There's a lot of pressure on a child when growing up to be groomed for the position. When our twins turn eighteen," Elio said as took a seat next to me and rested a hand on my thigh, "they can decide who will run the family business, or they both can. If they wish to know the truth, we'll share it at that time."

"But until then, they'll be raised as equals to the Don or Donna title," I added. "That way, they'll both be prepared for the role, and gender won't matter."

"That's incredibly forward thinking." Scott beamed at our family's choice.

"Thank you." I nodded, liking him already.

Scott covered his mouth and looked over at Wyatt with excited eyes.

"I know!" Wyatt nodded, and Elio and I exchanged a quick glance. "They're going to rock it."

"Rock what?" Elio sipped his drink, making me laugh as he mimicked Wyatt's words.

"Your story." Wyatt leaned forward and filled us in on what would turn out to be an interesting opportunity.

We were called to dinner late that evening, and Andrea, who had been missing for most of the afternoon, came outside to greet us.

"Wyatt!" She wrapped him in a big hug. "It's so good to see you! Vinni, dear, please call your brother." She stopped when she realized she wasn't speaking to Vinni.

I laughed out loud and nearly tripped as I followed the path that led down to the beautifully decorated table.

"I hate you so much," Wyatt called to me, and it just made me laugh even harder. Then I heard him introducing them. "Andrea this is Scott."

"My apologies. I'm Elio's mother. It's lovely to have you join us," she said in her softly accented English.

"The pleasure is all mine." Scott looked at Wyatt and then at me as she led the way to the table.

"Hi, Ugo." I kissed my cousin on the cheeks, happy he was back. "How was your trip?"

"Good. It was nice to visit some college friends." He motioned for us to sit.

Andrea had chosen butterflies as her theme this time. I was sure she'd asked little Marabella for her input, as she loved all things *bsflies,* as she called them. The rich blues, pinks, greens, and purples of the swallowtail butterfly peppered the centerpiece bouquets of lavender. They were fastened on with small clear clips, and when the wind blew, they swung up and down like they had just landed for a snack. Mason jars held little tea candles, groupings of wild grasses were held together with twine, and a spring of rosemary was laid diagonally across each of the off-white plates.

"I feel like I'm at a Joanna Gaines party," Scott whispered to Wyatt.

"You think this is nice, wait for the food," Wyatt breathed, and I giggled.

Suddenly, a flurry of activity made us all turn. Niccola rushed to the table holding up a hand.

"Sorry, sorry, we were helping Francesco—"

"We have a guest," Elio interrupted him so he wouldn't blurt out something that wasn't meant for all ears.

"…finish off something." Niccola's voice trailed off. He looked at Elio to let him know that Francesco had dealt with Oscar, who had completely gone off the rails and needed to be handled. "Nice to meet you." Niccola reached over and gave Scott a handshake then cast me a funny glance as he sat.

I knew he'd seen it, too. Scott was Vinni's long-lost twin, and at this point in our lives, I wouldn't be surprised if he was.

"Needless to say," Ugo lowered his voice, "Oscar is now at the bottom of a lake neatly tucked inside a tire, and, to answer your next question, no, I'm not upset. Our relationship, if we had any at all, was always in question. We certainly were never close."

"Glad we're on the same page." I squeezed his hand. During the time Ugo and I had spent together at the Coppola house, we'd had a lot of time to talk. Oscar was always someone I wanted to like but never really did. His first impression always sat heavy on me, and any time after that I'd never gotten a good vibe from him. The man had spent nearly his entire life watching me from a distance along with my mother. It didn't take a genius to realize he loved her. He certainly never made any attempt to help me to like him. He'd manhandled me without thought when given the opportunity.

"Where's Vinni?" Andrea checked her watch.

"He's been held up by Gain. Something about a girl not wanting to leave. You know my brother." Niccola shrugged.

Vinni came up behind me, and I knew the moment he did, because Wyatt suddenly sat up tall and guzzled his glass of wine. Elio pointed to Wyatt's glass, and a server quickly refilled it. I heard Elio chuckle under his breath.

Wyatt stared at me staring at him, and suddenly something clued him in.

"You know!" he mouthed, and I was like a deer caught in headlights. I never told a soul that I had seen the intimate moment shared between him and Vinni at my wedding, but of course my best friend could read my mind like an open book, so here we were. "Son of a bitch, you friggin' know," he whispered but loud enough for the others to hear.

I shook my head but stopped when Scott looked at me then at Wyatt.

"Why do I feel like I'm missing something here?" he asked.

"Welcome to my world." Elio chuckled again. "You'll get used to it. With those two, you never really know what's going on, and half the time you might be happier being in the dark."

Scott stood as Vinni approached the table. "Hi. I

think you're the last person I'm to meet this evening. I'm Scott. Wyatt's boyfriend."

"Oh, would you look at that." Niccola turned his head to me. "I think he just threw down the glove." It took everything inside me not to laugh. I hid a smile behind my water glass.

"You owe me, Si," Wyatt hissed at me, "and I know just what I'll use for payment."

"Nope," I shot back.

"Should I be concerned that I'm the spitting image of your ex?" Scott murmured as he draped his arm along the back of Wyatt's chair.

"Ex?" Elio mouthed to Niccola, who was having the time of his life enjoying the show.

"This is better than TV." Niccola grinned.

"So, Wyatt," Andrea spoke up to break the awkward silence. Vinni seemed stuck in time as he stared at his American twin. "I heard you and Scott brought up an interesting opportunity to Elio and Sienna. Would you like to share with all of us what it's about?"

"Yes," Wyatt leaned back when the server placed his food in front of him, "I pitched an interview with Elio and Sienna to talk about the rise of their empire. We think it would be a great opportunity to shed some light on a modern syndicate. It would be a chance to explain away some stereotypes that not all organized crime families are as ruthless as they were in the fifties through early nineties. That through respect, and maybe a little fear," he smiled, "a country can be run successfully. Of course, we'll keep all the business aspects out of it, but it would be nice to show how you support your people, church, other industries…"

"That actually might be a good way to show that you two are a power couple, and maybe you could flush out some old faces," Andrea said with a glance at Piero, who nodded.

"Yes," Piero said thoughtfully, "I would perhaps mention a location, give a date and time, a specific place to be."

"It could all work in your favor as long as Elio could," Wyatt eyed my husband, "tame his 'I'm going to saw you in half and sell your body on the black market' and add a little more 'I love my wife and I'm a good man' when talking to the host."

"Saudi Arabia," Elio corrected him. "I'd sell her parts in Saudi Arabia."

"Right there." Wyatt pointed his fork at him, making us chuckle. "You can be all nice and sexy mafia boss, and the next moment, bam! You've taken a dark turn." His face scrunched at the thought. "So, let's dial it up a little lighter," he lifted his hand in the air, "so I can keep this job and not have to take the one you so lovingly offered me last year."

"I thought you'd be good at crime scene clean-up." Elio shrugged, knowing Wyatt would rather eat dinner in a public restroom than clean body juice from a carpet.

"I can't with you," he muttered dryly than looked at me. "Would you, please?"

"Yes, yes, I'll keep him in check." I waved him off and looked at my husband, whose grin showed he was more than happy whenever he could get a rise out of Wyatt.

"What?" He shrugged.

"So, when will this happen?" Andrea asked, once again getting back on topic.

"Next week," Scott chimed in. "I hope that will give you enough time to prepare?"

"It's plenty," Elio assured him. "Mama, are you able to watch the kids while we're gone?"

"Is that even a question?" She smiled warmly, and we all went back to our dinner. I loved that I caught Wyatt as he glanced quickly at Vinni, who refused to look in his direction.

It was sexual tension at its finest.

Later that evening, after Piero and Andrea had retired and Ugo had left, Elio, Vinni, Wyatt, Scott, Niccola, and I swapped old stories about everything from New York, to the tour, to the wedding. It felt so good to laugh and relax with friends and family. A few times, Wyatt would drop a comment, and I knew the secret about which twin came out first was killing him. I also knew that from the day we'd met we had always had one rule. We never kept anything from one another. So, when Niccola and Scott were in the middle of a story, I reached over and took his hand in mine.

"Remember my first shift at the bar, and I spilled that really expensive bottle of whiskey down my shirt?"

"I do." He eyed me oddly, and the others felt the change in the atmosphere and stopped talking.

"Remember who came in to ask for a drink, and it

turned out they were shooting a movie down the street?"

"Oh, yeah, I forgot about that."

"Okay, so now you know."

"Oh!" He smiled wide, and I knew that our friendship just became that much stronger. "Thank you." His face flushed with emotion. "I love you."

"I love you, too." I grinned up at Elio, who just smiled back to show he knew Wyatt would take that secret to the grave.

The week flew by, and my time with Wyatt was just what I needed. I loved hearing about his new job, and I enjoyed watching Scott as he navigated around Vinni.

By the time we arrived in New York the day of the interview, we had pretty much ironed out all the dos and don'ts of what we could speak about, and as the interview was later in the day, I decided I wanted a little time alone with Elio. We excused ourselves from the others and walked down to a little café.

"Here you go." Elio placed a glass of juice on the long steel table then took the stool next to me. We sat facing the street. I loved to people watch. He sipped his espresso and then looked at me funny. "Are you feeling all right? I've never known you to pass up on one of those fancy coffee drinks that you and Wyatt love."

"It's probably best I skip caffeine for a while."

"Don't be nervous," he assured me. "You've covered much more than a simple interview."

"No, it's because caffeine isn't good for the baby."

He dropped the plastic lid of his coffee and turned back to look at me.

"You're pregnant?" His smile stretched across his face, and his eyes danced with excitement.

"Yes, my love, another little heartbeat is on the way."

"Whoo!" he shouted, and others in the shop turned to stare. He didn't care, and he grabbed my face and kissed me hard. "Oh, I need to call Mama. She's got to get started on everything. No, I should call the doctor first and have her be there when we return. No, Mama first." I laughed at his spinning head as he left to call Andrea from a quiet corner of the shop.

I caught my happy expression that reflected back at me from the window, and it warmed my insides with the knowledge that the man I loved wanted to have a big family so we would always be surrounded by endless love.

I loved being happy.

"Mama, guess what?" Elio's voice came to me as he talked on the phone, then faded as my attention was drawn to a familiar looking man. He looked as though he was shouting at someone, I leaned toward the window to see better, but with his beard and ball hat, I struggled to fully see his face. Then whoever he was yelling at got out of the car. The flash of sunlight as it caught on her cane had me jolt to my feet.

"Elio!" He was instantly behind me. "It's Rosa!"

Suddenly, a black tinted SUV came to a screaming halt, and three men hopped out and forced Rosa and the man into the back of their vehicle. People on the sidewalk scurried so as not be get involved.

"Who are they?" I couldn't believe what I was

seeing.

"The Cartel," Elio mumbled as the SUV peeled off into traffic and out of our view. "I guess Rosa's not going to be a problem anymore."

I turned and made a face at him and thought how wonderful karma could be at times.

"I guess not." I shrugged.

He grinned as he pulled me to him. His hands threaded into my hair, and he kissed me the way he always did to let me know he loved me. I felt a sense of freedom as I sank into him and allowed myself to let go.

Note to my readers:

I hope you enjoyed Elio and Sienna's story.

Oh, and not to worry, my villains cross over in the next series.

We haven't heard the end of Rosa and Tieri.

Acknowledgments

My mother, cheers to another series we got to enjoy together.

My husband, for always being my cheerleader, formatter, ad creator, and best friend.

My betas and proofers, Kim Kelchner, Kasey Griffin, Rachel Womack, Veronica Nelson, Maggie Savarese, Jamie Johnson, and Elizabeth Clark. I love you ladies!

Cody Hale, for all the photos, videos, treats, and a FaceTime call to help me dive deeper in Italy. I'm so glad this series brought us together.

Rachel Womack, for not only beta reading but for the Italian treats and your overall love of Italy. Someday we will make our plans happen!

My street team, for being amazing every single day.

My beloved editor Lori, for always being there when I need you. I really appreciate you.

For my readers who give me such positive feedback on my stories and for continuing to read them in spite of my dicky cliffhangers.

To my kids, Brooke and Parker, who understand why I

cry over the loss of a fictional character or why I laugh out loud sporadically over something I've written. I only hope someday the writing bug will bite you, too.

Thank you.

A look at what's to come next!

SHADOWS
DARK WATER SERIES

CHAPTER ONE

Present Day
DANIEL

"How bad is it?" Savannah stopped me in the kitchen after our morning meeting had run several hours over. "It must be bad, bcause Frank's assistant has called me three times wanting to know if Cole has signed off on the paperwork yet."

"It's bad." I warmed my hands around my mug and wondered how quickly we could make things happen. "Frank said his intel should be providing an update soon. Regardless, the Cartel numbers are growing fast, and it's impossible to keep up. What's happened to Captain Brent can't be ignored. It's a wakeup call that we need to step up our game."

"Agreed." She leaned against the counter with a

sigh. "I know Cole is nervous of changing the dynamics of the house, but what other moves do we have?"

I couldn't help but smile at how she looked at things. She reminded me so much of Sue at times. It was always our problem, never just the team's problem.

"I don't think it's so much nerves as it is just a lot. Between Shadows and Dusk, there have been a lot more plates to juggle than there used to be. Cole's focus is split in too many different directions, and bringing in another team to live here and train under Blackstone, well, it's a big decision to make. The way Shadows has been run for years now works well, but a new team will be less stress on Blackstone, that's for sure."

"You're right," she nodded, "it really will."

"We're not getting any younger, Savannah," I smiled, "and the Cartels are not only increasing in number, but they're getting smarter and more sophisticated all the time. I'm all for the idea of Blackstone training another team, though. We really need the help."

"Me too." She leaned her arms on the island and bent over, taking a deep breath. "I'd always thought that once The American was removed from the picture, it would give us all breathing room, but clearly, I was wrong."

"The use of fear builds an army quicker than anything else, and most of those poor people don't have much of a choice. Once you've been approached by the Cartel, they either accept the role forced on them or they or their family could face death."

"It's sick." She rubbed her face.

"What's sick?" Olivia asked as she dropped her

bookbag on the counter and looked at the two of us. "Grandpa, are you sick?" Her eyes bored into mine, and a fine line of worry, very similar to her mother's, appeared between her eyes.

"No, dear, it's just about work."

"Oh, yeah, did Daddy sign the papers yet?"

"How do you know about that?" Her mother shook her head.

"Mom, I'm a Logan. There's not much I don't know about what goes on in this house." She pulled out her binder. "If I'm going to run this place someday, I need to be in the know. So," her dark eyes took in both of us as she raised her pencil as though to take notes, "why is everyone looking stressed out?"

"No one is stressed."

"Mom," her hands went to her hips, "Uncle Mark didn't smile when I got home, and he always smiles."

"That means nothing." Savannah tried to assure her, even as we both knew it wouldn't work.

"Then why is there a full rack of cookies on the counter?"

I sipped my coffee to hide my smile. The little girl missed nothing.

"Olivia," Savannah cupped her face and stared down at her lovingly, "there are some things that are meant for adults. At this point, we don't have all the details. So, I'm asking you nicely to let it go until we have some answers. Then Daddy and I will let you know what's happening, okay?"

"Okay." She knew better than to argue with her

mother, especially when she used a certain tone. Her expression went from concern to a smile. "Since Uncle Mark isn't eating those cookies, can I have some?

"Of course, you can." Savannah planted a kiss her forehead then stepped back as Olivia jumped off the stool, grabbed two cookies, then raced off calling for the twins.

"She's quick." I chuckled.

"Daniel?" Keith popped his head around the corner. "The video chat is ready to go, and Frank should be logging on any minute now."

"Great, thanks."

"Savi?" Keith lowered his voice. "Is Lexi home?"

"I don't think so. I haven't seen her since last night." Keith nodded and looked away, then quickly turned back, waved goodbye, and disappeared as quickly as he'd arrived. Savannah looked at me, and I closed my eyes and shook my head slowly with a deep sigh.

"One thing at a time."

"See," Olivia popped her head around the corner, "Uncle Keith didn't touch the cookies either."

"Off you go." Savannah shooed her away, "here Grandpa take one for the road."

"Thanks."

I hurried downstairs and only just avoided a collision with Butters. The crazy dog was infamous for stealing socks, and his latest bright blue prize dangled from his mouth as he raced in the opposite direction to avoid being caught. Things certainly had changed around here.

My eye went to a grouping of photos on the wall,

and I took a moment to study them. When I'd first put together Team Blackstone, it had only consisted of four guys—myself, Frank, Zack, and Ray. A photo of the four of us put a grin on my face. We were together, heads thrown back in laughter, while Zack hung upside down from our homemade climbing wall. He clowned around, having lost a race with Frank. I moved to another picture, one of my son Cole. It had been taken the day I'd handed the team reins over to him. Cole was so happy to take over as team leader, and it showed in the pride on his face.

Then Mark, basically our adopted son, was brought in, along with Paul and John. Mike and Keith came into play later, and then York. York was never really a full-fledged member of Blackstone. I thought of him only as a filler and the one man who would never have his picture hung on any wall at Shadows.

I studied the photos along the wall, and nostalgia filled me as I walked toward the conference room. Over the years, we'd lost a few of our men, and each one hit us hard. One hit, in particular, had been really difficult for us all. It happened just a few years back. Staff Sergeant Paul. He was a great soldier and an even better friend. He'd been killed while trying to protect Savannah. We had his picture hung inside our conference room, not just to remember him, but to give us all the feeling he was still part of our meetings. I touched the frame as I entered the room. It had become a tradition for all of us.

As I sat down at the rectangular wooden table, Frank angled the camera and started in.

"Intel has confirmed that the Cartels have started a new movement. They call themselves 'Los Débiles.'"

The weak.

"That's a pathetic play on words. They prey on the weak, but they're hardly weak," Keith muttered.

"Agreed." Frank shook his head. "Los Débiles' purpose is to grab homeless women and children off American streets using soldiers they've hired. They are also targeting the rich, famous, and of course people like us."

"Just add it to the friggin' list." Mark rubbed his eyes.

I understood his feelings. We were all worn out and tired of the endless fight, and though none of us would ever stop fighting, we needed some fresh blood to join us to help carry the load. All the more reason I knew we needed to recruit some new men.

"The Cartels have made another push into the States and are spreading fast," Frank continued. "The border patrol is adding new agents, police are doubling their efforts in all their border towns, and now to follow suit, I think, like we've discussed, it's time we added some new people of our own." Frank turned his attention to me. "Daniel, I've sent over several files on men I've personally hand-picked. Some of them are still on active duty, and some are looking to try something new. I want you and Cole to go through their dossiers but pay some serious attention to Captain Ty Buckett. I've seen what he can do firsthand. I think he should be looked at for team leader." He nodded at me. "Trust me, read his file."

"All right, Frank." I knew Frank had always been meticulous when vetting anyone, and his suggestions would be seriously close to the mark, so I was very curious to see who he'd recommended.

"The money's already been approved for the new team's salary, so just send the list of what you'll need for supplies, and I'll handle everything else here."

"Frank," Cole spoke up, "has any intel been provided as to possible locations of where the Los Débiles are holding the people they grab?"

"Yes, they have two locations identified." A map popped up on the screen next to his head, and he circled where they were. "We know there are several more places and one main hub. As we speak, we're moving some of our inside men around, trying to understand who the ringleader of the operation is and where the other locations might be."

"Let me guess." Mike spun a bottle cap between his fingers. "We're to sit tight until we know all the locations?" A few of the guys groaned, and I knew they hated to sit still for long.

"I'll make Blackstone a deal." Frank clicked off the map. "I have Eagle Eye watching the borders. Once we bring in a new team leader, you can go in. But I want him to go with you. We don't have time to train on friendly ground, so we'll drop him in the deep end. We'll build the team from there."

"And if any high-profile cases come up?" Mike questioned again.

"That's different," Frank assured us all. "This hold

is merely for Los Débiles. Otherwise, it's business as usual." He checked his watch. "That's all the time I have right now. Daniel, Savannah will provide you with the files. I'll be in touch."

The screen went black, and everyone remained quiet, until Mark couldn't take the silence anymore.

"You know, a little poison in their water supply would take care of this entire mess."

About the Author

J.L. Drake was born and raised in Nova Scotia, Canada, later moving to southern California. Though she loves the weather in Cali, she would sell her left kidney for a good rainstorm. Jodi's love of the seasons back home in Canada definitely appear in her books.

When she's not writing, you can often find her sitting somewhere along the coast of Huntington Beach, reading, or at home curled up on a couch with her two children and husband, binge watching Marvel movies.

Authorjldrake.com

Books by J.L. Drake

Broken

Shattered

Mended

Honor

Escape

Trigger

Demons

Unleashed

Freedom

Omertà

Courage

Darkness Lurks

Darkness Follows

Darkness Falls

Behind My Words

Christmas at the Cabin

All In

Quiet Wealth

Quiet Secrets

Quiet Power

Quiet Empire

Shadows

Whiskey

Tango

Alpha